A YI

TWO LIVES

Tales of Life, Love & Crime

Translated by
Alex Woodend

This is a **FLAME TREE PRESS** book

Copyright © 2020 A Yi. This edition is published by arrangement with
the agency of People's Literature Publishing House and China National
Publications Import and Export (Group) Corporation.
Translation copyright © 2020 Alex Woodend.

FLAME TREE PRESS
6 Melbray Mews, London, SW6 3NS, UK
flametreepress.com

Distribution and warehouse:
Baker & Taylor Publisher Services (BTPS)
30 Amberwood Parkway, Ashland, OH 44805
btpubservices.com

Publisher's Note: This is a work of fiction. Names, characters, places, and
incidents are a product of the author's imagination. Locales and public names
are sometimes used for atmospheric purposes. Any resemblance to actual
people, living or dead, or to businesses, companies, events, institutions, or
locales is completely coincidental.

In order to retain the author's voice, we have followed his original intentions
in each story regarding style and punctuation. Any inconsistency or variation
among the stories is a result of that and is intentional.

Thanks to the Flame Tree Press team, including:
Taylor Bentley, Frances Bodiam, Federica Ciaravella, Don D'Auria,
Chris Herbert, Josie Karani, Molly Rosevear, Will Rough, Mike Spender,
Cat Taylor, Maria Tissot, Nick Wells, Gillian Whitaker.

Front cover image: *Seeing Red* © Polly Rose Morris 2020.
The font families used are Avenir and Bembo.

Flame Tree Press is an imprint of Flame Tree Publishing Ltd
flametreepublishing.com

A copy of the CIP data for this book is available from the British Library
and the Library of Congress.

HB ISBN: 978-1-78758-278-1
PB ISBN: 978-1-78758-276-7
ebook ISBN: 978-1-78758-279-8

Printed in the UK at Clays, Suffolk

A YI

TWO LIVES
Tales of Life, Love & Crime

Translated by
Alex Woodend

FLAME TREE PRESS
London & New York

CONTENTS

TWO LIVES

1

The low point in Zhou Lingtong's life occurred in his 26th year. At 26 some of his classmates had children, and some had graduated college a few years ago and were teaching high school, while Zhou Lingtong was still studying for the college entrance exam. Then after taking it again, Zhou Lingtong disappeared. He waited a long time for the results then secretly trudged back to campus. There wild grass grew long in cracks in the cement, terribly long, and a corner of the white paper on the wall hung down as if dozing. Zhou Lingtong smoothed the paper out and read the names one by one. When he came to his own name he couldn't help but cry out loud. When he was done crying he did not know how to go on. He wandered around – east, west – with no destination as the night grew dark like mud cruelly pouring, layer on layer, until he arrived at the river.

Its surface was full of light. From the fields he could hear all kinds of bugs having meetings. Zhou Lingtong walked straight into the cold. When he was nearly up to his neck the sound of a girl's voice came from the grass: Lingtong, what are you doing?

Bathing, Zhou Lingtong said. Then he hunched over and swam away. When he emerged from the water he saw only a figure carrying a laundry pail, dwindling into the distance. Then a flash of lightning streaked through the sky, lighting up the mountain summit. Zhou Lingtong took a breath and went ashore. Dripping with water, he headed for the summit alone.

At the summit, there was a temple called Longquan, which was built in the late Qing dynasty. When Zhou Lingtong arrived, the paint-chipped door was shut. He didn't knock but dropped straight to his knees. After a while, his kneecaps, numb and hurting, could no longer bear the weight of his useless body, so he lay prostrate on the ground. He stayed like that for a while. Many ghosts came behind him, many beds came before him. He lay down, lay down like a dog and fell dead asleep. Early the next morning, a rain shower swept over, waking Zhou Lingtong up. He straightened up and went back to his knees. When it got brighter the temple door squeaked open. The vitiligo-riddled monk, Deyong, walked out, head to the sky. When he saw a lump of breathing flesh kneeling in the doorway he jumped back into the door.

Zhou Lingtong slapped his head on the muddy water. What are you doing? Deyong said, pointing at him.

I want to become a monk, Zhou Lingtong said.

Deyong shouted, astonished, and shook his head violently. Zhou Lingtong went on: Master, I can't go on living. Please take me in.

Careful not to get his cloth shoes stained, Deyong made his way across the muddy ground to inspect Zhou Lingtong. He said: You're in the prime of life. Why do you want to become a monk?

Zhou Lingtong said: I've failed the college entrance exam eight years straight. I have nowhere else to go.

Hands behind his back, Deyong straightened up and said: In my opinion, you are still clouded by your senses and entangled in your obsessions. You won't make a Buddhist.

Zhou Lingtong suddenly clung to one of Deyong's legs, and said: Master, I'm dying. Dying.

Disgusting, Deyong said and pulled his leg free. Then he walked straight into the temple. Fuck your mother, Zhou Lingtong wanted to shout, but was completely drained. As the door squeaked shut he passed out. When he came to, bleary-eyed, it took him a long while before he managed to see the shriveled apple in front of him, which he then wolfed down. Then he caught sight of Deyong brandishing a huge door bolt at him. Away with you, Deyong said. Zhou Lingtong gathered himself up and began limply walking downhill. After walking some distance, he turned around and saw Deyong standing upright on the hilltop with a hand resting on the erect bolt. He gave another shout: Away.

2

At the foot of the mountain, Zhou Lingtong ate a whole field of potatoes the size of baby mice. Seeing a corner of the temple peeking out he got an itch to set it on fire, but it seemed too far away. After sitting for some time he decided to go home and give in to his parents. Then he saw a classy woman rolling down the paved road on a Phoenix bike. The woman, perm-headed and fair-skinned, threw him a disdainful glance.

What are you looking at? What the hell are you looking at? So what if I failed the exam eight years straight? Zhou Lingtong roared, raising his mudskipper face.

Psycho, said the woman, pedaling harder. It was an unnecessary move, riding down a slope. The chain came off, and with a clank, she hit the ground. Her palms were scraped, pearls of blood oozed out. She moaned in pain. Zhou Lingtong walked over and said: Who did you just call psycho?

Frowning, the woman didn't respond. Zhou Lingtong grabbed her by the collar, and said: Who did you just call psycho? The woman clenched her teeth, not answering. Zhou Lingtong began to drag her off the road and into the fields until they were behind a cluster of wormwood. The woman screamed for help, so Zhou Lingtong squeezed her throat. Her scream choked quiet. Zhou Lingtong started to peel off her clothes, letting her bare white flesh tremble and struggle a little. Then he pinned her down and thrust into her with brute force. Who did you just call psycho? he said.

This forced tears out of the woman. Meanwhile her head was scraping the rain-soaked soil beneath her, making a big mess. Zhou Lingtong said: Cunt, so tell me who the psycho is. In the distance came the sound of a car speeding down the paved road. Zhou Lingtong quickly covered the woman's mouth. The car slowed down as it neared the bike, and Zhou Lingtong's back broke out in sweat, but then it hauled away again. After quickly finishing up, Zhou Lingtong started to bind the woman's wrists and ankles with her clothes and gag her with her panties. He found the money in her shoes and walked back to the road. He took off the bike's chainguard, reattached the chain, and rode off. As he was pedaling through town, vendors of vegetables, meat, and steamed buns, restaurant owners, and radio listeners all turned to look at him, their mouths open, words not coming in time. Zhou Lingtong said, Do you want to say come quick and catch the rapist?

Zhou Lingtong passed through the town, panting, and continued on the run. It was an hour before the people and the police realized what had happened. By the time they hopped on two trucks, carrying guns and cleavers, to pursue him, Zhou Lingtong had already ditched the bike and boarded a ship. By the time they made phone calls to the police station on the other side of the river, Zhou Lingtong was on a truck heading farther away. The police station said the truck seemed to be a blue Liberation or a white Dongfeng. They couldn't say for sure.

Later, the pursuit team was streamlined. Three men, led by the head of the criminal investigation unit of the county public security bureau, headed for Nanjing to continue the chase. With their green Jeep parked at Nanjing station, the four watched the crowd flowing like a school of minnows, together in one direction, then in another, stupefying them.

3

Amid the flowing crowd, Zhou Lingtong felt desperate and afraid. He was overtaken by the persistent fear that a powerful hand would grip his shoulder, then a voice would say, Let's see you get away now. Every so often he looked back only to find workers, strangers to him, rushing about on their bikes. Days rolled on like this. Sometimes, Zhou Lingtong went toward the crowd, sometimes away from it. Then, exhausted from wandering about, he'd sit in the cool shade of a stone pillar and become a beggar. When the department store clock magnificently chimed, a ten-cent note floated through the air to him.

This desolate situation after a period of turbulence made Zhou Lingtong feel safe. His fear was gradually leaving him. But fear, like the tears shed that day, once gone, left one defenseless against reality. He was again overtaken by the plain, ugly truth: he'd failed the exam eight years straight and become a wanted rapist. With all hope gone, he had to kowtow and say thank you to passersby. And that was it: they walked on two legs, upright, while he was on all fours, a reptile. Two worlds.

After living as a beggar for only a few days, he noticed a problem. The concrete ground he slept on was damp and cold during the night, leaving him with severe back pain the next day. The healthy young man was helplessly sliding toward sickness and disability. The idle life of a beggar wore Zhou Lingtong out. Life was gloomy like he was slowly dying from blood loss. He thought he'd rather die right then; he'd already attempted suicide once anyway. Nevertheless, dying was not a pressing matter. Before then he'd eat soupy buns, Liuhe dry beef, and Baiyun pig feet. Having done so, he'd head to Mount Zijin to watch the sunrise. Only when he saw it would he bid farewell to this world. The *Nanjing Daily* he sat on read: For as far as I could see, mountains stretch away to meet the sky, green waves undulate toward the eyes. Amid endless mountains and countless woods, where can the tiny dust of the floating world rest?

The mountain, being three or four hundred meters high, was not difficult for Zhou Lingtong to climb. At one point, he followed a group of tourists and listened with a great interest as the guide introduced the area through a megaphone: What we are going to see is Sun Quan's grave; Sun Quan, or Zhongmou, was even admired by his enemies. At another point, he ran to an ancient tree and awkwardly put his arms around it. The tree had a huge top. He couldn't figure it out how a snake could shake it and make it rustle. Lost in thought, carefree, he suddenly caught sight of two men beating a lanky woman over the stone steps, which reminded him of the legendary Wu Song who pounded a ferocious tiger to death. Unsatisfied with the beating, they began to pull her curly hair.

When the woman turned to face him, Zhou Lingtong saw her nostrils and the corner of her mouth were bleeding. Her eyes flooded with despair, the kind of despair fish on a chopping block might show when at the very last moment their eyes meet the butcher's knife. Feeling a stab of pain at something they shared, Zhou Lingtong suddenly decided what he should live for. He thought he was going to die anyway, but it was worth it to trade his life for someone else's, so he grabbed a rock and ran toward them. Though those Nanjing men were terribly abusive toward the woman, seeing someone charging at them with a rock, roaring, they left her alone immediately, and ran straight into the primordial forest.

Zhou Lingtong came over to help the woman up, and after several attempts, the woman managed to stand in her high heels. The woman, horse-faced, eyes unusually small, ears and nostrils huge, was a horrible sight. After a short while, several young men in suits ran over. Some shoved Zhou Lingtong aside and took hold of the woman. Others ran to the edge of the forest, standing on tiptoe, observing. As Zhou Lingtong stood, stupefied, the woman was being escorted away, leaving behind indistinct groans.

Then she stopped and asked: Got a pen and paper? Her escorts presented them right away. She jotted down a phone number, and beckoned Zhou Lingtong. She said: Thank you, If you need anything in Beijing, call me. Zhou Lingtong scurried over, took the paper, and mumbled thanks but thought to himself, You wouldn't help me. For you, it's just a matter of a meal. City types are all like this. They immediately forget what they've promised.

Zhou Lingtong came back to his senses and headed for the peak. He ran up until there was no one around and sat down to sleep. He planned to sleep until dawn, watch the sunrise, and find a way to kill himself.

4

When the sun hung low over the horizon, like a huge red ping-pong ball, Zhou Lingtong woke up, his body prickly and itchy from insects running wild all over him. When the sun was high in the sky, he let out three roars to summon his courage and set about looking for a supple vine. A supple vine was hard to find. After he found one, he went in search of the right tree, not too big, not too small. With everything ready, he gripped the looped vine with both hands and pulled himself up. As he was about to put his neck inside the loop, he saw four people in green police uniforms coming over from the far end of the path. One of them said in a bossy tone, I told you to find us a guide. You just wouldn't listen. You said you'd been here once, but you've still managed to get us lost.

Zhou Lingtong listened and thought, Isn't that an Eshan accent? Tumbling to the ground, he looked around for an escape route, but there was none. At that moment the head of the criminal investigation unit cried out: Zhou Lingtong, let's see you get away now. Hearing each word clearly, Zhou Lingtong froze right there, watching the four men coming to besiege him, panting like jackals. The leader reached out his hairy arms, trying to grab him. As he was about to succeed Zhou Lingtong hardened himself and rolled down the hill. Countless little flowers, yellow and pink, and big patches of green grass started to spin, retreating toward the sky. He kept rolling down until a mound got in his way. He got up, head still spinning, and before the spinning stopped, a bullet thudded against the stone beside him, and bounced off.

Zhou Lingtong leaped behind a bush, where he could see the police coming down, hand in hand. Like a lunatic, he dashed into the darkness. He ran until there were only trees around, sunbeams slanting through leaves, insects humming out of sight. Then the pain kicked in; his left pinky toe was broken. Not daring to cry out loud, he screwed his eyes shut, letting tears trickle down. He was very sad. The sadder he got, the stronger his hatred became.

The monk's bolt, the classy woman's disdainful look, the leader's bullet made him go on living. He returned to bustling Nanjing. During the day he had his head down, begging. He slept awhile in the evening, then emerged in the alleyways after midnight, waiting with a brick for lone passersby. First he'd slap the brick on the person's shoulder, and say: Give me your money. The person would dig out ten-yuan notes, five-yuan notes, and change. Then he would say: Run. The person would run right away.

After some of these guerilla war games, Zhou Lingtong battled to Zhenjiang, Wuxi, Suzhou. When he was convinced that he'd shaken the pursuit team off, he decided to settle down on the street as a beggar and endure whatever life had to offer. To his surprise, Suzhou was under Hygienic Cities evaluation and vagrants were often rounded up in trucks and put into shelters. This put Zhou Lingtong in a dire situation again. That day the beggars at the far end of the street suddenly jumped to their feet, immediately followed by the rest, all fleeing. Ravenous, Zhou Lingtong couldn't make it far before he tumbled over. A uniformed young man rushed over and grabbed his arm. He had long thought about the scenario. If he were put into the shelter and sent back to his hometown he'd be sent straight to jail. With a rape and resisting arrest to his name, he could be shot. So he made a sudden snap at the man's wrist, biting through his sleeve and injuring his wrist. Then he dashed off down the lane. When he reached the end he turned back to see seven or eight uniformed men rushing toward him. He made haste again and turned down an alley. Having run in circles for a while, and with no one in sight, he flipped up the lid of a dumpster and squeezed in. He didn't come out until it got dark. Moonlight shone upon the stone road. The walls stood tall and formidable, warding him off. He plodded along miserably, feeling cold and hungry, tortured and frightened. He felt the world, vast as it was, offered no place for a person as insignificant as him. To console himself he began to recite a poem: When you hoist the sails to cross the sea, you will ride the winds and cleave the waves. You will ride the winds and cleave the waves, when you hoist the sails to cross the sea.

He recited it all the way to a corner shop at the end of the lane. Under the light bulb, he saw six words: long distance calls, domestic and international. He dug all his money out and piled it up. Then he took out the paper from Mount Zijin and dialed the number. The phone went beep, beep, beep for a while – no one answered. He wondered what she could possibly do to help him. *She may just say thank you, or politely lecture me with clichés like, There's always hope in life, don't give up, young man.* He asked the shop owner: Do you charge if it doesn't connect? The shop owner scornfully waved a hand in disgust.

Just then, a voice in the receiver said, Hello?

Zhou Lingtong said: It's me.

The woman said: Who are you?

Zhou Lingtong said: The one with the rock on Mount Zijin.

The woman said: Ah, my lifesaver. How have you been lately?

Zhou Lingtong burst into tears and said: Miss, I can't go on living.

The woman said: Why can't you go on living?

Zhou Lingtong said: I'm about to starve to death.

The woman said: Where are you now?

Zhou Lingtong said: In Suzhou. He tilted his head and wiped away the tears to read the street sign and said: I'll be in the dumpster beside the second electric pole north of Changrui Lane.

Wait for me right there. Don't move, the woman said and hung up.

5

After paying for the phone call and a biscuit, all of Zhou Lingtong's property was gone. He reclined on the dumpster and felt his throat grow bigger and bigger, stronger and stronger. He could hardly control his urge to swallow the biscuit whole. Hand trembling, he reached his lips toward the biscuit and licked it. His lips began to tremble, then his whole body did. The licking went on for a long time until only crumbs were left. Then he felt sorrow. The little biscuit was like bait, luring the big, fat, hungry monster out of him. He dug into the dumpster and found radishes. He started eating the leaves. When he got to something that couldn't be chewed he pulled it out – a plastic bag.

The night was cool and breezy. In the air he could still hear the sound of her hanging up. *Click.* The voice of the living person cut off, his connection disappeared. The woman would take her shower, go to bed, and pretend that she had forgotten all about it when she woke up.

But he also knew he had to wait. In fact, he had no other options but to wait. He pushed open the steel box, shoved the filth aside, and fell asleep in the stench. He woke several times in the middle of the night and clambered out. In the lane was only the wind leaping down the houses' roofs and darting over the stone road. The corner store's light was out too; there was nothing.

At dawn Zhou Lingtong faintly heard the dumpster being kicked. Not trusting his hearing, he went back to sleep. As he was slipping into a deeper slumber, he suddenly got up. Zhou Lingtong clambered out of the dumpster and looked around the lane. But there was still nothing. Rubbing his eyes, he looked again and saw a lanky figure walking past the corner shop.

Is that you? Zhou Lingtong shouted. The other stopped. Zhou Lingtong shouted again: It's me. The other turned around. Zhou Lingtong continued to shout: Rock, rock.

The woman walked over to him and said: It's me.

Zhou Lingtong felt as if a string of firecrackers went off at once in his heart. Bleary-eyed, he saw a black bag reach toward him. Inside were the things he'd always wanted: roast duck, ham, bread…endless food and Coca-Cola. He snatched the bag, tried to tear the packets open with his hands but failed, so he ripped them with his teeth, which worked. He began to eat ferociously with both hands. When his throat was clogged with pieces of bone he force-swallowed them down.

Zhou Lingtong finished the food and shook the bag. There was nothing. He glanced up at the woman. The woman shook her head. As they stared blankly at each other the woman tapped one of her high heels on the road and said they should go. Zhou Lingtong rose obediently. Before setting off the woman bent over to pick up that black genuine leather bag and carefully toss it onto the dumpster.

Zhou Lingtong wanted to say thank you, but couldn't get the words out. He followed her out of the lane and into the street where a worker was sweeping the ground with a bamboo broom. The rustling sound gave him the uncanny feeling of entering the world of ghosts. Zhou Lingtong knew that in his world, there were people with kidney problems, so there were those who tricked people into drinking, got them drunk, gave them an anesthetic, and cut out their kidney while they were still alive. Zhou Lingtong looked at the rear silhouette of the unknown woman and felt suspicious. But he also figured dying is just dying. He had long been dead; at least he was full now.

The woman led him all the way to a hotel. At the entrance, there was a guard in a red woolen uniform. He first bowed to the elegant-looking woman, then to the ragged, stinking Zhou Lingtong. At that moment Zhou Lingtong knew he was hers. After checking in, the woman led Zhou Lingtong to a room. She ran a hot bath, tested the temperature, and said: You have three hours to wash up.

Zhou Lingtong looked in the mirror: a ghost. He jumped in the bath and scrubbed himself hard. The water turned completely black, then it turned completely white. Again he scrutinized himself in the mirror: looking like a human now. He repeated this process several times until there was nothing left to wash. Only then did he realize he had nothing to wear. He ran to the door and listened. There was no sound outside. He gently opened the door a crack and saw a pile of clean underwear, a shirt, and pants in the doorway.

Zhou Lingtong got dressed, took a deep breath, and stepped onto the fluffy carpet. The strong morning sun shone like a projector on the woman, leaving a shadow on the white bedding.

The woman was facing the sunlight, smoking a cigarette. Her long, soft fingers tapped ashes into the trash can like a pianist's. At that moment, Zhou Lingtong could see her warmth, misty, forming layer by layer from her elegant back and bare upper arms, and suddenly broke into tears. He fell to his knees and said: I love you. I love you, Mom.

6

At 26, Zhou Lingtong also went from the bottom to the very top. That Beijing woman, Zhang Xina, who represented an impossible utopia, an impossible Bodhisattva, absolutely let Zhou Lingtong hold her hand, bite her tongue and became the guardian angel of his money and life.

For a long time Zhou Lingtong kept his beggar's instinct. When he went with Zhang Xina to Beijing he gripped her hand, afraid she would run away. Even with his penis inside her he didn't feel secure. Not till the day when Zhang Xina couldn't help but lick it like an ice pop did he completely relax physically and psychologically. He caressed her hair and said, Don't, babe, don't do that.

The first time they paid a visit to Zhang Xina's father, Zhou Lingtong was a bit nervous. He just perched on the edge of the leather sofa, not daring to meet the formidable eyes across from him. Having observed Zhou Lingtong for a long while, the old man held up his tea mug, took a few gulps and asked, Where you from, little Zhou?

Zhou Lingtong blushed and said: Anhui.

The old man waved a hand and said: I already knew that. I'm asking if you're from the city or the country.

Zhou Lingtong felt a little insulted, said softly, From the mountains.

The old man said: Speak up. Where?

The mountains, Zhou Lingtong shouted, humiliated. Then he heard a clap. The old man began to laugh. The laughter made Zhou Lingtong's whole body tremble, then suddenly the laughter stopped. The old man said: The mountains. I really like mountain folk. Down to earth. Then the laughter started all over again. Zhou Lingtong also started to laugh.

At dinner, the old man pressured Zhou Lingtong into drinking a lot. When he saw his face turn red the old man patted his shoulder and said: Down to earth.

After dinner, Zhou Lingtong thought he shouldn't stay long and started looking for an excuse to leave. Meanwhile, the old man went to the sofa, made a phone call, slowly spoke a few sentences, and hung up. The old man looked at cautious Zhou Lingtong, said, Come here, son-in-law, I'll give you a company to run.

Those were the words Zhou Lingtong wrote over and over in his general manager's office: Come here, son-in-law, I'll give you a company to run. Things were that unimaginable. Yesterday he was in the dumpster with plastic bags and dead rats, and now he had his feet up on a giant, glossy mahogany desk – twinkling, swaying.

Later, the company opened a branch in Malaysia. The first time Zhou Lingtong went there he checked into a hotel and asked a trusted assistant to make some calls. Soon prostitutes from England, France, Germany, Russia, America, Japan, Italy, and Austria came to his room. They bowed at once, smiling, then said in Chinese: Hello boss.

Zhou Lingtong pointed at them, counting, and said: Back then you guys were the eight allies that invaded my country's capital, Beijing. Now I'm going to set you straight. He spoke sternly. The eight girls looked at each other, not understanding his Chinese, and laughed loudly. They quickly took off his polished leather shoes and creased trousers, pulled the thing out, and tasted it one at a time. Soon the fluid was coaxed out. Zhou Lingtong got flustered and said, Really not fucking worth it.

For eight years Zhou Lingtong's life rolled along smoothly and peacefully. But one day as he was leaving his office he saw several men barging in, calling Lingtong, Lingtong. Security couldn't hold them back. He recognized their Eshan accent, panicked, and shouted: I have a gun too.

The leader grinned and said: It's not that, not just that. You just got slandered back then.

Zhou Lingtong took another look at them. They were all smiling flatteringly. Only then did he relax and wave for them to sit. After sitting and talking a little he understood they worked in Eshan's Beijing office and wanted someone to pull strings to get Eshan's status changed from county to city. Zhou Lingtong dismissed the idea, saying he had no sway. The director and deputy director immediately understood and said, Someone claimed you raped someone – what rape? Where's the evidence? We were after the wrong person.

Zhou Lingtong just offered them good tea, then offered them good alcohol, but didn't answer. A few days later, the head of the county criminal investigation unit, now Deputy Secretary of the Eshan County Political and Legal Committee, hurried over behind the head of the county, patted his chest and made a note that finally made things clear.

When Zhou Lingtong was drunk, he shook the deputy secretary's shoulders and said, You were a good shot back then. The deputy secretary turned white and changed the subject: You and I are related on your mother's side. I'm just thinking about everything Auntie and Uncle went through.

Zhou Lingtong thought, *What the hell kind of relative are you?* but didn't want to seem unfilial so instead asked, How are my mom and dad?

Not long after you left they died, the deputy secretary said sorrowfully. Zhou Lingtong looked around, stunned, picked up a napkin, and rubbed it back and forth a dozen times till his eyes were red. Everyone flocked around him: Don't cry, don't cry, it's been years. Only then would you say Zhou Lingtong began to cry.

7

Having fled his hometown eight full years ago, Zhou Lingtong returned for the first time. He did not take a plane or a train. He asked the driver to go slow in the Lincoln limousine with him and Zhang Xina in the back. When the car was a kilometer from the Eshan border he saw the secretary of the Eshan City Party Committee and the mayor waiting respectfully at the roadside, a throng of local officials and a fleet of Santanas behind them.

In the city proper were red banners on every building and red inflatable arches at the entrance to every street to celebrate the upgrade in status from county to city. Hydrogen balloons floated in the sky, firecracker residue carpeted the ground, Eshan citizens flooded the streets and lined up outside the public toilets. As the convoy went by countless hands reached for the jet-black limousine, ignoring the police cars honking at them to get out of the way. Zhou Lingtong sat in the limousine in his suit and leather shoes and watched pairs of bulging eyes rush toward him. They couldn't see him, but he could see them, see right in their hearts.

After attending some meetings in the city, giving some speeches,

Zhou Lingtong got sick of it and figured he'd just go tend the grave in his hometown and then go back to Beijing and never come back.

His wife was having a migraine, so Zhou Lingtong went alone in the county head's car to Zhou Village in Toushan Town. He handed a stack of red envelopes filled with money to the village head to distribute among the villagers for him. Then he went to look for his parents' grave. He looked a long time. Everyone bashfully said it was the one without a stone. Zhou Lingtong said, Oh, then tossed some cash to a couple cousins to take care of it.

After a few cups of Gushao baijiu at lunch, Zhou Lingtong left Zhou Village. Halfway back, he suddenly thought of something and asked the driver to head for the mountain. The 2000 Santana reached the foot in 15 minutes. Zhou Lingtong got out of the car and looked at the paved ramp and dry potato field, sighing, overcome by emotion. Then he told the driver, I'm going up the mountain to burn some incense. The driver wanted to go with him, but he refused – going alone was more sincere.

Zhou Lingtong was nastier than eight years before. Though he was fatter, he walked faster like he was burning with anxiety, in a hurry to find something. Only when he was soaked in sweat and discarded his jacket did he reach the summit. He stood where he'd knelt eight years before, in a patch of shade, looking at the dilapidated Longquan Temple. The temple door was shut. Wisps of steam rose through the tiled roof. Zhou Lingtong went and pounded on the door, shouting: I'm back.

The voice from behind the door answered, Coming, coming. Zhou Lingtong thought it sounded familiar but couldn't think of who it was. When the door squeaked open he couldn't help but take a few steps back. The monk's reaction was similar. He stumbled and fell on his butt. Zhou Lingtong watched the bald monk fall in his long robe, string of prayer beads around his neck.

Somehow he and the monk looked exactly the same.

Zhou Lingtong started to open his mouth, and the monk opened his mouth too. Zhou Lingtong let him speak first. The monk put his palms together and said, Amitabha. When the voice came, strange mold grew over the familiar face until finally they were completely different. The monk was the monk. Zhou Lingtong was Zhou Lingtong. The humble was humble. The noble was noble.

Zhou Lingtong relaxed and asked meanly, Where's Deyong?

My master passed away 8 years ago, the monk said then nodded and bowed. When he raised his head, his eyes gleamed with unconcealable envy. Zhou Lingtong tried swinging his Rolex hand to the right – the eyes followed it, swinging right. Zhou Lingtong said, Come touch it. The monk, embarrassed, came and touched it all over.

Zhou Lingtong said: What did Deyong say when he was dying?

The monk said: He cursed me. He said the temple could only feed one mouth. Me coming made him starve to death.

ATTIC

Thanks to Ms. C for the embryo of this story.

For 10 years Zhu Dan answered countless pointless phone calls from Mother. The only one she ignored was a warning about avoiding her own death. She was on her way to her parents' home, the afternoon sun making the face of the building shine. There were swallows and cicadas but no wind, like a panicked ghost town. Her mother was shuffling madly in a pair of slippers right toward her. The moment she glimpsed her, Mother turned down an alley. She stopped the shout rushing to her lips, sensing the other had not seen her. No need to make a fuss.

The second person she ran into was the owner of Sheyuan Restaurant. He was squatting by the bridge, plucking a chicken. The restaurant had more than 10 years of history. After nightfall, he and his wife would pour the swill into the city moat. He was a craven but excitable fatty. He threw a glance at Zhu Dan, but she ignored him. When she was a few meters past him, she cursed, as always: "Die sonless."

"What?"

"Die sonless."

"I'm not the only one dumping trash in this river, everyone does."

"Do it one more time if you dare. Do it."

"Fine."

He held up the red plastic tub and threw the feathery water into the river. Then one by one, he tossed down the rotten vegetable roots. But she'd already arrived home. For 10 years, every time they met she cursed him and listened to his pushback but he never got retribution.

As he said, he would dump trash into the moat if he had any, and if he didn't, he'd make some.

For a long time all that had been left of the river was a stagnant trickle. The swampy riverbed overgrown with weeds gave off the abhorrent stench of excrement, swill, pads, dead animals, and even dead babies. A secretary of the county party committee once convened a meeting to state that the river, being the eyes of the city, mother river, must be restored without delay. Zhu Dan was thrilled at the time, but as soon as the assessment was done the project was abandoned. It would have required 1.5 million yuan.

★   ★   ★

Ten years prior, the Zhus built their house by the river because it was the main route to the city for the farmers of the eight nearby villages and towns. Just before the house was completed, Mother had a quarrel with the contractors from Fujian, because the stairway to the attic was narrow and steep. "What good is it?" Mother said. "I won't pay for it. If you think it's a bad deal tear it down." Being no match for Mother, the contractor quickly finished the house. A day later he came back with a trowel and said: "If you live through the year, I'll take your last name." At the time Zhu Dan's father was standing in front of him. He looked stupefied.

Father was a genial person. Geniality made him offer to name the contractor's son and made him unable to stop his wife's unjust behavior. It was almost Spring Festival. Apparently waiting until after Daughter's wedding, and apparently in order to make clear that as a man he felt ashamed about those Fujian contractors, he left a fish basket, fishing tackle, and cigarettes he hadn't finished smoking at the river on the outskirts, and went to another world.

The smell of spent firecrackers from the wedding hadn't completely left when new firecrackers were lit again. Guests again poured in, tidying up, making arrangements, eating, drinking, jostling like a flock of penguins. Facing the sky, Zhu Dan cried aloud. A few times she nearly passed out. Women took out their handkerchiefs, now and then wiping the tears rolling down her face. When the women had all dispersed, her crying continued like it was a shield or something worth indulging in.

Since Father's death, Zhu Dan, already a wife, went to her parents' home at noon every day for lunch to keep Mother company. You could also say it was a duty Mother made her perform. She and her elder brother Zhu Wei had been under Mother's control since they were little. "Don't think about leaving me," Mother often said but then would add, "It's all for your sake, isn't it?"

The control bore two fruits:

Zhu Wei was an idler, Zhu Dan a nervous wreck.

Zhu Wei knew he could do nothing and Mother would still protect him, so he just let her take care of everything. He quit high school his sophomore year and was forced to work in the police traffic division as a temporary worker before going pro some years later. Mother bought him a house and let him marry the movie ticket seller he was secretly in love with. He was responsible only for getting fat. At a young age he puffed up like bread. Back home he'd sprawl on the sofa and say: "You're nagging me again. What's there to nag about? Can't you just leave me alone?" Zhu Dan knew whatever she did, Mother wouldn't be satisfied. Life was filled with choices of one kind or another, from whether or not to join the Party to what vegetable to buy, all of which terrified her. When she had to make a choice she did so covertly, reassuring herself all the while that Mother had no idea.

"Everybody gets married sooner or later. I've had my eye on that young man for six months," Mother said one day. It was already decided, but Mother pretended she was discussing it with her. Of course, when she showed slight hesitation, Mother scolded her loudly. "You know what, a lot of people are introducing girls to him. Who do you think you are?" Later, Mother took her to the county police chief's house. There was sitting a fair-skinned young man who worked in the township government and whose father was the vice-secretary of the county Political and Legal Affairs Committee.

After the elders left, he kept his head down, rubbing his hands. Zhu Dan said, "I recognize you."

"How?"

"I just do."

Leaving, she heard the police chief ask the other in a low voice, "What do you think?"

"I have no objections. It depends on her."

Soon they got engaged. Trying on her wedding dress, Zhu Dan showed unusual satisfaction with herself as a woman. In front of the mirror, she turned this way and that, over and over. "What do you think?" Mother asked. She suddenly bowed her head, weeping.

"Not satisfied?"

"No."

"Then why the tears?"

"Happy tears maybe." Zhu Dan gave an ugly smile. Mother did some more sleuthing afterward and was sure Daughter was satisfied. But as the wedding banquet approached things suddenly changed. Zhu Dan went numb. It became a shadow weighing on the hearts of the two families. A few months after the wedding, unable to tolerate it any more, Mother-in-law came to the Zhu house in a rage and said to Mother: "I know you're a tough woman. But I have to say this today. There's something wrong with Dandan."

"What could possibly be wrong with her?"

"She won't have marital relations."

Mother shouted that it wasn't possible but felt completely crushed. "If Father passing away made Dandan sad we understand, but she can't be sad so long. If it's that Dandan despises Xiaopeng, we won't be ashamed. I won't tell anyone, but if it continues, they'd better separate, better sooner than later," Mother-in-law said. Mother thought of the misfortune that affected two generations of women in her own family, fearing frigidness could be passed down. After she married the good Zhu Qingmo, they had marital relations no more than three times a year, all at his constant requesting and pleading. The first time she pushed and shoved, almost breaking his penis.

When Zhu Dan came home Mother said: "All women have to do it. It's women's fate." Zhu Dan lowered her head, scooped food. Mother went on with uncharacteristic sorrow: "Just lie there and let the man poke, be good."

"I know."

"Take it, and it's over."

Later, after talking with Mother-in-law, Mother knew that Daughter vomited every time after marital relations – even once in bed. Though Mother-in-law said no more, Mother felt utterly disgraced. Mother frightened and coaxed daughter, studied *A Must-Read For Newlyweds* with her, made her eat cistanche and placenta, but there were no obvious results. Mother felt helpless and turned to a confidant for help. It so happened this sister-in-law, who seemed concerned when she was listening, rapturously told others about it afterward. Soon the whole town knew. Unable to stand the looks, Zhu Dan's husband, Chen Xiaopeng, had an affair with an intern at the agricultural school. Though the evidence was unequivocal, and the circumstances awful, Zhu Dan and Mother dared not make a scene. But the girl came to the Zhu house and called them out. Mother went and slapped her three times and got pushed to the ground. Mother called the police chief to take the girl away and lock her up a good 24 hours.

As it turned out, Mother was right to choose this husband for Zhu Dan. Though he never enjoyed a single night with her and was constantly urged to get a divorce, he guarded their marriage like a gentleman. During holidays he would come to the Zhu house, one arm full of presents, the other holding Zhu Dan's hand. He went with the Zhus to worship their ancestors and sided with the family on many things. In public he was agreeable. People had seen so many men who turned their noses up at them. Because he was powerful but unpretentious, they were unusually friendly with him. While Mother liked him at first sight, she found her own son, Zhu Wei, a disappointment. And she continued to regard him with great affection. Mother was grateful he attended to the interests of the two families rather than his own.

When Zhu Dan gave birth to a baby boy, Mother was relieved.

Being 1.57 meters tall and 40 kg, giving birth to a six-pound three-ounce son for the Chens nearly depleted her – it was enough wasn't it? Mother-in-law had been concerned about male heirs, not sex. Since she had gotten one, the family, off balance, attained balance, even more balance than families who love each other from the start. The three women reached a tacit understanding that as long as Chen Xiaopeng didn't bring a woman home, everything was good. They arranged among themselves roles and responsibilities for the newborn:

Mom, Grandma, Grandma;

breastfeeding, changing diapers, putting him to sleep.

But once the breastfeeding period was over, Zhu Dan went numb again, not only numb but also scared. Sometimes, she would suddenly become possessed in her seat, pressing her breasts, panting, forehead breaking out in sweat. "What's the matter with you, Dandan?" Zhu Dan stood up, grabbing a bag to go. "What are you doing?" Mother asked.

"Going home."

"Isn't this your home?"

She suddenly stopped.

"What's this about?"

"I am going to die," she said irritably, then added, "I won't die. It's just I felt a bit unwell all of a sudden."

This symptom came every few days, or a few times a day. Mother asked questions but found nothing. She got insomnia and thought she heard the sound of a man pacing upstairs. He went back and forth a few times, then the sound stopped. Mother thought there was nothing to be afraid of. She was a good person. So she felt her way upstairs. When she switched on the light on the landing, she didn't see anyone in the attic. In the corner lay the furniture she and Zhu Qingmo bought when they were first married and a four-post bed.

"Old Zhu, Old Zhu," she called several times, but no one responded.

Mother didn't dare sleep, so she turned up the television, which disturbed her all night. The next day she hired a maid to live with her. When the fuzzy-lipped maid began to snore in the living room,

Mother finally felt at ease. Later she took Zhu Dan to worship their ancestors' graves and burn incense in the temple. Though the stomping never came back, Daughter's panic continued.

Once, Daughter seemed to make up her mind and walked into the kitchen mumbling to herself. Mother asked: "What are you doing here, Dandan?" She went numb again and shook her head violently.

"Why'd you come to the kitchen?"

"I don't know."

"Don't be afraid, Dandan. If there's something bothering you, tell Mom." Mother's tone softened. Zhu Dan tossed a pained look at her, and dropped her gaze. "Don't be afraid, child. Just tell me. Whatever it is, I won't blame you." But Zhu Dan just walked back to the living room. Mother turned off the gas stove, walked over, uncharacteristically took Daughter's hand and said: "How can I get you cured if you don't speak. If there's a disease, we cure the disease. If it's in the body, we cure the body. If it's in the heart, we cure the heart. Every woman has a disease of one kind or another. You're not the only one."

"It's fine. I mean, I even gave birth to a child."

"Right, even gave birth to a child. This means you have no problems."

"Even got the next generation."

"That's right. Don't think too much. The more you think, the more you can't think straight."

Mother said no more. Later she went to Mother-in-law, and Mother-in-law found Chen Xiaopeng, and said to him, "Don't fool around anymore. You're disgracing us." Mother said, "Don't blame Xiaopeng. They're husband and wife. Husband and wife should look after each other."

"I know."

Chen Xiaopeng was a passable husband ever since, or at least appeared to be. He saw Zhu Dan off and picked her up, put his arm around her shoulders at night. But the latter did not improve at all. She took Alprazolam and Prozac, but she just didn't seem to get any better.

Then one day, Mother took her to the provincial capital to see a psychiatrist. The psychiatrist said: "Breathe deeply." Zhu Dan breathed deeply a few minutes, and sure enough felt dizzy, unsteady.

"Do you feel like you're dying?"

"Yes."

"Afraid of dying?"

"Yes."

"Before you die, do one thing for me. Put your hands behind your back, squat down, and jump forward."

Zhu Dan was a bit confused. Mother said: "He asked you, so do it." Zhu Dan put her hands behind her back, squatted down, and stiffly took a small leap forward like a frog. This made the psychiatrist laugh out loud. He said: "Do you think someone dying could still long jump? Have you seen it?" Mother joined in the laughter. Zhu Dan looked at Mother and laughed too. "There's nothing wrong with you," the psychiatrist said.

"Right, she's always been skittish. Doctor, please give us some medicine," Mother said.

"Hell no. I'm telling you, the problem with your daughter is that she keeps implicating herself. When she feels uncomfortable, for example short of breath, a tight chest – these are such common things – she immediately thinks they are signs of death then gets panicked. The more panicked she gets the more she feels she might die soon, if not why such panic? Dying my ass, can dying people long jump?"

Mother thought this over a few days; when she saw Zhu Dan she'd viciously say: "Dying my ass." Daughter would immediately bow her head. This only worked a couple of weeks. Sometimes walking and seeing no one was around, Zhu Dan would hunch over and take a leap. Gradually this became compulsive.

★　　★　　★

As her condition continued pain turned into boredom, boredom into numbness, slowly becoming a constant part of life. Only on the day of her retirement, seeing the bleakness in everything, Mother suddenly realized that Daughter had grown old more completely than herself. She hadn't noticed the changes from one day to the next. But that day it was like she hadn't seen her in years. She was astounded to see a woman in her thirties with hair like snow-covered coal, so gray.

"Why don't you dye it?"

"It turns black at first. When the roots show up, they'll still be white and uglier."

You've still got a long time to live, Mother thought and started to follow Daughter. Daughter never looked around and swung her arms like a goose as she walked in silence. Mother was a bit disgusted. When she fell off a bike the first time she was learning to ride it, Daughter never rode a bike again. Other women rode electric scooters on the street. She was the only one walking, unable to carry anything with her, like an illiterate person. In the morning Daughter walked from home to work; at noon from work to her parents' home; at dusk from work to home. She paid no attention to anyone, and no one paid attention to her. Nobody knew what had been torturing her, or who.

Just let her be. One day Mother realized her following would be noticed sooner or later, so she walked back. She walked and wept then sat down on concrete stairs by the road, watching the bustle pass before her. These, those, the going, the coming, the joyful, the sorrowful would all be gone in a hundred years. She was in a daze for a long while then she glimpsed Daughter zip by in a taxi. She hesitated for a moment, then as if propelled by something, stumbled down to the road and grabbed a taxi. If Daughter was out on business she would have had a company car at her disposal. Mother called Daughter's office. As expected her colleague said she had left for her parents' house, which was in the opposite direction.

The car drove out of town, covered six, seven kilometers of paved road, turned onto a country road, drove through a big rapeseed field, bamboo grove, and pond, and arrived at a village called Erfangliu. She looked around and saw cottages in tight rows with tiled facades and aluminum window frames, three or four stories tall. The one Daughter went so familiarly into only had one story, gray brick walls and an old tiled roof. Daughter went through the gate as if dissolving into a black hole. Five or six minutes later she came out followed by an old couple. The old woman, short, smiling, regarded Daughter with sincerity. The old man was scrawny. All that was left of him was a big, dark-yellow face with the eyebrows, nostrils, and corners of the mouth pressed firmly down. He put his big left hand on the old woman's shoulder, straining to haul his right leg over the threshold.

"Dad, Mom, no need to see me off. Get some rest."

The old woman turned around and said, "Old man, Little Zhu is saying goodbye to you." Daughter walked up, took his paralyzed right hand, called him Dad, whispered softly. His face of tightly welded scrap iron suddenly relaxed and gave a wholehearted smile. "All right, all right," he said.

At noon Mother sat at the dining table and watched Daughter go upstairs. Like a mime, Daughter changed into slippers, put down her bag, went to the toilet, washed her hands, prepared vegetables, washed rice, and straightened up the tea table. She didn't ask Mother why she hadn't cooked, nor did she want to know where Maid was. How many years has she been lying to me? Mother thought. A tinge of terror flashed in her heart, but she sat still, face grim. Eventually Daughter gave a frightened look.

"Put the bowl down," Mother said.

Daughter's body shuddered. Then she heard Mother say, "Give that to me." She regarded the feather duster on the tea table with terror and confusion then passed it to her. Mother pointed at her and said, "Tell me, what have you been doing these years?"

"Haven't done anything."

"Nothing?"

"Nothing."

"Then why did you call that strokey old man Dad?"

"I didn't."

Mother swung the duster down at her, but she dodged it. "Kneel." Daughter moved around the table, hands on its edge, seemingly about to cry. "Kneel, you shit. I'm telling you to kneel." Daughter did not obey. Mother held up the duster and chased her around. Just then Zhu Wei returned, said: "Why are you trying to hit her? All you've done since we were kids is hit us. Haven't you hit us enough? Aren't you ashamed of yourself?" Then Mother said: "Ask her. Ask her if she has another man on the side."

"I don't."

"You don't?" Mother swung the duster down again, which Daughter took with her head up. Mother didn't hit her again, just saw daughter's nose twitching, weeping and sniffling as she grabbed her bag to leave. Mother grabbed her, and said: "You're not going anywhere. Come clean now. If you don't come clean 'cause you'd rather die then die here." Daughter couldn't break free, angrily said, "Isn't it all because of you?"

That was how Mother realized she had broken up a loving couple years ago. She thought she had just given Daughter a warning, but it had unintentionally broken them up. She once lectured Daughter for no apparent reason: "You have to think it through when you're in love. You only have one life, which like money, if spent on an impulse, is gone for good. You tend to be rash, and like sweet talk. Just remember if you're not careful with your life, your life won't be kind to you." Later Zhu Dan's cousins brought men home, each elegantly dressed and polite. "Look at them, either wealthy or have parents who are officials, an honor to have them," Mother said.

Zhu Dan thought Mother already knew. For three years, she'd been in a secret relationship with a classmate. After he retired from the army, he came to work in his relative's battery factory as director of sales. Though people called him Director Liu, which sounded nice, he was, in the end, a rural resident. "But regardless it was my own choice. I decided. I couldn't have no feelings," Zhu Dan said. "Now I think if I'd stayed with him things would be a bit harder but better than now. Now I'm not a human or a ghost."

"Why didn't you say this back then?"

"How could I?"

"You just try to go against me in everything. Think about it. If I died, didn't exist, didn't interfere, would you still want him? Would you be willing to spend your whole life with a man like that?"

"At least it'd be better than now."

Zhu Wei interrupted: "I understand what you're thinking, Dandan. But the ruling party is always at a disadvantage. Once the opposing party takes power, you understand it's even worse than the predecessor. Politics is not reliable, neither are men. I don't think you could have stayed with that man."

"It's not like that," Zhu Dan said.

That was how they learned about the terrible night Zhu Dan had gone through. Only two weeks before her wedding. Mother was on business, Father took the chance to travel and accompanied her. Big Brother was in the hospital taking care of his wife. She was left alone in their big new house. Like a rabbit she locked the door as soon as she got home and tried to reassure herself that her boyfriend Liu Guohua had no idea about her upcoming wedding. But the latter heard about it at a party. "Your woman took engagement photos with some other guy."

The looks put a lot of pressure on Liu Guohua, driving him to do something reckless. "Let it go," a friend said.

"Whatever."

He grabbed a Mongolian blade and headed for the Zhu house. Rumor had it that people at the party all panicked. Apart from one, who thought it over and called the police, the rest fled home on their motorcycles. The officer on duty said: "Verbal threats aren't considered crimes."

"Will it be if he kills someone?"

"Theoretically speaking, yes."

That special forces veteran, Liu Guohua, 1.8 meters tall, walked all the way to the moat in a rage, howling for a long time like a wild wolf. All the lights around went out, and the one in the Zhu house hesitantly turned off. At that point, Liu Guohua's strength was completely depleted. He threw his palms against the security door and began sobbing. "Dandan, open the door. My heart hurts like hell."

Over these two hours, Zhu Dan's head buzzed incessantly. She felt there was no way to shake it. The discontent and agony of her life gushed up like she was being flogged by countless whips or cornered by a ferocious tiger slapping its sharp paws against the fragile bars between them. She wanted to bang her head against the wall or have a gun aimed at her temple and shoot a bullet in it. She wanted lucidity, the kind that chases darkness away. "I was about to lose my mind," she told Mother. "I didn't know what to do." She opened the door. Liu Guohua tumbled in and hugged her legs. Besides crying, he just kept asking: "Why?"

"My mom disapproves. I've tried to persuade her for years. No use. She disapproves."

"Then do you still love me?"

"Don't know."

"Don't know. You don't know." Liu Guohua slapped the table, tears rolling down his face. "Obviously, you don't want me anymore. You despise me."

"There's nothing I can do."

Then she added, "I tried. Sorry."

"You despise me."

"I don't."

"Then why are you marrying someone else?"

"Everyone gets married sooner or later. I'm not young anymore. Don't speak. Listen to me. I waited for you. You always said you'd make money. Where's your money? Where's your house? Do you expect me to live in Erfangliu when we get married?"

It was the right moment to break up. "All right, all right," Liu Guohua repeated, waddling downstairs. She never thought it would be so easy. Covered in sweat, she followed him down. He slammed the door behind him, which was what she had hoped for. Then she pulled herself together, leaned against the doorframe and watched him leave to show that she wasn't heartless.

"No. I still love you." Liu Guohua came back out of the dark. "I can't stop myself from loving you. I can't live without you." Then he willfully acted like a lunatic. He found a new weapon which he used so smoothly that his weaknesses were hidden, and all his unreasonable demands were fulfilled.

"Either you die, I die, or we die together."

"You know what? You're scaring me." She shook her head.

"I don't care."

At first, it seemed like he was acting, then he lost himself in it. "Kill me. This is the only way. See, I can't help loving you." She went to the kitchen to get him water. When she came back and saw him dramatically return to his grief-stricken state she couldn't conceal her contempt at all. She said: "Drink some and stop the crazy talk." He drained the water, and looked at her with the silent, frightening eyes of an animal, and said: "Do you really love me or not?"

"You're drunk."

"Do you really love me or not? I'm asking you."

"No." Suddenly she entered an unusually calm state, said, "I'm telling you. I don't love you and never will. I won't love you in this life or in the next. Even if you try to kill me I'll say the same."

"You think I'm afraid to?" Liu Guohua said as he drew the knife.

"Come on then."

She shut her eyes. Waiting in dead silence, she felt like a martyr cloaked in a sense of autonomy she'd never felt before. She said, "Go ahead." Liu Guohua roared in despair and to show his attachment to her suddenly stabbed his palm.

"What are you doing?"

"Fuck off."

Like an excellent executor, that beast began to draw lines with the knife, first on his belly, then arms, knees and forehead. The lines appeared white at first, then red beads of blood oozed out from them. "What are you doing?"

"Fuck off."

While she was bewildered he shouted again, "Fuck off, you bitch."

She saw him put his left index finger on the table and chop it like a vegetable then say: "I want to make myself remember. I have all these scars just to remember to never be sweet with you. The scars will remind me that I hate you. From now on all we have is hatred.

"I swear one day I'll come back and set you straight. I might come back at any time, I might ruin you, and might ruin your parents, husband, or children. You might get killed or paralyzed, maybe one of you, maybe all of you. It's all up to me to choose one or all, to kill or to paralyze. I'll wait till your life is like a ripe peach then pick it. I'll do what I said. When the time comes and you beg I won't forgive you either. I swear with this finger that I'll never forgive you."

Then, he disappeared for good.

Zhu Dan went numb after that. Everyone knew she was panicked at her wedding. She turned back from time to time to look at the doorway or hide behind Father. Once the wedding ceremony was over she rushed to her room and locked herself in. At the time people thought she was just being shy. "I was afraid that he'd come throw acid," she told Mother. When the latter took her into her arms, she cried out loud, "Since the child was born, I've been afraid he'd suddenly show up, snatch the child, and drop him to his death. These years he's been like a steel plate jammed in my head, keeping me from relaxing. Mom, it's like I'm standing in an isolated temple, the sounds of hooves everywhere in the rain. I turn around and around, no idea where the danger is coming from. I'm afraid."

"Don't be afraid. I'll save you. I'm here to save you. Has he come?"

"No. He disappeared. For a time, I thought he was bluffing, and time would change everything. Time could lessen his anger. I even thought the threat was a joke. The joke was the purpose, he used it to punish me. This country has laws after all. He terrified me, terrified me to the point of being unable to live my life. He got what he wanted. But just when I was thinking this he had someone deliver me a package. Inside was a plastic bag dripping clear butter, a moldy finger inside. It was the one he chopped off.

"He will come back."

Though Mother wasn't completely convinced by the story, she nevertheless furiously summoned her relatives in town. They all hurried to Erfangliu Village. "Liu Guohua? Where's Liu Guohua?" they shouted as they arrived. The young and middle-aged were all at work. They found the little house. As usual, the old man put his left hand on the old woman's shoulder and came out, dragging his crippled right leg.

"Who do you think you are?" Mother said. Drool suddenly ran out of the old man's mouth as he said, "What are you talking about?"

"She said Guohua has wronged her daughter," the old woman said then turned to Mother. "Please be fair. Our family has been farmers for generations, and I know you're townspeople. Though they didn't get married, we never blamed the girl. Not the same class."

"Never blamed? Your son said he'll kill my daughter."

"Impossible. My son's so well-behaved."

"How is it impossible?" Mother got mad, screamed. A big tear rolled down from the old man's eyes. Fighting the tears, he said: "You should go away."

"We're not going anywhere. I've come all this way to tell you the Zhu family has never been afraid of anyone."

"Go."

"I'm here to tell you my daughter came to your house all these years, begging you, serving you so that your son would change his mind and not harm her. Does she deserve it? Do you deserve it? What did you do to deserve her kindness?"

The old man got so angry he shakily took out a glass from his bag and threw it. It landed a meter away from Mother. The old woman started crying. "They must all be dead, no one's coming to help." Mother wasn't afraid of any villagers, just afraid the two would have a stroke. After some more bitter words she calmly got in the car and went right back to town. She found the police chief. The police chief immediately put Liu Guohua on the wanted list.

★　　★　　★

Two more years passed, smooth and calm. In her old age Mother suffered the loss of her toughness and fell into loneliness. She joined a qigong group and clapped vigorously every evening. One day she overexerted herself and came to an epiphany that the world was a cannibalistic world. From then on she was barely lucid. She also happened to be a born atheist, so she could control her outside appearance, keep others from noticing for a while. But insanity, like savory meat, tempted her to dig in willingly. The instant she stopped it would feel like countless ants were eating her heart.

Zhu Wei knew the situation and seldom came home. Unlike sons, daughters were a parent's down coat. Zhu Dan still came home every day. Mother began constantly hounding Maid with the suspicion of poisoning her. The fuzzy-lipped Maid was an illiterate country lady. She couldn't stand the humiliation and packed her bag to leave, but Zhu Dan stopped her and raised her salary by two hundred yuan. Zhu Dan said, "Auntie, you've served her for eight years, after all. Just treat her like a child and play with her." When Maid heard this her heart softened and later she might even joke: "Boss, you say I'm poisoning you, if I wanted to poison you I'd have done it long ago, wouldn't wait till now."

Mother said: "Hmph, you eat first. Better if you poison yourself to death first."

Maid drank big bowls of alcohol, and ate big pieces of meat. Then they played games in the house day and night. Mother always hid money scribbled with strange patterns in the corners when Maid wasn't paying attention and pretended to forget them. Maid would gather them up and give them back to her. Mother would wet her fingers and count each one; if any were missing, she'd shout: "I've always known you were lying scum. You're so greedy you'd even steal such a small amount of money from your boss." Then Maid would look for the money with a flashlight and soon found the five-yuan note.

One day, Mother suddenly came up with the idea that Maid had lodged her country relatives in the house. Restless, she started searching everywhere. She searched from the first to the fourth floor and found nobody, so she went up to the attic. The stairway to the attic was narrow and steep. She protected her head with one hand and climbed the stairs. As soon as she unlocked the door she saw a curtain of dust, a big crow flapping its wings as it flew out the window.

There were two wooden chests lying there, sealed with tape, and wrapped in rope, perfectly coated in crimson paint. It seemed to her they were waiting to be moved elsewhere but were left behind like poor children. Mother wiped the dust off the lid and thought, "I've never organized the things in these two chests."

She went downstairs, looking for Maid, but couldn't find her, so she went back with scissors. She cut the ropes, tore the tape, and opened the lid. A moldy stench nearly knocked her over. What she saw stunned her. First she thought Maid's father was a butcher but then decided the bones didn't belong to animals. She was amused. At the time, her feeble mind was absorbed by two memories swimming toward each other. Once they met she understood everything.

Bones...Daughter.

But just then from downstairs came Maid's hearty laughter. How can you still laugh? What have you done? You killed someone, hid the corpse here, framed the Zhu family! She stumbled downstairs, leafed through her notebook, and found the telephone numbers of Zhu Wei and Zhu Dan. Zhu Wei didn't answer the phone. Zhu Dan didn't answer either. The second time she called, Zhu Dan's phone was off. Mother walked downstairs through increasing terror and into the sunny afternoon. She walked across the city moat and down Zhishu Lane, nearly running into Daughter before turning onto a side street. *This is a serious matter.* She took the shortcut to the police station. Meanwhile, Zhu Dan came to the end of Zhishu Lane, crossed the river, and bickered with the owner of Sheyuan Restaurant, before going home. The lazy maid quickly appeared, knitting in hand, and said with a fawning smile, "Dandan's back?"

"How's my mom today?"

"Same as always."

"I saw her run out."

"Don't worry. She'll run back. She's afraid I'll steal her stuff."

Not too long after, Mother shouted, "Stay where you are" as she ran up, followed by a group of policemen. There was something fishy about this: the police had never paid attention to reports from madmen, but the old police chief was Mother's lifelong sweetheart. They had been close since middle school, never held hands, hugged, or kissed. They were like the closest siblings in the world. He'd always been tolerant and accommodating of her domineering personality. That day when she kneeled down, sobbing, the police chief teared up. "If it's a game, I'm playing the game with you. I'll be stepping down soon anyway." He brought a policeman and two trainees with him to the Zhu house. Going up the stairs, they saw Zhu Dan rushing down, sweating all over, so they hugged the corner and let her go down first.

"What's going on, Dandan?" he asked.

"Nothing."

She forced a bitter smile and leaned against the handrail as she glided down the stairs. Ten minutes later, as the four policemen investigated the scene, they suddenly understood everything. They rushed downstairs; one of them even drew his gun. They saw Zhu Dan had just reached the bridge. In 10 minutes she had only walked 10 meters. Her footsteps seemed held back by giant globs of chewing gum. She seemed to be hopelessly fleeing in a nightmare.

"We found Liu Guohua's business card in the victim's suit. He was your first love wasn't he?"

"Yes."

"How many years has he been dead?"

"Ten years."

It is said the moment Zhu Dan was handcuffed Mother suddenly became lucid. She threw herself between Daughter and the police, howling very normal phrases: "It was me who did it, it was me who did it."

"It was me," Zhu Dan said.

The police chief easily pulled Mother away like a rabbit. She then hugged his legs tightly, and shouted: "I killed him. I stabbed him to death, chopped him up. I chopped him up into pulp."

"It was me," Zhu Dan said.

After that Mother seemed lost in an endless, thick fog, never to be normal again. She once waited outside the prison, without knowing she was waiting for her daughter. Maid took her there. When the prison van drove by, through the barred window, Zhu Dan saw Mother smiling at her – a rather nonchalant and detached smile as if they weren't related by blood at all. The incident caused a stir in the town, even the entire county. Every day a crowd came to the door of the Zhu house, hands in pockets, and looked up to examine it. Some even pulled out cameras to take pictures. Liu Guohua's relatives had long since covered the facade with white placards reading *Blood for Blood*; they hung a banner too. Mother was like one of the onlookers, curiously observing every detail. Sometimes she would stroke the white paper and, using the vague knowledge in her memory, read a few characters.

The case was heard in the county's people's court. Surprisingly, Chen Xiaopeng suddenly ignored his mother's disapproval and tapped all of his and his father's political and legal connections to exonerate Zhu Dan. He hired a nationally renowned lawyer who pushed the trial to an impasse with a single sentence:

"The deceased committed suicide by ingesting a large quantity of sleeping pills. After he passed out my client felt for his breath and found he was already dead. In a panic, my client dragged the body beneath the bed and concealed it. Later, out of fear, my client dismembered the body in an attempt to move it elsewhere. In accordance with current criminal law, her act constitutes corpse desecration, but at the time, the law had no regulations regarding this crime."

"Bullshit."

Liu's relatives, who had already made trouble, clamored in the public gallery. The judge slammed the gavel and asked with the compassion of an elder: "Defendant, is that the case?"

Zhu Dan turned her head and saw Liu's mother was gripping a

white handkerchief over her nose and mouth and crying. She cried and cried, then pinched the tip of her nose with her right thumb and index finger, and blew her nose loudly. Then, head swaying, she went on crying. On her lap lay the portrait of the deceased adorned with white flowers. Sensing Zhu Dan was looking at her, she stood up and shouted: "That nasty woman came to my house these last years, either lied that my son was in Guangdong or Fujian, and said he wouldn't come back until he earned enough money to buy a whole county. You lied to us so long. You liar."

Zhu Dan said, "Sorry."

Then she turned back and said to the judge: "Now I breathe steadily, feel relaxed. The doctor was right. When I turn and face the fear, the fear just is what it is."

Later, the prosecutor requested permission to exhibit evidence, and the two chests of white bones were carried into the court; one of the lower limbs wore a leather shoe. The majority of the bones were chopped open before the public, the cracks like blooming morning glories. "We may gather how much force was exerted at the time," the prosecutor said.

"This proves nothing. You have no proof this is a murder case," the lawyer said.

"We have eight incriminating statements from the defendant."

"I think we should rely mainly upon evidence rather than oral confessions."

"Defendant, what do you think?" the judge again said with compassion. His attitude caused an uproar in the public gallery. The group of Liu's family and friends slapped the table, railing against the unfairness of the trial. But then they heard Zhu Dan say: "If I say I killed him, you'll find me guilty. If I say I didn't kill him, it'd be very hard to determine I killed him. Now I intend to say I killed him.

"You know there is a scratch on my house's floor, it's from his leather shoe scraping. You can see there is a scrape on his sole. When I strangled him, his feet scraped the floor out of instinct. After he drank the tea I mixed with sleeping pills, he fell asleep. Then I pulled out the telephone cord, looped it around his neck, and strangled him to death. His head leaned against my ribs on this side, this rib still hurts.

"I killed him. There is nothing else to say. You Lius want compensation, I've saved up these years, saved seventy thousand, as repayment to you."

After she finished a hush fell over the court. Liu's mother held up the portrait. She wanted to say something but didn't know what, so she just shook it. "Don't make me see him. Disgusting," Zhu Dan said. Prior to her execution, she wrote a brief letter saying: *Xiaopeng, You must believe I love you. I've always loved you. Our son is yours.*

In prison, she was constantly kneeling and she desperately kept her eyes shut like a firing squad was on the way but in the end was executed by lethal injection.

SPRING

1

"Take a good look." The young man stared a long while, suddenly covered his bulging mouth, hunched forward, and ran away. I even saw tears fall diagonally to the ground. The guard raised his eyebrows and ogled me. *I told you not to look, what's there to look at.* He pulled up the shroud, and she was just an outline.

I walked right out of the funeral parlor. The young man squatting by the road had vomited thoroughly, but his fingers still pressed the ground, arms shaking incessantly. I patted him, and he turned, tears streaming endlessly like blood from a wound. I completely understood this pain. "Don't be sad. You came and saw her," I said.

The corners of his mouth moved.

I helped him up, and slowly we walked. He turned and looked at the funeral parlor. "I'm taking you to wash your mouth," I said. "Just to wash your mouth." We ended up at a corner store. I let him lean on the counter while I paid for a bottle of mineral water. I said: "Let's go out and wash your mouth." But he seemed asleep. I yanked him, he reacted, followed me out. His gargling was very mechanical like an old man chewing food. A dusty Santana raced over, passing us with a sudden swerve, almost brushing against us.

It stopped at the entrance to the funeral parlor.

A man in his forties squeezed out of the driver's side and hurried into the funeral parlor. He wore a yellow jacket and baggy jeans that only an obese person would wear, a bunch of keys dangling at his hip. Soon a short woman got out of the back seat. She wore a black robe, black pants, black leather flats, a piece of black gauze was pinned to her right sleeve, another piece clenched in her hand. She carried a black bag over her shoulder, ran after the man like a duck.

"Let's go inside," the young man said when it was almost dusk. I felt that for a long time he didn't know what had happened in the world. He didn't know a girl had died and didn't know why he came. But when he finally woke up, he started crying again. I walked him into the funeral parlor. The temperature was very low, the hall cool, the guard mopping the cement floor. He said to us: "I really don't understand."

"It's been a long day for you," I said.

The guard had been mopping a clean spot back and forth for a while. He gestured for us to take the seats on the east side. I could then see the man and the woman sitting on the west. Unlike us – the young man was leaning against me mumbling nonsense – they sat two seats apart, arguing nonstop. They argued more and more bitterly, and their droning voices hovered overhead, making everyone dizzy.

"Stop arguing." The guard thumped the mop on the floor. The man raised his head, and the woman pulled out a handkerchief, sobbing. When she got too excited, she stopped and blew her nose with her thumb and index finger. The guard bowed and continued to mop. I guessed the excessive boredom had so wrecked him that he saw the floor as some kind of piece of art he had to wipe over and over.

I saw the man was wearing a crimson T-shirt underneath, a gold ring on one hand. He sometimes rubbed his hair, sometimes scratched himself. He picked up the black gauze from the empty seat and pinned it to his sleeve then turned and said to the woman: "I'm wearing it now. I know she isn't just your daughter, she's mine too." Then he looked at his watch and asked: "How much longer will it take?" The guard was still mopping the floor. "Do you really have to rush?" the woman said. The man glared at her, fierce light in his eyes. *If we weren't here, I'd have long beat you to death.* But after some silence passed, the man's eyes turned red and snot hung from his nose.

"I only have one daughter." Sobbing, he dug out a pack of

cigarettes from his pocket, shook one cigarette out and held it between his lips. Then he dug out a lighter and lit the cigarette. He smoked and coughed, tears dripping on the cigarette.

"Please put out your cigarette," the guard said.

"Put it out where?" The man scanned the floor, the chairs, and the cupboard where various cremation urns were kept. The guard was still mopping the floor and seemed about to finish. The man tilted his head, regarding him somberly, then he took a long drag.

"I told you, no smoking in public places." Even the young man in my arms was startled by the roar. The guard stormed over.

"If it's not allowed, it's not allowed. Can't you be more polite?"

"Don't you understand smoking isn't allowed in public places?"

"Can't you just be more polite? Did I offend you?"

"You didn't offend me."

The guard walked up to him and continued: "You haven't offended me. If you want to smoke, could you please smoke outside?" The man rubbed his eyes, holding the cigarette in the other hand. The ash, which had grown quite long, dropped to the floor. The guard's eyes followed it to the floor.

"I'm just smoking, what are you gonna do?" the man said.

"What am I gonna do?"

Probably to his own surprise, the guard gave the man a slap in the face. Now things got heated. The man straightened up, and grabbed the scrawny guard. "You know what, they're cremating my only daughter. I only have one daughter, and she's being cremated. Do you understand?" He pounded the guard in the face. "Do you understand?"

The guard screamed and shouted. The man took a look around him, then threw the guard to the floor, and gave him a kick. "Fuck you." Then he took off the keychain and strode to the door. First I heard the Santana chirp, then the car door slam shut, and the engine start up, then came the sound of the tires scraping hard against the ground as the car turned. He fled.

The woman sat shaking. When the guard got up, she said: "I

have nothing to do with him. He hasn't been my husband for a long time." The guard glared at her, and she shrank back. Then a worker in a white flame-retardant uniform rushed over with a shovel. She repeated those words. The shovel was smoking. Imagine, it must have been burning red when first taken out. Now it was gray. I remember seeing a blob trickle down the shovel, the way plastics trickle when burned. Then the woman made another remark. It was this remark that woke up the young man. He stood up straight, kept clenching his fists, then he walked toward the crematorium at the end of the hall. Before I rushed ahead, he had dropped to his knees and spread out his arms, babbling. I guessed he was begging them not to turn the body of the dead girl into nothing. Though it was inevitable, I still wished they wouldn't burn her up real fast.

His face looked like water kept being poured over it. I wanted to fucking cry too. That woman, that is the deceased's mother, said: "Spring, it was your dad who made you this way."

She kept mumbling: "I'm always the one who cleaned up the mess. Not one time did I not. What responsibility did you ever take for your daughter? Where was your responsibility? You sized me up, you knew I was a softie, you knew when you ditched Spring by the road, I'd no doubt go carry her back. You were so heartless. Spring wasn't just my child. Weren't you supposed to take some responsibility as a father? Why did I have to clean up your mess every single time? Was I born your servant?"

When the guard and the worker scurried to their boss's office, the mother, who wore a black blouse, black pants, black leather shoes, and black gauze like a black duck, walked out clumsily but resolutely. She followed the footsteps of her ex-husband. She walked and said: "I will not come back no matter what. I've had enough. I've long had enough. I've decided if you don't come back I won't come back. You think I will, I definitely won't. Let's see who comes back, who's more heartless. You leave her alone. I'll leave her alone too. Let's see who comes back."

2

He took out the letter of introduction of no more than 30 words. Judging by its format, the letter was originally addressed to the prison, but the addressee had been changed to the funeral parlor. Where it said REASON FOR VISIT, the police officer put a slash. "You'd better write something specific here, like, 'assisting investigation and interviews'". He looked troubled. "That's enough," the police officer said. "We've never issued an introduction letter like this."

He spent two days handling the matter. He called the journalists in his newspaper office, asking them to contact the journalists who covered the city's political and legal news and ask the latter to get in touch with their contacts in the local public security bureau. Each link further than the next. His fellow journalists promised to do it right away, but he waited from morning to afternoon. In the end, he broke into the office, and called their names.

"Can't you see I'm busy," one of them said.

"I just want hurry to there to see her, brother," he said more and more softly. "She's my girlfriend, my woman."

"Look, the sub-bureau will be off duty soon."

Waiting, he thought: If this doesn't work, pour petrol over the abandoned hearse at the corner of the parking lot. The only tire is flat anyway. The car is rusted inside and stuffed with damp wood sticks. Set them on fire to create smoke. When they rush over, slip into the funeral parlor. But this isn't a wise move. Just grab a club and knock them down one by one.

The first time he walked into the funeral parlor, the guard stopped him. "Look at you." He saw his shoes had left marks on the freshly mopped floor. "What are you doing?" the guard said.

"I come to see my woman. She died."

"How many days ago was she moved here?"

"Should be seven or eight days."

"Got your household registration?"

"No."

"Marriage certificate?"

"We're not married."

"What do you have to prove you're her boyfriend?"

"I'm her man."

"Then so am I." The guard continued: "You have to have a way to prove it."

"Why would I lie to you? I still haven't gotten to see her."

"Everyone says so, that they're the dead's relative or close friend. Don't you know the funeral parlor is also a place of business? You come when you want, leave when you want. Don't you think you should follow the rules?"

"Look, there's no one else here."

"Rules are rules."

"Please do me a favor."

"Why do I have to do you a favor? I work here, and this is what I do. I have to ensure the dead are not disturbed."

"She really is my woman."

"No one says otherwise."

You know what, in this world I only love her. If I can't see her, I can't go on living. If I can't, don't ever think you can. He took out two notes from his wallet and looked pleadingly at the guard. But the guard shoved his hands into his pants pockets and walked away without turning back. A while later, the guard came back with a mop and started to mop the floor under the young man's feet.

"I have no time to get sentimental with you," the guard said.

"I'm a journalist." He thought a long while and said, "I have the right to investigate the cause of her death."

"Didn't you just say you were her man?"

"I'm a journalist and also her man."

"Then your press card?"

"Didn't bring it."

"Go away."

He took out the introduction letter of no more than 30 words and handed it to me. "I didn't even know if this would work. I just stopped by to say goodbye to you. You're a good person."

"You have to rest first. You can rest at my place."

"I have no time."

"Let me go with you. I have nothing to do anyway."

I have to thank you. But it's better to do this myself. How can I express my rejection to you properly? I have to thank you. You are a good person. He seemed troubled. "I have to see her off anyway," I said then put my arm around his shoulders, walked toward the garage. I drove him toward the outskirts to the west. The afternoon sun came through the car window; he got drowsy. He slept very little. Even if he had time to sleep, there were probably various nightmares mingling in his mind. A short while later he woke up and asked: "Where are we?"

"Still a long way to go."

"I must have slept long."

Then he looked ahead vacantly. Finally a big smoking chimney came into view. "Right there," he said. And we drove to the funeral parlor beneath the chimney. In front of it was a cracked cement parking lot and a small flower bed with two rows of plastic flowerpots with plastic chrysanthemums inside.

The guard wore a uniform in the honor guard style, white from head to toe, including the leather shoes and gloves. Only his epaulettes and the decorative strips around his cuffs were red. He tapped the seams of his pants, looking at us as he walked over. The young man took out a pack of Chunghwa cigarettes and for a long time couldn't figure out how to open the seal. He wrinkled all the filters, said, "Have a cig, boss." The guard raised a hand to his lips, waved. "Don't smoke." *He really should die.*

"Read this please."

The guard took the letter, turned and studied it in the sunlight. Then the young man clenched his right fist and raised it to his chest. He was ready to give the guard a blow on the back of the head. I pulled his shirt, but it only made him angrier. He waited until the guard waved and said: "You know, I act according to the rules. I do what the rules require me to do."

I said, "Of course, of course."

We followed him inside. Before entering the guard said: "Wipe them clean." So we wiped our soles back and forth on the red doormat. Although the young man had been full of inner courage, as soon as he was inside the huge quiet hall, he became shaky, and sweat broke out all over his pale face.

The guard led us through the hall to the boss's office. A man with glasses was reading a newspaper. When the introduction letter was handed over to him, he signed it without reading it. Then we went back to the hall and walked out through the small door on the north-western side. At the end of the path was the crematorium. They say the incinerators there shimmer, are neatly arranged like bread ovens. The mortuary was halfway down the path to the crematorium, adjacent to cold storage on the left. "The refrigeration is broken. We tried to fix it but failed. So we have to burn her today no matter what. Gah, we'll have to cut the corpse open, otherwise it'll burst," the guard said.

The young man stopped, unable to walk on.

"You insisted on seeing it," the guard said.

The young man gasped, took several deep breaths, before managing to keep walking. The guard pushed open the frosted glass door; a pungent smell of formaldehyde rushed out. There were 10 or so iron beds inside. Some were covered with shrouds, showing the outline of the corpses. There was a ring of moss six inches high around the corners. *Where there are corpses vegetation flourishes*, I thought. The guard walked straight to one of the corpses. Like a magician he lifted a corner of the white shroud and said: "Do you really want to see it?"

The young man nodded seriously.

Slowly, the guard raised the shroud. Ah, it's still so disgusting to think of now. Spring lay there, swollen to twice her size, but her belly was shriveled, the opening in her shirt revealed rough stitch marks from the autopsy; the skin was one part brown, one part black, like tofu going moldy; only her face retained some slight traces of her former image, but her ears stretched out from her cheeks, eyeballs protruding, lips swollen and turned out, showing teeth like sharp stones. I twisted my face and closed my eyes in agony. I'd already vomited hard because of the corpse once. The young man kept standing stiffly. The guard asked him:

"You look?"

"Yes."

"Take a good look?"

"Yes."

3

I entered the apartment block where my home was. The elevator door opened at the fourth floor. A young man was squatting in the opposite corner. He met my gaze and wanted to say something, but I stopped him. I walked over, and opened the door of my home. I heard a slight rustle; it was him standing up. I turned to look. His lips opened again, again they closed, like a tent put up with difficulty suddenly falling to the ground.

"What's the matter?" I said.

"Are you Mr. Chen?"

"I don't feel well, and I won't give an interview to any of you." I shut the door. After a while, there was a knock on the door. I pulled the door open and shouted: "Enough, buddy, I said enough."

"I'm Spring's ex-boyfriend," he said.

"What?"

"I'm Spring's ex-boyfriend."

"What are you up to?"

"I'm wondering if she left anything here."

Helpless, he let the tears pour out. I was waiting for that thing called a sudden realization. *So this is the guy.* He said: "Really it's all because of me." But I didn't think so. He was supposed to have the dangerous look women like, and a cold, cruel temperament, but whether it was his face or his demeanor, he seemed too honest. Only the modest scar on his forehead seemed to indicate that he'd had a violent experience, but I prefer to believe he was the one who got beat up.

"Come in," I said.

He thanked me quickly and bent over to untie his shoelaces, but I stopped him. I went to the small bedroom to fetch Spring's belongings, found he was still at the door. "I read the news in the paper, so I came, couldn't believe she died," he said.

"It's been hyped up for a while. It was a suicide, but they have to say murder."

"I know."

"Spring was not some prostitute either."

"Mm, really I hurt her."

"Don't say that."

I thought I was, after all, friendly to people, and so softened my tone. "I haven't shown it to anyone outside. Take a seat." He bowed and took it. On the title page of *Lady of the Camellias*, there was the line:

Margaret feels sorry for Spring.

The moment he saw it, like a criminal facing ironclad evidence, he suddenly dropped his head. This was his handwriting from the old days, innocent, confident, and casual. Driven by love, he blindly believed the other was the one and only. Now he'd walked across the river of time and faced numerous consequences to be checked against his past promises and praises. In the journal he was about to open, every page had a big, nasty cross drawn in ballpoint pen, some to the point of being torn, as if making visible the hysterical actions of Spring that day. I walked into the kitchen to get water, while the young man kept leafing through the journal, finally held his head tightly, and broke into sobs. I saw his back slightly heave, then his shoulders, arms, and clothes clearly heaving, as if his whole body was participating in the crying.

Spring wrote:

I can't find anyone to talk to. I've thought of all the people I know, none are right. Maybe right is not the word, but no one is willing to listen to me. I'm dying. I'm dying but they keep asking: "What's the matter with you? Do you want some hot water?" You're not here too. Even if you were here, you would cruelly walk away. I can't trust you anymore. I'm sick and dying. I could die somewhere desolate where it rains for days on end. My corpse would be soaked through, but none of you would come. I'm not on your list. I deserve it. None of you sympathize with me. None, none, none of you care about me. Who the hell am I?

Other than this, the rest of the journal is gibberish from a patient with persecutory delusions. I'd long since ripped out the pages about me where she wrote how I seduced her deliberately – passing by, I brushed against her, hooked her chin with my finger, grabbed her privates with my hand, and so on. She slandered everyone.

"Never happened," I said.

I know. Lili knitted her eyebrows, and kept shaking her head. *You'd better rip them all out.*

I walked back to the living room with water. The young man raised his head, his eyelashes wet. "I have to go. I've bothered you enough."

"No problem."

"Can I take it?"

I nodded and put down the tea I'd prepared for him on the table and let him walk out. "If you need anything, you can come to me," I said.

"Mm," he answered quickly.

I shut the door, walked to the window, and waited until he appeared on the ground. He walked the wrong way, and it took him a long while to realize it and walk back. He held his head to the sky, arms hanging, and cried uninhibitedly. A few passersby stopped to look; he almost ran into one of them. I guessed even if someone spat in his face now, he wouldn't care; even if someone stabbed him in the chest, he'd still walk on. He'd have to cry for a long time for his sins.

Afterward, I was alone again. For a long time, I put a drink between my legs, and sat dully on the sofa. Morning left and afternoon came. When the gray thing pressed down from the sky, it got dark. Then an indistinct moan came from that small bedroom. Maybe just a cold, but Spring, like a seasoned old lady, was silent when her surroundings were silent. As soon as she heard footsteps, she quickly moaned again. When we were at the door, the moaning was even louder.

"What's wrong with you?" we asked as we walked in.

"I'm dying. Look, there's no color in my face," she wailed, tears tumbling out. *Cunning.* Lili looked at me. I nodded, and said: "Drink some hot water. I'll go get it." Afterward, we never stopped when passing the room, she just moaned in vain. Now she was dead, but I could still hear her like a weaver weaving her moans in the room.

"Enough." Drunk, I kicked the door open. There was just a small crimson mattress inside. I found a broom, and swept every corner. I shouted: "Enough, enough, stop your fucking moaning." She stopped. But when I looked down, she had floated elsewhere. I hurried to look, and she, like debris blown by breath, scattered silently away.

I called Lili and said: "I've never missed you so much." But she was still wrapped in sorrow. "Sell the house, I really can't keep going."

"Okay, after the New Year."

"Sell it as soon as possible. I've never been this bad."

"So you'll come back?"

"I won't."

I left the lights and TV on all night and more than ever looked forward to morning. During the day, I walked street after street, mimicking the sound, *um-ah, um-ah, um-ah.* But there was always a gravitational force pulling me back. Even with my back turned to the door of my house, I'd walk home backward. *Um-ah, um-ah, um-ah,* I mimicked, and was forced back like a donkey.

★　　★　　★

"Isn't that him?"

The guard pointed his finger over the young man's shoulder at me. The young man turned, his gaze hitting me like a club. Within a few days, his hair had become unkempt, face whitish, lips colorless, even his eyebrows graying. He looked like he'd been doing drugs for years, or staying up night after night playing mahjong, extremely exhausted physically but extremely excited mentally.

"I came here to say goodbye to you." He bowed to me.

"Is everything settled?"

"Not yet, I'm about to go see Spring."

"You haven't seen her?"

He clenched his fists and started to curse the funeral parlor guard. In fact, the fury of this decent man, *um-ah*, since it wasn't acted out, was expressed as nastily as he could verbally. He searched for the introduction letter in his bag, cursing.

4

The police didn't reply and summoned me into the conference room. Someone drew the curtain closed. The cameraman carried a video camera on his shoulder. The rear of the machine had a cable plugged into a speaker. Holding the speaker, the TV reporter recited the opening. "Was it suicide or murder? Death. That is certain. Welcome to Mysterious Situations."

"Can I leave?" I asked again.

"Wait. They'll probably ask you something." The police officer gazed at the video camera.

The boatman sat in a corner, his hands resting on his knees, eyes fixed straight ahead. I heard someone say, "Record first, record first," then the lighting man held the incandescent light up to the boatman. The latter's face froze immediately. The TV reporter walked over, grabbed the boatman's hand, and gave it a powerful shake. "Don't be nervous," he said and withdrew the hand. The boatman didn't know whether to close his fingers or to leave them apart, so he just let his hand hang in the air. When the interview finished he withdrew his hand and squeezed his clothes.

Then the TV reporter started to shake the cable. It was my turn. I panted. Nothing was more tormenting than the wait; I'd never experienced anything like this. When the TV reporter held the smoothed-out cable and walked toward me under the incandescent light following him, I stood up. He was like a commander exuding an authoritative air, armor clinking.

"No need to stand up," he said, smiling. I sat down. My face turned thoroughly red.

"Are you ready?"

"Yes."

"We all know the deceased lived in your home for a period."

"Yes."

"Who is she to you?"

"She was my wife's classmate."

"Why did she live in your home?"

"She was my wife's classmate, and they were very close. She was poor and couldn't afford a house. Maybe."

"What kind of person do you think she was?"

"She was friendly with people, and polite."

"Could you be more specific?"

"She was very decent."

"For example?"

"She was friendly with everyone."

He winked slightly at me. I said: "Ah, I never expected she would pass so early." He turned to the camera and made some comments, then he turned to me and said, "Thank you." He held my cold hand, but my sweat was pouring out.

"Can I go?" I walked over and asked the policeman.

"Wait, who knows what else there might be."

A while later, the forensic scientist pushed the door open. He tossed a blue file folder onto the table and put on a pair of white gloves. He was followed by a bunch of noisy newspaper reporters led by a short man wearing a red V-neck sweater. He nodded at his acquaintances, smiling hypocritically. Then, with a beastly, almost barbaric arrogance, he sat down across from the forensic scientist.

"Are you filming now?" the forensic scientist shouted at the cameraman.

"Can I?"

"Sure, why not?"

The forensic scientist shook his clothes, settled in his chair, pulled a picture from the folder, and said: "Look, there were mushroom-like bubbles under her nostrils, indicating death by drowning. This is the result of cold water getting into the respiratory tract and irritating the mucosa of the windpipe." Then he pulled out another picture showing Spring grasping muddy grass. "This is also an important indicator of death by drowning. We can at least eliminate the possibility that she was thrown into the water after being murdered. She died directly from drowning."

The dumpy journalist raised his hand.

"What is it?" the TV reporter asked him.

"May I ask some questions? I'm afraid I may slow down your shoot."

"No problem. They'll edit it," the forensic scientist said.

"All right then. The two pictures can't rule out murder. Death by drowning doesn't necessarily point to suicide. Someone may have pushed her into the water to kill her."

"That situation is quite rare."

"I've seen it in movies. Golden Triangle drug lords always push people into ponds to kill them."

"That's a movie."

"Movies come from life."

"Let me ask you this. If you were a murderer, would you push an adult into a river?"

"Why not? No trace left behind."

"Have you taken into account his swimming ability, his survival instinct, the depth of the water and the direction of the current? Have you ever considered that? What do you do if he doesn't die?"

"I'd take precautions."

"What precautions?"

"Tie his limbs together, or tie heavy objects to him."

"In that case, did you see any ropes or heavy objects?"

"Of course." The journalist put down the camera, pulled up a picture. "Look, her hands were tied together." The forensic scientist waved a hand. The journalist continued: "It's simple. If I'm trying to commit suicide, how do I tie my hands together?"

"This is not uncommon in suicide cases. You just haven't seen it." The forensic scientist gestured. "You can either ask someone for help, or make a rope loop by yourself first, and use your teeth to tighten the knot," he said, regarding the journalist mercifully as if wasn't he who was defenseless, rather the other had to take the final step and fall into the trap he himself had set. The journalist said, as he expected: "You can't rule out the possibility that someone tied her hands together and pushed her into the river." The forensic scientist clapped, and the police brought in the boatman.

"Ask him yourself," the forensic scientist said.

"Right, I was the one who tied her hands together," the boatman said.

"What?"

"I was the one who tied her."

"Why did you do that?"

"We all do that."

"You tie the hands of the corpse together?"

"Yes, that way we can pull it onshore."

"Can't you get it on board?"

"Bad luck."

The boatman added, "When I tied her, she had already died and bubbles were coming out her nose." The journalist took a big breath, and his chest puffed out. *I really want to stomp you to death, you old shit.* The forensic scientist walked over, smiling. He fished out a cigarette, tapping the cigarette pack with it, and said: "Writing news isn't writing novels. Right, little He?" Blushing, the journalist put the notebook away and said: "Don't I have a job to do?"

The cameraman gestured once again. The forensic scientist took two quick drags, squished the cigarette out, and sat back down. "I don't know if you have any idea about the width of the river?" He gestured. "Only this wide, roughly four to five meters. You swim a little. Well, let me put it like this, you paddle a little, and you reach the other side."

"Mm," the journalist said.

"Would be very hard to kill someone."

"Does that also mean the difficulty of suicide increases? Make the success rate of suicide low?"

"No, not the case for someone determined to commit suicide. Give him a small puddle, and he can drown himself. A person who is fed up with life can drown himself by sticking his face into the toilet. And there are people who manage to get water into their lungs lying drunk on a mountain trail after a heavy rain. All evidence shows that the party in this case attempted suicide. She drank pesticide first."

The forensic scientist took out the autopsy report:

"We've extracted prepared organic phosphorus from her body. She drank the pesticide voluntarily. This was the suicide method she'd intended to utilize. If someone fed her pesticide after killing her, since her metabolism had already stopped, we wouldn't be able to extract pesticide from her liver and other organs." The amber wine bottle, uncapped, was placed on the chair. The wine, mixed with DDVP, gave off a stench. The river, which hid fabric scraps, leftovers, used pads, black mud, and rotting dead cats and dogs, really stunk. The river flowed very slowly, carrying them and depositing them. Spring had drunk four bottles of wine. The fifth bottle was mixed with pesticide. Sitting on the roadside bench, she looked up at the dull night sky, then automatically grabbed the fifth bottle. She only took one sip then bent down vomiting. But she still took two more gulps to make sure she had ingested pesticide.

"She didn't drink much, not enough to kill her, but her body reacted violently." She held her head, walking limply. Her right leg swung right, and after it became the supporting leg, her left leg swung left. She swung a few steps forward, then a few steps in a row backward. She turned halfway, and continued to swing. Her head was the source of the swinging that made her body turn around. She felt sick and sweated profusely while turning around and around. After a while, she felt like she had entered a world of fog. The streetlamps, benches, and branches all became slightly darker shapes, some small, some big. She held her head tightly, panting.

"Her body had been damaged partially but not completely. She couldn't live and she couldn't die either — worse than dying." She was halfway between life and death. The human world was at the mouth of the well which gave out a faint, ironic glow. She had no strength to rise another inch. The bottom of the well where the infinite darkness dwelled was like a mother waving an encouraging handkerchief to her. *Jump, Jump down.* She considered it again and again: *In a flash, everything will finish, no more physical pain or mental torment. And if I don't decide now it will be too late. I'll be like a badly wounded wild pig caught in mud, twitching endlessly, horribly.*

"So she jumped into the river a few steps off. She no longer cared that it stunk so bad. This is very common in suicide cases. Many suicides give up their initial method of suicide in the end." Spring started to walk. She walked a long while, but as if in a nightmare, she couldn't move. She was anxious, frightened, and furious. In the end, she made out the rustle of the river. She climbed onto the floodwall, moaning, and plunged into the river. When she was falling down, everything in the world flashed clearly before her eyes like racing numbers. Everything veiled began to take shape — oh, she was about to have an epiphany. Then she was swallowed down by the river. The river, like icy blades all around, pierced her body and cut in and out of her thoughts.

"And here." The forensic scientist presented another picture, which showed Spring's bruised, scraped palms, the bones of her right index and middle fingers sticking out. "She was trying to climb onshore, to grab something, but in the end the only thing she could grab was the water grass." Spring reached the floodwall, her hands shaking incessantly. She had no more strength, not even enough to keep her body from falling back into the river. Her body was like a wild bull, pulling her cruelly the opposite way. Finally, she was like a lonely shell, falling back into the river. For a while, she stuck a hand or half her head out of the water, but then we could only see the slightly swelling water surface. Her face started to appear in the vast, dull night sky. The face of her soul lingered alone in the empty sky, watching her body sink deeper and deeper until it touched the bottom of the river like a weight, and stuck there. Then, the soul was gone too.

"Can we say she had a very strong desire to survive?" the TV reporter said.

"You may say the person eager to die had already died, but her body was still reacting out of instinct."

The forensic scientist lit a cigarette. The cameraman left with his machine. The crowd, which had been holding their breath, started to talk. The dumpy journalist walked over and said: "You can't prove she wasn't persuaded to drink the pesticide. She was drunk."

"Do you have any evidence?"

"No."

"Why do you bring it up if you don't have any evidence?"

"I still can't rule out the possibility of murder."

When the journalist walked back, he tugged at the nylon rope fastened around the boatman's waist. "None of my business." The boatman shook his head.

"You're fine."

"None of my business."

"Why didn't you tie one of her hands? Can't you pull her onshore with one hand tied?"

"It depends."

"Isn't it less troublesome tying one hand?"

"I have no idea. I'm going back."

The journalist scornfully let go of the rope. Then the policeman said: "Don't you have questions? The ex-landlord of the deceased is here." That bunch of journalists turned and stared at me at once like I was carrying some conspicuous weapon.

"I have things to do," I said.

"It'll just be a moment," one of them said. But the dumpy journalist said: "What's there to ask?" He walked off alone.

"We'll just keep you a moment." The rest kept following me. "Who is she to you?"

"She was my wife's classmate."

"Why did she live in your home?"

"She was my wife's classmate and was very close to my wife. She couldn't afford to rent a house."

"Did you know she was a hooker?"

"No."

"Really?"

"Really."

"Did any men come to your house for her?"

"No."

"Anybody call her?"

"No idea."

"How long did she live in your house?"

"Three months."

"Three months. How could you have no idea?"

"I really had no idea."

"You didn't even know she was a hooker?"

"She may not have been one back then."

"Then you didn't know she stole things?"

"No. I have to go."

"We only have this one question. Did she ever steal anything from you or anyone else?"

"I have no idea."

"Did you ever charge her rent?"

"No."

I walked on, and they, like parachutes tossed out of a plane, became farther and farther away. They said, "No rent charged. She probably paid with sex." I stopped immediately and pointed at them. "What did you just say?"

They threw up their hands, and looked at me mockingly.

"Let me tell you this. You keep calling her a prostitute. What about you? Aren't you a bunch of scum?" Sometimes anger made people eloquent. "Has it ever occurred to you that she is a human being, and has human dignity. She's already dead. Why are you still fussing about all these things?"

"It's an undeniable fact that she was a hooker. We just speak facts."

"Fuck your facts. You just choose the facts useful to you. Is there a single sentence in your reports that expresses sympathy and concern for her? You only care about the filthy minds of your readers. To ingratiate your readers, you sell the pitiful woman out. Is that the journalistic justice you've been bragging about? What's the difference between you and the terrorists? Aren't you the desperados of corrupt news reporting? Have you ever tried to understand her as a human being?"

"You have, so tell us about it."

"Fuck off."

I walked toward my car. But couldn't dampen my anger so I turned and roared: "With you everything is made into pornography. Pornography, pornography, pornography. Is there anything else in your minds except this? If it isn't pornography, you recklessly make something up. You have pens to write, and nobody cares about your outrageous lies. You're not afraid of retribution."

They laughed together. *Look at him. He's being so eloquent.* I got into my car, feeling much better. I felt if I lifted the steering wheel, the car would fly into the sky. But in a moment, my head started to buzz. I went to a gaming café. Gunshots rattled everywhere. I was bad at it, so I went to a bathhouse. Columns of water thudded against the floor, making the same rattling sound. So I went to a club. The club was good, as if there was something leading us, thump, thump, thump. It made my hand turn involuntarily, and as my head and shoulders turned, it made me turn the other way. Nobody told you how, you just knew yourself how. This way I had no time to pay attention to the maddening sound of *um-ah*.

Later, I stuffed my head into the breasts of a prostitute and said: "Just hold me like this for one night."

"No." She kept pressing my penis.

"Just hold my head like this, I beg you."

I put my arms around her waist and went on: "I'll give you two thousand yuan."

I went back to my apartment block the next day. The sun shone brightly, but I felt sick from fatigue. I parked my car at the entrance, and slammed the door. I saw that group of journalists waiting inside a car. *He's coming. He's coming.* They nudged the dumpy journalist in a V-neck sweater. He rolled down the car window and said: "Do not underestimate our ability to get things done."

"Fuck you."

I walked toward the little supermarket. I heard the car door slam shut and felt he was staring at my back like a jackal. He must have had one hand tucked in his pants pocket, letting the other dangle. With his eyes he said to his associates, *Watch me*, then sloppily walked over. Finally he patted my shoulder and said: "I've heard you and she had a pretty shady relationship."

"Who?"

"The deceased."

"I mean who told you that?"

"None of your business. Just tell me if it's true."

"Who slandered me like that?"

"This person, you know him, and he knows you." His hand motioned toward all the residents through the air. "Of course I know him too, though not for very long. But from my point of view, it's better to believe the party involved."

"It's not true."

"I'm doing this for you too." He looked at me. *You'd better think it over, what to write and how is up to me.*

"Fuck off."

I continued to head to the small supermarket. He walked over and slapped my car, said: "Don't you know you can't just park anywhere on the side of the road?" Then he said to the journalists: "He's just a regular resident who thinks he's a spokesman." After I paid and got out of the supermarket, he was still talking: "Don't you think you're acting very suspiciously?"

I wanted to give him a good slap, but I figured there was nothing else he could do.

5

The train finally pulled out silently like God gently moving a building block. A total of 15 coaches slid away in a moment, and I saw the empty platform across from me. It seemed to take Lili alone, its sole duty to take her away from me. I felt a kind of shattering loneliness. It seemed our family had fallen apart.

I grabbed a bite, bought the newly shelved morning and city papers, and sat in the station to read them one word at a time. They devoted a good deal of space to cover the latest developments in Spring's case, which were summed up by one of the headlines:

New Doubts Cast on Unsolved City Moat Case.

Dead Humiliated in Post-mortem Body Search.

They were based on the account of a KTV prostitute and peppered with comments. The prostitute went by the name Greeny, the one who wore a qipao and lipstick and was constantly chatting by the river. She was bold and outspoken, shoved aside her partners grabbing her, lifted her dress, walked to the journalist that had just been turned down by them, and said: "She was killed by them."

"Don't say that."

"Don't say what? If they haven't done anything against their conscience, why do they run away?"

"It's been a month."

"Exactly because of that, exactly." She found the qipao constricting, so she parted her legs and stood like a compass. "Come. I'll tell you everything I know. Don't stop me."

A platinum ring bought at Chow Sang Sang, worth about 1,500 yuan. Maomao couldn't wear it and asked: "Who'd you buy this for?"

"For you," Ma Yong said with a fake smile.

"Why didn't you take me to try it on? Did you know my ring size?"

"I had money with me, and I just bought it on a whim."

"Who would believe that?"

"Then forget about it. Give it to me."

"No, tell me the truth."

"Give it to me."

"Let me try it on." Now Spring walked over. Angrily, Maomao passed the ring to her and said: "Try it on."

"Go away," Ma Yong said.

"Let me try it on."

"Try it, come on try it."

"Don't cry, you're the one who stole the man from me. I never cried, why are you crying?"

Spring held it to the light. The moment the man tried to snatch it away, she turned and put it on her right ring finger. It fit perfectly, not too small, not too big. She gave the hand a shake, but the ring seemed to have grown there. "Take it off," Ma Yong shouted. Spring turned, saw his raised palm, said: "Slap me, slap me." Maomao was so furious she kept stomping her high heels.

"Slap me, just slap me. You said you would buy me this ring, but then you gave it to someone else." The slap came but not hard. "What the hell do you think you are?" Ma Yong said.

"I'm nothing. I just miss being sick, someone coming, making soup and giving a massage." Spring took off the ring. She threw

Maomao a glance and gave it back to her. "I just wore it for fun. He wouldn't buy me any rings and never took me to the jewelry shop to measure my finger size. I was just teasing you."

At least in this round, Spring's sisters thought she won beautifully. The ring was like a filthy thing ever since. Maomao couldn't put it on her finger, or in her heart but to provoke Spring, she always took it out and played with it. "What if you lose it?" someone said.

"So what, is it a big deal?"

But when she did lose it, she broke out in a sweat, frantically searching closets, counters, and KTV rooms. It was dim in the rooms so she got an emergency light and later used a broom handle to probe beneath the sofa. "If he finds out he'll beat me to death." She regarded her sisters. "I just don't know who could be such an awful bitch."

"Think carefully, when was the last time you saw it?"

She cursed, trying to remember. When Ma Yong came, she still couldn't come up with anything. "What's wrong?" he said. Head down, she mumbled. *Toilet. It must be the toilet. I went to the toilet, and then it was gone.*

"What the hell is wrong?" Ma Yong asked irritably.

"Spring stole my ring."

"Are you sure?"

"I remember seeing her when I came back from the toilet."

"Are you sure you saw her?"

"Eighty per cent it's her. No, a hundred."

"Spring," Ma Yong shouted.

"What's up?" Spring walked over.

"You took Maomao's ring?"

"No."

"I'll ask you one more time. Did you take it?"

"No."

"I'll give you a chance to give it back to me."

"I didn't take it, how can I give it back to you?"

"This is your last warning."

"I didn't take it."

"All right, everyone get in the dressing room. Get in now."

Ma Yong chased all of them like ducks into the changing room. He asked them to open their lockers and let Maomao check them one by one. Now in retrospect, it wasn't that Maomao had any evidence. She was just afraid and wanted to place the blame of losing the ring on someone else. She chose the one she hated the most. Spring started to tremble. When she couldn't find the silver thing in any of the lockers, Maomao shouted: "Strip off Spring's clothes. Search her."

Spring shrank and moved back to the wall. Maomao walked over and gave her a slap in the face. "I didn't steal your ring," Spring said. She shouldn't have said that. Maomao squatted down, pushed up Spring's top, and dug her hand into her bra, searching. "I didn't." Spring looked up, dazed, her breath weak like swaying silk.

"You didn't?" Maomao took the ring out of her bra. "What's this?"

"That's mine."

Maomao tried the ring on. It didn't fit. "Take a good look, whose ring is it?"

"Mine."

Maomao slapped her, and was about to slap her again, but Ma Yong pulled her away. Spring's eyes flickered with joy. But Ma Yong rolled up his sleeves, bent over, and grabbed her hair. Spring started to jump. Ma Yong hadn't held it right so he grabbed it again. He lifted her up, and pinned her head with his elbow, weighed her, then said, "Up," and in two or three steps ran to the other side. Spring's body followed her hair, and her hair followed the chunky arm tattooed with the dark-blue dragon to the other side then hit the wall. Fortunately, the wall was covered with heavy fabric, and made of slats, otherwise she would have died.

"Did you steal it?"

"I didn't."

Ma Yong switched his hands and grabbed her hair again then he repeatedly banged her head against the wall. "You psycho," Ma

Yong roared, but Spring still said: "You said you would never beat me. You said that."

"You're a fucking psycho. Ever since I met you you were a psycho."

Ma Yong was stubborn. We thought he would stop after a few slams, but he kept going and going. We pulled his arms back, but he used his remaining strength to bang her head one last time. The wall was dented, her neck crooked.

Because of that, many people thought some strange things that happened could be explained, such as a missing earring or five hundred yuan (in the blink of an eye) turning into three hundred. They suddenly understood everything. But I didn't think Spring was that kind of person. She did steal the ring, but it was nothing compared to stealing a man. You stole my man, and I stole your ring, isn't that fair? Besides, the ring was originally bought for me. Who's more shameless? Spring left that day.

I sat there until nine o'clock. Then I bought a bottle of beer. I grabbed the steering wheel in one hand, the beer in the other, and drove home. I saw passersby pointing at me and exclaiming in silence. Traffic policeman also looked confused. It would be better if I'd been arrested. I really couldn't manage my life.

I feel deeply asleep at home, until there was a knock at the door. It was someone from property management. "The public security sub-bureau called, asking you to be there at 2 p.m. this afternoon," he said.

"What is it?"

"He didn't say."

"Are you sure he asked for me?"

"Yes."

"Do you know whether it will be an inquiry or an interrogation?"

"I have no idea. You'd better hurry there."

"They must want to ask me for Spring's family's contact information," I said. "That must be it."

What right do they have? I sat down on the sofa, and kept changing channels. *What right do they have?* But in the end I went out with my car. At a crossroads I saw the sunshine was warm and seemed to cover the sidewalks with a glistening layer of water. Tree branches and leaves, all gilded, swayed brightly. This was what freedom looked like. You could escape right away, escape to somewhere far away. But still, I drove toward the sub-bureau. I told myself over and over: Inquiries target witnesses, victims, and knowledgeable parties. Interrogations target suspects. If I were considered a suspect, they wouldn't have called, they would have come knocked down my door.

After I drove into the courtyard of the sub-bureau, I didn't immediately open the car door. I was still thinking, had I done anything wrong in my life that I myself didn't know? Or had I ever offended someone? I waited until I was sure there wasn't any smell of alcohol on my breath, and I got out. I think I was afraid of the public security bureau itself, like someone hospitalized for the first time, whose head is crammed with legends of open bellies.

"It will be all right," I heard a man walking in circles in the corridor murmur. He was wearing a white vest, a white shirt, black pants, and sandals, with cracked mud between his toes. It was the boatman. He said to himself, "I just hauled her out under your orders, what's wrong with hauling?" I looked at him sideways, but he looked down, avoiding my eyes. I followed the instructions in the note, knocked, and opened an office door. A pale, fat policeman wearing a pair of glasses was sitting inside. "Sit down, sit down." He stood up with a natural kindness and poured me a glass of water. This reassured me greatly.

"Can I ask the reason why you wanted me?"

"Nothing serious. Just trying to figure something out about Spring."

"She was my wife's classmate."

"Why did she live in your house?"

"She was my wife's classmate and was very close to my wife. She was poor and couldn't afford to rent a house, so she lived in my house. Stayed three months."

"What kind of person do you think she was?"

"I can't say she was a good person, but at least she wasn't a bad one. She was very polite and rarely caused anyone trouble."

"Do you know what she did in the KTV?"

"I learned of it recently from newspapers."

"Did she say anything to you or your wife?"

"Like what?"

"Like someone hurt her."

"Never said that."

"Think back a little."

"Never."

"She didn't mention it when she lived in your house?"

"Never."

When it was done, he walked over and showed me the written record. I stuck out my right thumb, pressed it lightly on the inkpad, and left a fingerprint the size of a soybean on my signature. "Why does everyone leave such a small fingerprint? Is the public security bureau that scary?" he said but didn't ask me to do it again.

"Can I leave?" I said, scrubbing at my inky thumb.

"Heard you're a painter?"

"Just a hobby, no big deal."

"What do you think of this case? Take a seat."

"Nowadays, death is fucking humiliating." I was getting revenge for my prior timidity. "In any previous century, death was a private matter, a solemn curtain call. But now, you look now, it's become material for sensational news. You have no idea how many readers masturbate every day as they read the news about Spring."

"What you've said is very unusual."

"There's something even more unusual. There something I didn't believe before, but I believe now."

"What is it?"

"Once in a public security bureau, even an innocent person can feel guilty."

He looked elated. I said: "Can I leave now?"

"Wait."

Hands behind his back, he strolled out into the corridor, and poked his head into the conference room. Through the door open a crack, I saw a bundle of dusty electrical wire tangled on the floor. "Can I leave now?" I said.

6

It was just a thought like the *um-ah* I heard was a thought. It's rooted in the mind, but Lili tried to escape it through the displacement of her body. "Let's get out of here quickly. I can't stay another second," she said. Unable to open the car door, she just slapped it. I turned the key, and the door opened. She got the car started, but then it stalled. So she just kept slapping the steering wheel.

"You haven't released the handbrake," I said.

She hissed angrily then shouted: "Don't just sit and stare. Come over and drive the car." I got out of the car. As we passed each other, she didn't look at me or speak to me. Her face, fully powdered, looked stiff and cold, her body gave off a smell I'd never smelled before. It was a sign of weariness. She sat back and said with her eyes closed: "What do you see?" I knew she didn't need an answer. Along the river, the journalists and onlookers were all gone. The prostitute in the qipao had finished her impassioned speech and was now burning paper money alone. She stirred the faint flame with a twig, weeping. She wept for Spring and for herself, most fundamentally she wept for herself. I didn't tell Lili this. I didn't say anything.

When we reached the farm, she was still sleeping. As soon as she woke up, she said: "What is this place?" She must have seen what I saw, dusk hanging over the corner, cool ground, a bunch of strangers. They regarded us with a calm, animalistic look. *Didn't you pick this place?* I thought.

"Let's eat first," I said. But Lili followed the staff into the room. It was a room with a large bed-stove.

"Didn't you tell me you had single rooms?" I asked.

"I'm sorry. Look, it doesn't change anything," the staff said.

"Do you still have a single room?"

"We don't."

"What the hell is this place?" Lili shouted.

"Men and women sleep on two separate bed-stoves. It's been like this for seven or eight years." The staff member bowed and left the room.

"How can I sleep here?" she went on shouting.

"I didn't know it would be like this."

In fact, she was the one who booked the place. After venting her anger, she hugged me from behind, acting flirtatious. Not anymore now it seems. "Let's go eat," I said.

"I don't want to."

We went to the dining hall, and she just ate a few pieces of spring onion. I sensed an unsettling air lurk. When the staff put several tables together under a bright lamp, men put down their chopsticks and gathered around. They were going to do some simple, quick gambling. The owner shuffled the cards, and a visitor drew a card. If he got a nine, and the preceding player got a seven, he won two hundred yuan from the preceding player. If the following player got a six, he won another three hundred yuan from the following player. Everyone believed they would win. I drew a card and won one thousand yuan.

"Stop playing," Lili said.

"Don't be shy." The owner faked a smile. Now my blood was pumping hard and free, making my whole body itch. "Just a few more rounds," I said.

"I said stop playing."

"Last five rounds, just five."

Lili fell asleep on my shoulder. If I hadn't suddenly jerked my arm to throw a big card on the table, she would probably have never woken up. She said: "How are you still not done?"

"Soon. Just three rounds."

"How are there three more rounds?"

"Last three rounds."

I meant it, but I just played three rounds after three rounds, until I looked around the room and didn't see Lili. Then I stopped. I thought really I deserved to die. I walked to the bed-stove room and opened the curtain, looked for her in dim light, didn't find her. One of them looked a bit like her. I moved her shoulder gently and she turned over, still snoring, a bubble hanging from her nostril. *Where'd she go?* Anxiously, I walked to every corner of the farm. *She couldn't possibly have been raped and ditched in the well.* It was totally dark out. I called her phone, but no one answered, and I couldn't disgrace myself by calling out loud. I asked people passing by. They tried hard to remember, looked thoughtful, but ended up shaking their heads. I walked out of the entrance; the car was still parked there. I slapped the door and lit the interior with the cell phone's faint light – no one.

It was just like a nightmare.

I finally ended up shouting frantically. Staff quickly ran over and led me into the kitchen. A female chef was scrubbing a pot, she pursed her lips: *Look how soundly she sleeps.* I saw my dear child leaning on a wooden post, fast asleep beside a blazing brazier. I carried her out amid the female chef's chuckle.

"Go play, go play again." She struggled, and I giggled. Then she actually, rudely, maliciously pushed me away, and got down on the ground.

"I want to go back. When are we going back?" she said.

"We just arrived."

"I want to go back."

I regarded her nasty face. "Fine, if you don't go, I will." She turned to go. "You stay here playing cards until you die." My heart was slashed. But I followed her to the locker to get her luggage, then I followed her to the car. I said: "We didn't get a refund."

"Whatever, get it yourself if you want." She snatched the key from my hand, pushed me away, and opened the car door. I grabbed her, and she jumped. "What are you doing?"

"Let me, it's too dark. Let me."

When we got home, we still hadn't said a word to each other. She nodded off in the passenger seat, while I drove, my eyes fixed on the ground lit by the headlights. It seemed the car wasn't running, instead the asphalt road was sending itself along the tires. Again and again the road rolled out what I wanted to say:

You can't reason with a woman.

You can't reason with a woman.

You can't, you can't, you can't.

You can't reason with a woman.

I carried her to bed and pulled the covers over her, then I held her hand and sat falling asleep. I felt like I'd slept for centuries when a rustling sound woke me. Lili was stuffing things into the big duffel bag, furious, it was loud.

"What time is it?" I asked. She didn't answer. I looked at the clock on the wall. It was 2 a.m.

"What are you doing?" I asked.

"Going home."

"You're going home this late?"

"I'm going home, I can't stay another second."

I stood up and sat down on the sofa, getting a bit closer to her. Watching each of her movements and their huge shadows on the wall, I said: "Driving back?"

"Train."

"Ticket booked?"

"Of course."

"What time is the train?"

"Five a.m."

"Why so early?"

"I told you already, I don't want to stay here for even another second."

She kept banging the bag on the tea table. I mumbled. I could anticipate the vast loneliness. I would live here alone. It would be better if we could live together for a time in a hotel. "What the hell?" She couldn't find what she was looking for, so she pulled all her clothes out of the closet and jerked them all over the floor. "What the fucking hell?"

"Don't, take your time."

"I know," she said. She looked up and cried. The hardened thing in my heart was soft again. I heard her say, "Tell me, dead so many days, still um-ahing?"

"You hear it?"

"Yes, endless *um-ah*."

"It's the old man next door moaning, been moaning two years."

"Hope it is."

Then to the air she said quizzically, "I never hurt you in this life, nor harmed you in the previous life, why can't you leave me alone? I invited you to live in my house, is it my fault? Did I ever offend you somehow?"

"Don't do that," I said. I wanted to hold her and whisper in her ear: *I love you, I love you now more than ever, I love you so much, right now, I saw you as a relative before, but now I love you so much I've never loved you this much*...but my legs, as if trapped in rumbling currents, couldn't move. She was wrapped in her sorrow, didn't look at me. When I held her hand tight, she was still wrapped in sorrow. She drew her hand away and cruelly uprooted herself from the room, the house, and the city. If only she'd said, "Remember to take care of yourself."

Through dark fog, I drove her to the train station, went with her to get the ticket, go through the security check, go down to the platform. I clenched the ticket like a defeated general, composed outside, desolate inside, just watching my rivals loot everything. For a long time afterward, I lived alone. Moonlight seeped through the window, the bedding freezing cold, westerly wind blowing making paper scraps dance. Home was hardly home, I hardly a man, free time filled with masturbation.

Lili walked into the car.

She never turned, didn't wave, didn't engage in anything

important. She completely ignored me. She sat down dully and placed the bag on her lap then she closed her eyes and let out a long sigh. She couldn't wait to return to her mother. I covered my mouth with my hand, feeling the sting in my nose. I felt like I ate wasabi. The train had 15 coaches in total.

7

I walked down the slope then across the cement road. There was a willow at regular intervals and a long bench after every two. It was the green belt between the road and the floodwall. The stench of the river wafted through the air. People watched that prostitute taking paper money out of a plastic bag. The green belt looked like it had been repeatedly trodden by a bull, the edges of the soil sticking out like daggers.

"You just love watching."

Lili said that before I came. But she never questioned why she herself was such a dawdler. Women were like that, no matter what kind of outing it was they would make it into an important diplomatic affair, making scrupulous preparations, especially with their face. I said: "I'll wait for you there." From the balcony I saw another dozen or so people gathering by the river.

The prostitute gripped the lighter and shook the paper money. She wore a qipao so couldn't squat down, and therefore bent over. A large teardrop quietly fell to the ground. The small patch of land before her was level and smooth, the withered grass dancing slightly. I seemed to see the depression the body had left on the ground. The small stone was still there.

When the corpse was first thrown there, it was covered by a rotten, blackish straw mat, showing the wet hair and one leg. The boatman squatted there, coughing, smoking, and blowing his nose from time to time. His eyes were fixed dully on the corpse all along, as if he couldn't believe it was the result of a morning's work. People rode bikes, eyes fixed straight ahead, riding past the cement road. They came and went, until someone suddenly braked, jumped off the bike, and ran a few steps with it. One of her feet stepped on the pedal to get the bike going again but suddenly she stopped. Sure enough, she'd been watching. The newcomers put their toes on the ground and turned their bikes. They watched with her, stunned.

"None of my business," the boatman said, eyes fixed on the ground.

A leg stuck out from beneath the straw mat. The ankle was eerily pale, the sole shriveled. The pants were drenched and dripping with water. One platform shoe that was tossed aside was unusually swollen from soaking. People were struck by the sight of the death of their own kind, saw their own destiny. They mumbled, their faces taking on a pure, philosophical look. But not long afterward, as the sun brought heat, they became restless. Those in the rear jostled against those in the front, and those in the front strained against them. Then within the crowd, a hand reached up, waved incessantly, and the newcomers who lingered on the cement road resolutely hurried. At the far end of the main road, many more were cycling over. One of them rode an electric bike whose battery was dead. He pedaled twice, and the wheels turned, the bike wriggling as the man burned with impatience. When people gathered their black heads were a horrifying sight like a bunch of starving vultures, continuously pushing and jostling.

"What's the matter?" one of them said.

"They asked me to recover it. None of my business." The boatman walked away. He tucked his shoulders and restrained himself from walking too fast. The speaker regarded the boatman for a while, then he turned and raised a finger. *Oh.* He took out a business card. "A story on this is worth at least 50 yuan."

Then three women rushed over on a pedicab. They wore gaudy clothes and heavy makeup. People all knew what they were and from their anxious looks, what the deceased was. They walked in through the path people automatically made for them.

"Unlikely," one of them said.

"Why not? Look there," another said.

They all looked at the platform shoe. "Her little thing is still tied to the shoelace," the second one added. Then the prostitute in the qipao who had been silent, opened her mouth, twisted her face, and broke into dramatic laughter. Only when a choking sound came did I realize she was crying. Her wrist was tattooed with the character for loyalty. People regarded them scornfully, the way city folk regard country folk or human beings regard animals. Their scorn didn't diminish when she started crying. They just had a new perspective: even hookers have feelings. They exchanged looks to confirm one another's opinion. Their looks were like a hand that pulled the arms of the newcomers, making them focus on the heavily made-up women. When the women left tearfully and the journalists came, they reported noisily: "They are from the nearby KTV. Prostitutes. Pussy sellers."

The journalists jumped over. The cameramen stood straight, squinting one eye, moving their cameras this way and that. The photographers sometimes got down on one knee, sometimes stood on tiptoe, sometimes ran somewhere higher, snapping and snapping without pause. The writers scribbled away in their notebooks, finishing a page then flipping it over violently. Onlookers gathered behind them, tiptoed, necks craning. "Go away." The journalists waved at them.

Only the dumpy journalist in a V-neck sweater remained silent, squatting by the corpse, contemplating. When someone called out to him, he reached a hand to hush them. Like a prodigy, he frowned, tilted his head, remained still, as if listening to something from the corpse. He found a twig and lifted a corner of the straw mat. The onlookers tilted their heads too. They wanted to see something. There was only shadow. He stared awhile then suddenly threw the twig aside and lifted the straw mat. He lifted it as he stood up then put it to the side. He took out a camera and kept taking pictures. When he was done, he put his hands in his pants pockets, turned, raised his head, and went on contemplating.

Spring lay there, clothes clinging to her body, showing plump breasts. In places they weren't tight water collected. Her exposed skin was horribly pale like a pig thoroughly bled and shaved. Around her neck, back, and waist, there were light-red speckles. They didn't bulge from the skin but were hidden under it. Word was pressing them made them disappear, but when the hand was removed, they would reappear. On her waist there were three triangular holes with smooth edges from the corpse pressing against a small stone when it was thrown there. She was like someone snoring in an eternal sleep, lips pouting, a bubble hanging from her nose. Her eyeballs slanted, a blood clot on the eyelid membrane. Her hands grasped the muddy grass, and the bones of her right index and middle fingers stuck out. Though tied, her dead hands still grasped muddy grass.

I found it unbearable. Although I'd known all along the ending would be like this, knew this would be the inevitable ending of this deranged girl – even still, I found it unbearable, threw up. I vomited like a man whose belly is cut open and can't stop his bowels from pouring out. I pressed my palms on the ground, squatting, vomiting like a high-power pump. The onlookers dashed off. A white-haired man with a walking stick vomited too. The filth gushed out, some clinging to his clothes around the chest. "You insisted on looking." His wife was furious, kept wiping him with a handkerchief. "You're addicted."

"I'm not looking anymore." Tears rolled out of the old man's eyes.

When I had nothing more to vomit, I walked back to the cement road, up the slope, and sat down there until a beat-up truck drove over. The policeman got out of the truck, asked everyone to step back, and kept taking pictures of the corpse. The boatman sneaked up out of nowhere, and said: "You finally came."

"No cars want to move it."

The police tipped his head toward the truck, then turned back and went on shooting. "Don't worry about the money. I'll get it for you." The boatman nodded. He couldn't decide whether to leave or not, feeling restless. A long time later finally said: "Didn't you take pictures in the morning?"

"The lighting wasn't good."

"They gathered themselves, I couldn't stop them."

"No problem, go on home."

The boatman walked away. The policeman finished shooting and called the transportation crew. Wearing black gloves, heads raised, they carried the corpse stiff as furniture onto a stretcher. Before they transferred it to the truck, they leaned the stretcher against the bed. Spring, dead, leaned there, still, the hem of her pants dripping with water. The driver rushed over to help and got her into the truck. Then the truck sped off like a wisp of smoke. The crowd immediately felt depressed and soon dispersed.

The prostitute in the qipao kept clicking the lighter – today she brought paper money. The lighter clicked, faint sparks leaped up. When the journalist in the V-neck sweater came, she still couldn't light the paper money. "They told me to come here," he said. The prostitute tossed him a glance.

"I want to interview you," he said.

"For what?" she said.

"I've heard you were close to the deceased."

"Yes." She stopped clicking the lighter and looked up at the sky.

"Can you say something?"

"There's nothing to say." Two of her associates grabbed her.

"I want to say," she said calmly.

"There's nothing to say."

"No, she was killed by them." She shoved aside the partners who grabbed her, lifted her dress, and walked to the journalist.

"Don't say that," they said.

"Don't say what? If they hadn't done anything against their conscience, why did they run away?"

"It's been a month."

"Exactly because of that, exactly."

She found the qipao constricting, so she parted her legs and stood like a compass. Her associates stepped aside. When she was telling the story, she turned from time to time and said emphatically: "I must speak." People gathered around, the journalist tried to stop them, as if only he had the right to hear it. But everyone could hear her. The prostitute spoke more and more excitedly.

In the end, the crowd dispersed, and I heard an impatient car honk. It was the secret signal to me, someone ordering me. Our old car was parked at the slope leading out of town. Lili stepped out of the car, pacing back and forth, very impatient. We were going to a farm. I knew in a moment she would say: "I can't stay another second."

8

News:

Exclusive report by He Fang – Around 6 a.m. yesterday morning, a female body was recovered from the Zhaojia Sluice in the eastern part of the city moat. According to Mr. Li, who was doing his morning exercise nearby, the corpse was discovered and reported to the police by him and his exercise partners before dawn. Civilian police from the Zhaojia Pass public security sub-bureau rushed to the spot, arranged for recovery, and removed the corpse before noon. According to the observations of the journalist at the scene, the female was in her early twenties, about 1.62 meters tall, wearing a white top, black capri pants, and white platform shoes. She was pale-skinned with some goose bumps, her hands tied together by a rope, already dead. Journalists have learned from police that the female is still unidentified, and they have yet to determine whether or not it was murder.

9

I'd never seen Lili fly into such a rage. Her hands were shaking, and relentless roars, like a barrage of cannonballs, were fired at the closed elevator door. *Fuck off.* She was compensating. She'd just been choking back her anger in Spring's presence. I clamped her arms tightly, holding her, and we walked home. She kept breaking away. "Do you think that's how it is, yes or no?" she said.

Since then she never forgave Spring. That's the essence of relationships between women, once torn apart, forever torn. We sat blankly on the sofa. The room was like wreckage after a tornado. In the morning, the three of us ate together, but by midmorning, one had left. We couldn't have predicted that result at the start of the day. We'd thought it would go on for a while. I walked toward Spring's bedroom. The pillow had been left under the lamp, the bedsheet and blanket a mess, revealing the crimson mattress. There wasn't really anything else left. A few paintings hung on the wall, the air conditioner plug dangled, the narrow closet open, only one sock inside. I wasn't surprised Spring had managed to pack everything up so quickly. The place we lent her wasn't big, not big enough for her to breed her own world and things.

When Lili came out with a mop, I slipped into the bathroom. I'd been holding it a long time but now I can't go at all. The more I want to the less I can. Writing this may make you uncomfortable, but nothing can better explain what I've been suffering from. I feel I'm occupying someone else's bathroom. Outside Lili and her man are shuffling around in slippers. You don't know whether they're reminding me or just want to walk around. They make my whole body stiffen up. They are watching me through this thin door. I'm occupying their toilet. Shame on me. I think only with no restrictions in a hotel could I go.

I sat on a corner of the mattress. When I stood up, I felt many odds and ends bounce. It felt surreal, but I still lifted up the mattress. God, hidden under the mattress were shoelaces, a button, a pin, a toothpick, a screwdriver, chopsticks, scissors, a mirror, a cell phone, a battery, electrical wire, a tin, a business card, some paint, a lighter, an ashtray, the top of a can, chewing gum, a condom, a discount card, a shopping bag, a sticker, a wooden carving of Guanyin, a book called *Lady of the Camellias*, and a journal crowded with thoughts. Things we'd used and ignored and the little treasures she'd collected at some point, made a kingdom there.

I pushed the door with my index finger, leaving it open a crack. Then I riffled through the journal. Sometimes she wrote stroke by stroke, but a great horror was hidden in her composure – she was convicting everyone in the world. Sometimes she wrote quickly, from standard to semi-cursive, from semi-cursive to cursive, eventually filling the whole page with exclamation marks like she'd stabbed the page again and again. In the end every page was covered with a big, nasty cross. I heard footsteps. She must have said bad things about me. It was impossible to hide it on me, only pants pockets, it would bulge strangely. Lili walked in. "Look what she's done." I lifted up the mattress. Lili's eyes popped open. *Like I said*. She held the mattress. *Like I said*. She tutted.

"Her journal's here too."

Before I really knew what I'd said, the journal had been handed to Lili. Perhaps in the rush I thought it would make me seem a little more forthright. I buried myself in reading *Lady of the Camellias*. Small-format, white cover, a female silhouette with eyelashes curled up, by Alexandre Dumas of France, translated by Wang Zhensun. I read this over and over. A runaway runs, naturally, but as a result, those who chase them gain more and more confidence. If he turned and walked toward the latter would the situation change? "Oh." *I'll say that soon.*

Lili read the journal line by line, and page by page, eyebrows crooked, nostrils flaring, cheeks twitching. I waited for her to drop it, stand up, and interrogate me. But she just said casually: "This cunt." Then she went on, "Come read this." I obediently went and sat, turned my head to read.

No need to be like that, cheapskate, no need. I just used your water heater for a little while, just a little while. It won't cost much. Lili, you didn't have to turn off the water heater when I was in the shower. You didn't have to. I will leave five yuan on the table as compensation for you. I will pay for every shower I take, and slowly compensate you for the showers I took before. You don't need to act generous to my face. No need, cheapskate.

"Did I fucking turn it off? Doesn't the water heater often break on its own?" Lili said. I nodded. "Did I offend you somehow? Can't you tell good from bad? I offered you face but you didn't want it," she went on.

"Forget it."

I took the journal and leafed through it again. I saw the recruiting manager's lewd look, passersby who followed her around all day long, attempting to snatch her bag, and all the cars trying to kill her – I felt I was standing on a crowded dock, filled with a sense of security being a part of the hubbub. I certainly saw how I deliberately seduced her. Passing, I brushed against her, hooked her chin with my finger, grabbed her privates with my hand, and so on.

"Didn't happen," I said.

"I know." Lili frowned, and kept shaking her head. I'd meant to say I didn't really have the chance to spend much time with her alone, but I thought it was unnecessary. I ripped out the page where she slandered me, and the pages where she slandered Lili. "You'd better rip them all out." Lili was looking at me, but still, in front of her, I put the journal and *Lady of the Camellias* into the open closet. She didn't speak aloud, so I couldn't throw it away. I've left it there ever since. It wasn't anything wrong. If Lili looked for it one day, and it wasn't there, I would have to give a long explanation, so I just left it there openly.

This cunt. Once in a while, Lili would curse the person who had left. Then she forgot who the cunt was. Due to this forgetting, she was caught off guard upon hearing of Spring's death. But I had long anticipated the ending. Such anticipation, like hidden cancer cells, grew larger and larger, greater and greater, tormenting my soul.

I'd thought this was humanity one would have even for dogs. But when we lived together we held such a grudge against each other we were dying to ask her to leave right away, but when the bedroom was vacated, my heart started to ache. I didn't have a heart of stone after all. We'd lived together for a period after all. I once got bit by Mom's dog. Holding it tight, Mom retreated to the corner. I said: "You want the dog or me?"

"Both."

I snatched it away and threw it out the window. "You're nuts," Mom said, crying. "I'm not." I pulled up the hem of my pants and let her look. "I'm going to have an injection, otherwise I'll die." I heard the pup moaning in pain from upstairs. Dragging its broken hind leg, it crawled to the door, and in the end was picked up by a butcher. Head poking out of the pocket, forelegs clinging to the edge, it looked upstairs toward us. I suddenly felt guilty. Not because of Mother, but because I thought of the butcher's weighing motion. I felt as if I'd executed it.

I'd been thinking I was responsible for Spring ending up like that, but then I thought, yes, it was really good, but a good heart can make you a defenseless puppet who can be controlled or used by anyone. Although Spring had only said such a thing to me once – you could tell she'd said it to a lot of people and probably couldn't remember to whom she'd said it – it became a sharp claw gripping my heart. She only said that one thing, and I've been enslaved by it ever since. Though she left us and set us free, I was still firmly controlled by that threat. Even though what she'd said made no sense.

"I'll let you watch me die."

Because of that sentence, when she walked toward the window, I would think of her jumping; when she picked up a knife, I would think of her cutting her throat; when she trimmed her nails, I would think of her stabbing herself blind; was there anything she wouldn't do? When she left I was relieved, thinking she would be out of my mind from then on, but in the end I failed to guard myself against the fear of the possibility of her death. I imagined that she died and people found the suicide note on her corpse, in which she blamed me for everything. Morally speaking, I was the murderer, the scum and degenerate. She was firm and determined when she said that sentence. She regarded me maliciously and as if using a knife to carve the words into my heart. She probably left to make the horrible promise easier to carry out. I wondered if I should look for her and follow her for 24 hours in case she killed herself. *You can't get away. I'll let you watch me die, I definitely will. You're like rice waiting for me to harvest at any time, you just wait.* She gazed at me for a long time.

I went to a classmate of mine who was a therapist. We'd been like brothers in the past, and he still saw me like that, but I regarded him, white-robed now, as the father of my mind. I expected him to stroke my head and hold me in his arms. I said: "I'm always worried."

"About what?"

"Other people dying."

"Why?"

"I'm a softie, always worried other people will die. I'm kind."

"Not true," he said, laughing affably. "That is not kindness. You don't really care about other people. What worries you is not that others will die, but the consequences their death would bring on you. You're afraid of taking responsibility."

I thought this was goddamn right. He went on: "What you've got is an obsession. People are more or less hypocritical. So am I. You should say to yourself: if you die, you die. Just die, I can't wait for you to die."

Later I called Spring. There were countless times I almost dialed the number but gave up. This time I clenched my teeth and dialed the number. The beeping sound was long and steady, like streetlights going on one after another, then out one after another until they were all out. I dialed the number four times. She finally picked up the phone. I could tell she was in the middle of something.

"What is it?" she said.

"How have you been?"

"Same as always."

"That's good."

"That's it?"

"Yeah, that's it. Just called to ask."

Then I heard a man's voice on the other end of the phone. "Who are you talking to?"

"A friend," Spring said.

"Man or woman?"

"Is it your business?"

"Must be a man."

"Shut up." Spring turned back to the phone and said, "I'm hanging up."

I heard her horsing around as she hung up. I was greatly reassured. I didn't know why I was so reassured. She was finally accepted by someone. The time bomb was finally taken by someone. I was free. I started to live with Lili with true fondness. I'd never liked her body like that. It was as if our life had just begun.

10

The fifth time. The last time. Before executing a prisoner, they let him have a proper meal. We set aside chopsticks, a spoon, and a bowl for Spring and waited for her. We'd made her favorite minced pork congee with pickled egg and a fried egg. But this was only an attempt to ease the pain of us still living together. We didn't know she would leave that day. We only hoped she would keep her promise to leave in 10 days or so.

"Not eating."

Lili walked out. Creamy light shone from Spring's room. "She sat there stupidly, said she won't eat," Lili said. Then she sat down, picked up the bowl and got some shredded turnip. I did the same. We ate in silence like workers on break. I'd never heard a sound as odd as our mouths made. We ate slurping. In the middle of this, I walked to Spring's bedroom. I leaned against the doorjamb. The light fell on Spring, left a shadow on the floor. She squatted there, leather suitcase open, inside a neatly arranged makeup case, tweezers, pads, and other odds and ends. There were also some things on the bedside table. She transferred those in the suitcase to the table, and those on the table into the suitcase. Over and over again. Her voice was calm and serious, deciding which belonged to Lili and which belonged to her. "Eat first," I said.

"Not eating."

"The congee is getting cold, be good."

"I told you I won't eat, are you deaf?"

She kept fiddling with those things. I turned and shook my head. Lili responded with a pained look. In silence, we cleared the table, leaving the portion for Spring there. I rinsed the bowls and chopsticks. Lili wiped them with a dry kitchen towel and put them into the cupboard. After we finished, we went back to our bedroom and lay down on the bed. I heard my bowels rumble. From the living room came Spring's voice. "I won't eat your meal. I said I won't eat, and I won't eat." Lili gave me a little kick, I sat up. I saw she was looking at me. She held the congee in one hand and the side dish in the other, looking stunned, but she quickly tilted her head up, and strode toward her room.

"She ended up eating it," I said.

"Don't provoke her."

"She seems to be in the middle of packing."

"Yeah, it won't be long, bear with it a little longer."

Later I heard the sound of Spring rinsing the dishes. I still hadn't slept. I thought Lili had fallen asleep, turned to look. Her eyes were open, fixed tightly on the ceiling. I got up and went to the bathroom. Spring sat on the sofa, holding a handbag tightly. She flicked the cigarette ash in the ashtray. She didn't look at me.

"Going out?"

"Can I not have a bag if I'm not going out?"

She held the handbag closer and let out a puff of smoke. Smoking women are so beautiful, cold and dreamy. She turned her body to the other side and continued to smoke with her head held up. I went into the bathroom and sat on the toilet. I liked reading the paper again and again until I got bored. I heard Lili shuffling sluggishly out of the room in slippers. In the meantime Spring walked back to her room in high heels. As if there was a rule: only one woman allowed in the room at a time. Lili walked into the kitchen, turned on the tap, stirred her toothbrush in the cup, and squeezed out the toothpaste. She mucked around her teeth on the right side, then the left, mouth full of foam. She could brush her teeth like that all day long. *Everything will pass. It seems hard to pull through it but it will pass one day. You can see the present as the future. Spring isn't here in the future.* She gargled on and on.

She would walk back to our bedroom. I would also go back there. We would continue to lie there. In the meantime she slid open the knife drawer. She found something missing again. "Spring, did you hide the kitchen knife?" she roared.

"No," Spring responded louder.

The knife drawer banged shut. Lili hurried to the living room, then into Spring's bedroom. I pulled the bathroom door open and followed. Lili opened the closet and rummaged through the neatly folded clothes. Spring faced her, retreated toward the head of the bed. Whenever she tried to hide something she always led people to the place she hid them. She sat down on the pillow. "Move." Lili pulled her. She wiggled her body.

"I said move."

Lili gave her a hard push. She slid down sadly and instantly stood up. Hidden under the pillow were a fruit knife, a cleaver, a kitchen knife, a spatula, and a rolling pin. "What's this?" Lili grabbed the spatula — I felt I should thank her for grabbing this. One person holding the wooden handle and the other holding the iron head, they started to argue. "Stop, this is mine, you stop," Spring said. They would probably snatch a knife later. Lili would shove it forward while Spring gripped the edge, blood trickling between her fingers. It was terrifying. The moment they dropped the spatula simultaneously, I grabbed the pillow and pressed it against the knives.

"Enough," I roared. They grappled. I grabbed three knives and ran away. When I returned I saw Lili pointing the rolling pin at Spring's shoulder, saying: "Take a good look, this is my house."

"It's not."

"Is this yours then?

"Yes. Pack your stuff and get out now."

"How can I explain this to you, psychopath?"

Lili tapped her collarbone with the rolling pin. "How can I explain this to you? Don't you remember I invited you to live in my house?"

"This is my house."

"Look, whose leather suitcase is this?"

"Mine."

"It is yours. People with a house like us don't need a suitcase."

Right. *I have a house, so I don't need a suitcase. I don't have a house, so I need a suitcase. I walked around with the suitcase and arrived at your house.* Spring understood and broke into sobs. She wanted to hold Lili but was pushed away.

"Now please leave my house," Lili said.

"I'm begging you, Lili."

"Please leave."

Lili pointed to the door then grabbed Spring's clothes and dumped them in the suitcase. Spring knelt down on the floor, and picked them up one by one. When a platform shoe was tossed over, she quickly shuffled on her knees, picked it up, and held it to her chest. She looked at us pitifully, and we looked up. "Please," Lili said after a long silence. Spring stood up and said: "Who cares. I'm leaving."

At this point the matter was settled.

Spring started to stuff the things into the suitcase and soon finished. She buckled the suitcase and dragged it out. Everything went as fast as she intended, and also as we intended. She dragged the suitcase out the door. The elevator was going up from the first floor to the top. When it returned it would take Spring away.

I stood behind Lili.

Head down.

Spring was looking at the changing number. She held her forehead, shaking it. She was trying to find a way to counterattack and almost came up with one. *Your man comes so fast.* I hoped the elevator would take her away before she thought of it. Just before the elevator arrived, she turned. I met her eyes and breathed quick. But she directed her gaze at Lili and said: "Look at yourself, so black." That did surprise me. She broke into hearty laughter like a swordsman and walked into the elevator. There was no one inside. The silver door closed. She definitely saw Lili shaking when the door closed. She'd won.

"Don't be angry." I put my arms around Lili.

Then the elevator door suddenly bounced open. She pressed the close button and added: "No wonder we called you Wild Boar Lin. A person like you could only match with..." The door closed again. If I hadn't held Lili fast, she would have jump kicked her. I was somewhat relieved like an anxious criminal finally getting his punishment. What Spring hadn't gotten out was: "an old shit like Chen Qing."

Spring didn't get back at me that day. Her mind was muddled. "Didn't you say you loved me?" she probably should have said. I wouldn't have been able to explain it, because she'd asked me again and again before: "Do you really love me? Tell me the truth."

And I said: "Yes."

11

The fourth time. She'd been refusing to eat with us lately. When I walked out I saw her putting food in her bowl. I waved a hand. Her eyes immediately stiffened, then she grabbed the bowl and ran to her room, bits of pickles falling to the ground. She slammed the door. For a second the sound pinched my heart.

Lili walked out, looking apologetic. She was apologizing for Spring's insensitivity. There was also a certain bitterness in her look, indicating she was on my side, she was my wife, and we were fretting together about the unpleasantness the guest brought. I wanted to curse, but I just stroked her hand and patted her shoulder to make her feel magnanimity.

The door suddenly opened a crack, and Spring's head poked through it. She saw we were there and hurried to close it again. I was amazed that she didn't jam her head. Probably fearing the door hadn't been secured, she closed it again, turned the latch, and turned the key twice to lock it from the inside. "Fuck," I said nastily. Lili grabbed my arm. "Fuck," I repeated.

"Don't get mad."

"I'm not."

"She will leave."

"I know, I'm not mad."

Only when Lili was around did I dare vent my anger. Lili released the hand that had been gripping my arm. "I won't get mad again," I said. She walked toward Spring's door, eyes on me until she was almost there, then she faced the door. She knocked, then knocked again. There was no response. *She's probably sleeping, just leave her in peace.* Lili looked at me.

"I just need to calm down, then I'll be all right."

"I know."

Lili looked at me and continued: "I couldn't bring it up."

We walked toward the sofa. My hands were open. Lili picked one up and held it. We turned on the TV but didn't watch it. Then from the small bedroom came a sound. It was the click of the latch being turned, then the key inserted into the lock cylinder and turned. Spring pulled the doorknob. *Boom, boom, boom.* It seemed like she was going to yank it off. "Turn it, don't pull it," I shouted. She did that, but the door didn't open, so she kept kicking the door. The damn woman cursed. "Let me out. I want to get out."

"Nobody locked you in."

I walked over, and tried to insert the key into the lock cylinder but couldn't. "Pull out your key. Let me open the door," I shouted. No sound came from the other side. "Pull out the key," I continued to shout.

"You locked me in," she said, wailing.

"Why would we lock you in?"

"You just did, you did it on purpose. What right do you have to lock me in?"

She cried, slapping the door, then banged her head against it. I got agitated by her despair and started to yank the door too. "Let me." Lili pushed me aside. She tried to put the key in then pulled the doorknob. It didn't work. She thought for a moment and said: "Spring, turn the key one more time."

"I did."

"You only turned it once. Turn it another time, to the left. Just listen to me."

It rattled inside for quite a while before the lock clicked. The door was pulled open and a gust of wind leaped out. The window of the room was open. She'd probably thought about jumping, piece of shit. Lili scolded her, and she threw her arms around Lili. Her head was bruised and swollen, as if she had just escaped from a savage dog. She held Lili, crying and crying.

"It's all right," Lili said. She cried harder. Lili pushed her away and said: "Take a good look, did we hurt you? Did we?"

*　　*　　*

"We should have thrown her stuff out and asked her to leave," Lili said.

"Mm."

"I'll try to ask her in the next couple days, see when she's leaving."

"That's not what I meant."

"Have to ask anyway. I'm so fed up, beyond fed up."

*　　*　　*

When we got up the next day, we found Spring's door locked. I remembered she slept with it open, with a chair by the door to keep it from closing itself. But now it was closed. We knocked and heard a calm response, "Come in." We pushed the door open and saw she was sitting on the edge of the bed. The morning light poured in through the window, casting mysterious shadows on her face. Now she was like our younger sister, our little friend. She turned her face and regarded us cheerfully. Her eyes rippled like bright warm water. She held her head up, slightly slanted-out white teeth showing in an unbegrudging smile.

The smile, so beautiful and innocent, was like tranquil, supple sunshine after a tornado, shining on our hearts.

We had a cheerful breakfast together, then we played cards. She followed the rules. Lili asked her about the shop. She said the owner was going back to her hometown, so the shop would close for a time. Lili flashed me a look, seeing that I didn't press her, and didn't ask Spring when she would leave. But Spring said: "I'll probably leave at the end of this month."

"Leave for what?" Lili said.

"I found a room there, stop bothering you and Mr. Chen."

When she said this, her feet under the table moved toward me, and when they touched me, they gently rubbed against one of my shoes. I drew my feet back and concentrated on my cards. She lifted her head and unscrupulously regarded me. The corners of her mouth sneered. *She's laughing at your playing skills, look what you played.* Lili, the generous woman, pushed the cards in my hand.

I was thoroughly embarrassed, the more I wanted to hide the blushing, the more I blushed. "Awful play," I said. Spring leaned over, the upper part of her body almost touching the table. She regarded me squarely as if to dig something out of my face. Then she extended her legs and kept tapping my knees with her toes. *She is so unrestrained.*

Like her, Lili regarded me with curiosity.

Without thinking, I drew a card from the deck. The toes drew back suddenly from my knees. In less than a second, she stood up straight, and threw out a joker. "Bigger than yours." She laughed. Her breasts swayed from her sudden motion.

12

The third time. She suppressed her anger and went out. Hit hard by something emotional. In the afternoon, she came back, panicked. She stayed in the bathroom for nearly an hour. After she came out, she grabbed Lili's hand, weeping.

"Don't be sad, men are all like that," Lili said.

"No." She broke into sobs.

I was in the bedroom, restless. I should probably find a rope and sneak out the window. I could hardly breathe. But in the end, I pulled the door open. Spring raised her head and regarded me pitifully like a dog who got kicked out. I was trembling with fear at the sight of her. Her hair was unkempt and shaggy. Her eyebrows droopy. Her eye shadow had been washed away by tears, leaving charcoal streaks on her face like someone had used a wet kitchen towel to smear ink back and forth. Her pouty lips, painted remarkably red, were completely dissociated from her face. She was like a sad clown standing helplessly on stage.

She was looking at me. Lili was looking at her. And I was looking at the floor.

"Am I good-looking?" she said.

"Good-looking, good-looking as you can be." Lili stroked her shoulder. I hurried to the bathroom. The beauty had found the reason: it wasn't that others didn't love her but that she wasn't good-looking. I couldn't bear her pleading look anymore.

13

The second time. It's said that before a boat hits a reef, the crew has a premonition, but the boat hits it anyway. Before an earthquake, chickens and dogs flee, but people go on living. Also scary things are not scary in equal quantities, they can be grouped as slightly scary, quite scary, and very scary. Each scary thing comes with a degree of adaptation, making people numb.

We started to feel the things in our house were dwindling.

I asked Lili, she asked me, but it wasn't us. It was as if a gust of wind had swept them away when we were asleep. I couldn't believe the possibility that burglars had broken into our house again and again. One morning I got up early and saw Spring dropping an old mobile phone into a garbage bag. I reached out but said nothing. The thing belonged to me, but was it still of use to me? She lowered her head and continued to clean. She was going to throw the stuffed garbage bag into the garbage bin downstairs later. She was taking liberties, but why did I want to discourage her? She didn't disassemble the phone we were using or take down the clock that was ticking. She was just like a gardener cutting off unnecessary branches for this family.

Really I thought she was sick, but I couldn't say that.

14

The first time. Dinner. She came over and sat down. She picked up the chopsticks and put them down. "Eat," Lili said. She turned her head away, snorting. "Eat," Lili said. She picked up the chopsticks but wouldn't eat. She glanced at me. At this point, I knew eating was a private matter, shouldn't be watched by anyone for long. She wasn't in a good mood that day.

"What is it, Spring?" Lili said.

"He's using my chopsticks," she said.

I froze and looked at Lili, but she didn't get it either. I continued picking up food. "I'm talking about you, you're using my chopsticks," she shouted. Lili and I were stunned. I wondered if she was getting back at me, if so then bring it harder.

"Sorry, here you are," I said.

"Forget it." She waved, disgusted.

"How do you know these are yours?" Lili said.

"I marked them with a knife."

"Where?"

"Here."

To my surprise, Lili regarded the cut seriously, and said, "No problem, we'll remember next time."

"Forget it, just chopsticks."

Spring didn't eat and drifted back to her room like a ghost. Lili and I looked at each other in dismay, like we weren't sure she'd just shouted. We sat across from each other in silence. Only the wall clock ticked. It ticked steadily, making our hearts dull and despondent.

"What on earth is it?" I said.

Lili pointed at Spring's bedroom, then at her temple. *There is something wrong here.* I shook my head and stood up, walked to the bedroom. I was completely terrified by this, I needed to be alone for a moment. Lili followed me in. She grabbed my hand and put it on her breast. Her heart was thumping wildly.

"I'm sorry," she said.

"For what?"

"I didn't know it would be like this."

"Like what?"

"I want to ask you for a favor."

"What is it?"

"Don't kick her out."

"Why?"

"Promise me first."

"I never said I would kick her out."

"I have a younger sister, and I competed with her since we were little, always competing. She died when she was 13."

"What does that have to do with this?"

"There's no use competing with her. She's dead."

"That has nothing to do with this."

"I know, but this is my punishment." She started to cry. "This is my punishment, you know, Chen Qing?"

"I know."

I stroked her shoulder. A moment later, I stood up and paced back and forth. I said in my heart, *I know, I know, I fucking know.* "Don't be like that, Chen Qing," Lili said.

15

This is pointless. I put down the paper and found she was watching me. She'd been watching me for a while, then like a smoothly sailing boat suddenly hitting a reef, she shuddered. I couldn't read on. When I stood up, her eyes followed me.

"What are you looking at?" I said. She smiled affably. "What's there to look at?" I said. When I came back from the balcony, she said: "I just like watching you." Then added: "You don't like it?"

"It's all right."

"Hug me then." She opened her arms. I didn't reply, walked past her. "Hug me." Her voice became soft and weightless. I found a shoe brush and tapped the shoe shelf with it like I was choosing a pair of shoes to wear out. "Hug me," she said.

"We can't do this," I said.

Her arms weren't exactly open but being held up with effort. It was awkward. But did I have to send myself into her arms? I didn't love her. "I'm sorry." I tried to be sincere.

"You love me," she said.

"I can't."

"I know, I just want you to hug me."

"This can't go on."

She put down her arms, and some tears came out. I went to the bedroom and lay down. I thought I should have said we can have a relationship like relatives. You're Lili's god sister and mine too. Later when I pulled the door open I found her standing at the door.

"But I love you. You know that?" she said.

I wanted to go back and close the door. She went on: "I don't want to ruin your relationship with Lili. I don't want anything, don't want status, you know. I just need you to love me."

"It's not that." I pushed her shoulders away and walked out. She kept following. "Do you hate me or something?" she said.

"It's not like that."

"Then what? I don't want anything from you. I just want you to let me love you."

"It's not like that." My voice grew louder.

"Then what?"

I pushed her away and walked back then closed the door. I thought this was clear enough. But ever since then, whenever Lili was away, she would pester me. "Don't you love me?" she always asked. "Not at all?"

No. But. How can I put it? I faltered. Speaking was difficult. Every word should neither make her hopeless nor hopeful. I did want to say: stop dreaming. Yes, I fucked you, so what? Fucking you doesn't mean loving you. In fact, I didn't really fuck you. I didn't stick it in your vagina. I didn't get it in so it doesn't count as penetrating you. Since I haven't penetrated you, why do you think I should be responsible? You should go to those who have penetrated you. You women are like that, seeing that thing as special property, whoever penetrates you is responsible, but I didn't penetrate you, right? My penis didn't go into you.

Sometimes she didn't come back for days. She would call from a phone booth. In front of Lili I asked with exasperation: "Who is it?"

"It's me," she always answered with sorrow.

"What is it?"

The other end would fall into an annoying silence. "Who is it?" Lili asked. "No one," I told Lili and hung up. A moment later, the phone would ring again. "What the hell are you doing?" I shouted. It was always silent on the other end. When Lili wasn't there, I could hear her crying. She cried and said, "Chen Qing, let me tell you something." Then she went back to crying. I dared not hang up too soon. That could be the prelude to her going to her death. I coaxed her and sometimes shouted, "Enough, enough, enough. I really don't understand why you like an old man like me. I have no money, and I'm no good at sex." Or, "I'm dying. I feel short of breath, ah, I'm begging you, I'm begging you to stop torturing me."

If I turned off the phone she would rush over.

"What's the matter with you?" Lili asked, stroking her dry hair. She neither washed her face nor ate, eyes sunken, completely wrecked herself. I thought Lili was going to find out. But when I looked up to steal a glance, I found Spring wasn't looking at me but at the floor, sighing. She felt wronged, tears trickling down. "What's the matter with you?" Lili said.

"Nothing."

"Who hurt you?"

"No one."

I wished she could take this chance to make some oblique accusation. But she just kept sighing without saying anything. "Poor you." Lili settled her down and walked toward me. I nodded. I felt it was all unreal. But what is reality? Lili looked at me, pupils gradually dilating. Anger and fear, like two armies, converged from all over her body and rushed to her face. She looked at me, then at Spring. *You did this? Even you are capable of this? Are you conspiring to kill me?* She kept backing away. When she believed we were blanketed and totally dominated by shame, she broke into sobs. She slammed the door and left, leaving us behind, then brought more and more people to visit us. More and more police, more and more people from the residents' committee, more and more neighbors. Or she just kicked us away, ripped everything off that wasn't locked or nailed down or stuck tight and smashed them up one by one in front of us. Then she cried and cried, then had spasms and epileptic fits, then lay back down on the ground crying without pause, then stood up and banged her head against the wall, then used the knife to cut her throat. The two sternocleidomastoid muscles, like two strings, broke with one cut. Then her head dropped down.

Spring's lips opened several times. From the shape of her lips I could even guess what she was about to say. She had stolen her friend's man and felt too ashamed to speak. I hoped she would spell it out right away, I couldn't stand it anymore. I wanted to kill someone. But when Lili walked over, her lips closed at once. She waited until Lili went to the bathroom and started to mumble again. Unlike me, Lili could stand the humming of the exhaust fan. She had it on. Spring suddenly whispered:

"I just couldn't get over you."

She had wanted to fucking talk to me. I scowled at her. Sitting, she kept trembling. I'd thought of myself as the lamb waiting to be slaughtered, but in fact she was. I had a sense of being in control. She'd made up her mind to handle the reproach and wait for me to take her in. I was silent. The exhaust fan in the bathroom was humming. She started to cry and said: "You don't love me at all?" She gathered up the last bit of strength of her body, which only kindled a faint flame in her eyes.

"No," I said.

In a daze she walked toward the balcony. I glanced at her sideways. She pulled open the window. I went over. Her hands clung to the windowsill. I grabbed her elbow, got pushed away.

"Don't do something stupid," I said.

She looked at me then at the ground under the window. She took a few breaths, took down the clothes from the clothes hangers and walked back to her room. A moment later, she emerged, carrying a bag, then opened the door and left.

A few days later, she summoned me to the city moat and cried hard every few minutes. I sat beside her like a rock. She talked on and on. In the end I couldn't tell what she was talking about. She put her tears away as if putting away an object, said: "I'm asking you one last time, do you love me or not?"

I shook my head. *You wait.* She regarded me nastily and with determination said: "I'll let you watch me die."

16

I didn't like her, but I still knocked on her door. I knocked to the tempo of one, two, three: one knock, pause; two knocks, pause; three knocks. There was no response. I was a bit disappointed and walked back to my bedroom. I didn't like her, but my privates started to expand as soon as Lili left home. I touched it as if touching a sulky little monster lying on the ground. Bound to finish what it wants to finish.

She had a change of heart, or was hopelessly ashamed.

I heard her walking out of the bedroom in slippers toward where I was. I swallowed. But she turned to the bathroom. She gargled, brushed her teeth, gargled, sprinkled water on her face and used the toilet for a while then walked back to her room. My door was open a crack. I couldn't jump over and push her down. She would change out of her nightgown, put on her outside clothes, and go out. That was the end of it. I was very down. But that's all right.

She fussed for a long time. Women are like that, comparing two garments over and over before an outing. *If you want to go out, go out now.* I rolled over to the other side of the bed, facing the window. Though the curtain was drawn tight, light seeped infinitely in. In fact human beings are like mindless animals led about by sexual desires, walking and sniffing, head down, for the smell of women. *Just go now.* When I turned around, I saw her standing beside the bed, hands in her pockets. She was barefoot. I sat up and ripped open her nightgown. The white light of her smooth belly and slightly arched groin flickered, hugged by her arms, covered.

We didn't say anything. Everywhere was the sound of my breathing. She pushed me away and lay down. She twisted left and right, seemingly settled, then she sat up, removed her nightgown, and lay back down. I pulled down my underwear. But she still twisted left and right, as if trying to find the right way to lie. I bent down and stared at myself down there and her down there. *Don't. Don't do that.* She held my cheeks and pulled my head down. She opened my lips and teeth with the tip of her tongue and stirred in my mouth. Although she'd brushed her teeth, her mouth still had the foul smell exclusive to the malnourished. I almost stopped at some points but was held by her. I opened my eyes. *Damn.* Her face bulged, heaving, and her tightly shut eyelids twitched slightly. She was like a stupid pig savoring my saliva, forgetful and drunk.

"Let's talk awhile," she said.

"After."

"Let's talk first."

She let me lie beside her and held my hand. Her body gave off dry steam. I placed her hand on my privates. We lay like two innocent playmates for a while. She turned her face and said: "Do you really love me?" I didn't reply. She went on: "Tell me the truth."

"I do," I said.

My hand wandered over her body. She let tears out. When her tears came, I knew it was bad. There's no such thing as a free lunch, or a free woman. "Okay." Teary-eyed, she clenched her teeth, spread out her body as big as she could and let herself be exploited like a detached torturee. She lay there like that, her body dry. I couldn't get it into her no matter what. "I'm sorry," she said and shut her eyes, another pearl of a tear coming. The thing started to ache after a few thrusts. That clump of hay, dry and spiky, covering the inaccessible crevice. I figured even if someone managed to poke into it he'd be scraped raw. Lying on her was like lying on a rough bundle of firewood.

"There's no such a thing as rape," I said.

"Sorry."

"If a woman doesn't co-operate, a man can't possibly get in."

"Sorry. I don't want this either." She started to cry. "I thought it would work this time."

"Has it ever worked?"

I crawled out of bed and put on my underwear. She came over and grabbed my hand, was shaken off by me. I put on pajamas. Whether it was for subjective reasons or objective ones, I had to punish her. She lay there pathetically. She didn't get wet. She couldn't help it. This man did nothing to conceal his disappointment, anger, and disgust. She was shivering, every part of her body in the posture to hug me, but I was going to walk off mercilessly. I looked at her one last time. She looked down and hid herself in a sea of guilt. But when I turned around, she stumbled down, hectically stripped off my pants and underpants, and held the thing in her mouth.

This felt much better. I closed my eyes. Soon it was my turn to be useless – for maybe 10 or less than 10 times back and forth. I wanted to grab her head to stop her sucking, but half had already gushed out. I could only rock her head to make her suck faster. "Too much hassle in the beginning," I said. She raised her head to look at me and licked some off the corner of her mouth. "Hard so long then out in one punch," I said. She found tissues and carefully wiped me. I stood there, shrouded in an overwhelming sense of emptiness. Everything was meaningless and boring. I watched her pull up my underpants and pants, gripping the ball of semen-soiled tissue. I watched her tidy up the bedding and fold it back into shape. I let her do these things. Then from the door came the sound of a key being inserted. I woke up from the inexplicably and deep-rooted sense of emptiness, legs shaking. The key would turn around twice. The two bedrooms in our house were four to five meters apart. Like a naked rabbit, Spring grabbed her nightgown and leaped back to her room, clenching the semen-tainted tissue ball. Lili opened the door and habitually regarded herself in the wall mirror. She turned left, then right, tipped up her head, and brushed the dust off the tip of her nose. She kicked off her shoes and changed into slippers. Spring let the door shut.

I remained standing. When Lili walked over, I sat down. If she had been smarter, she would have associated the strange rustling and behavior with adultery. Women have that inherent ability.

"I'm feeling a bit feverish," I said feebly, blushing. Lili touched my forehead then hers. The same temperature, she couldn't tell the difference. She said: "Right, look at yourself, you can't take care of yourself at all." Frowning, she went to get me hot water. Water gurgled into the bottom of the cup. She raised her head. There was time for her brain to think about what was wrong. But she couldn't come up with anything. She saw the cup was full and walked over, holding it. Spring's door was quietly closed. In fact, until Lili went out again, she didn't know if Spring was home. Watching Lili find the paper and go out in haste, I thought of Spring's shameless voice. Spring said, licking that stuff I ejaculated: "But I feel, no matter what, I like you so much."

It was so meaningless.

17

"All right." She closed the door. *Sorry*. Before I'd figured what happened, I just let it end. My soul was empty, as if being shaved clean by fierce wind. Even the ground I stood on began to come apart. I fell into the bottomless abyss as the ground became weightless. At the thought of my penis going into her body, I felt empty. Nothing was as urgent and necessary as this, for which I would give up everything. I hadn't had sex with Lili for a long time, hard to get up, we almost forgot about it. Thinking about it now wears me out completely. I wanted to lift up the beauty's skirt and get into her body. Her knees bent, trembling, her thighs giving a soft glow, her belly and breasts heaving slightly. She would suddenly cringe and moan as if stung by an insect.

But I pushed her way.

I fell on the deathbed of regret. I saw the dying self looking at the present self, unable to get over the night. The night when the golden chance came, but nothing happened because of unnecessary courtesy and morality was like a piece of steel piercing the heart of our life. The dying self, stubborn as a kid, with tears rolling out, kept moaning. But I explained to him by the bed that this was poison not to be touched. One night's pleasure would yield betrayal, a split, murder, and irrevocable destruction. But these eloquent words were only to cover the fear I had at the moment. What I was fucking thinking about was how to put it in her body and nothing else.

I strode toward her room. When my fingers touched the door, I grew wary. It wasn't that I wanted to back off. The door was louder than usual. It went squeak squeak. She lay sideways to the window, flicking the cigarette ash into the ashtray. She didn't turn around.

"Are you hungry?" I said. She waved a hand. "I'm a bit hungry," I went on.

This was different from what I'd imagined. She continued to flick cigarette ash. I'd thought we would quickly hug and tear at each other's clothes. "Are you unwell?" I asked. I could hardly stand. I allowed myself to sit on a corner of the mattress. I felt my weight sink down. "Don't drink too much," I said.

"I'm fine." Her speech was drunk.

"Fine is good."

She didn't speak, maybe getting sleepy.

"Try to drink a little less," I went on. I thought I'd made myself very clear. But she embarrassed me. I stood up. "Get me some hot water, would you?" she said. Although the last two words made me uncomfortable, I still saw it as the most pleasant task.

I poured in half hot water and half cold. The water was gurgling down, and the thing had become extremely hard. I waited for it to soften a little and walked back. My heart had never pounded so hard.

"Thanks," she said. She pulled the blanket to cover her bare thighs.

"How's business?" I said and sat back on the corner of the mattress.

"Same as always."

"I see you don't go to work much."

None of your business whether I go or not. She didn't speak. I went on: "Don't work too hard." She sat up to drink the water. She drank half and lay back down. "Thank you," she said.

"You're welcome."

"You know what, they say you meet the right person at the wrong time, or you meet the wrong person at the right time," she said.

"I know."

"Or the wrong person meets the wrong person, or the right person meets the right person. But when the right person meets the right person, the chance has already slipped away."

"I know."

"What do you know?" She sat up. From her face, you couldn't tell whether she was interested in you or not. "I know," I said and grabbed her leg underneath the blanket. It tried to pull away. I grabbed it tightly. It didn't struggle.

"Don't do that," she said.

I crawled toward her. She looked down at me. I felt I was a dog. "Don't do that," she went on. I found her breasts. My hands were big but they couldn't cover her breasts. They were good – like springy balloons. "Not right." She brushed away my hands. "Don't do that."

"I just want to."

"I'm not in the mood."

"You will be soon."

I pushed up her T-shirt. She could have tugged it down, but her head twisted, co-operating to pull it off. "Sorry, I'm not in the mood," she said sincerely. I lay over her, sucking her. I was about to lose control. When it was almost time, I stripped off her skirt and panties. The area wasn't different from other women's but I couldn't take my eyes off it. I stared directly until her knees bent and her thighs closed. It was giving off clean steam. As if the heat from drunkenness was evaporating there. I parted her legs. "Sorry," was all she could only say afterward. I knew why she said it. Her privates were dry and burning. Even with water poured over it every second, it dried up immediately. It was a fucking inaccessible furnace, a foolproof chastity lock.

"Sorry," she said.

"You really aren't interested in me," I said.

"It's not like that."

"Then what?"

"Such good things rarely happen to me."

"Why?"

"I don't know, just afraid."

"Don't be."

"I'm not, it is. I hate it."

"Don't be afraid, it'll be all right, you have to open up."

"I know. Sorry."

I lost interest. I'd say I had an affair, but I didn't really get anything. I tried to let her hold it in her mouth. She just shook her head in pain, so I gave up. When I was leaving, she said: "We could go to the bathtub."

"There isn't a bathtub in this house."

We went to the bathroom anyway. I turned on the showerhead, rinsing her, and hastily smeared some shower gel over her, then some over me. Drunk, she started to cry. I said don't cry and pushed her against the wall. I was much taller than her and didn't know how to get in. I couldn't push her to the floor. I tried many times but didn't get the hang of it. I was afraid both of us would fall and die.

"Stop crying," I shouted.

She stopped, grabbed my thing and tried to put it into her. She tried a few times. When she almost made it, I sighed like I was really sick. The thing bounced and dense fluid gushed out. It spilled out like pus along the mouth of the urethra. I lowered my head. We were like two losers also able to blame each other. I filled with resentment. "I could do it for an hour with someone else," I said.

"Sorry."

She held me. We were slippery like fish, but she still made an effort to hold me tight. "Sorry," she said. I didn't know why, with the same shame, hers felt somewhat stronger. She could have said, "How useless." Or just sighed, then I would have been completely crushed. But she just blamed herself. *Mm*. I started to act impatient, I tried to break away from her arms. Before I ejaculated, there was just your enchanting body and its halo in the whole world. Once I ejaculated you became an annoying woman. Everything was boring, deadly boring, you made me so disappointed.

Later on the sofa, she tried to grab my hand, and my hand kept pulling away. She grabbed it back a few times, then stopped and sighed. She was old, though she was only 20. Some women don't blossom until 23 or 24 but she had already withered and declined.

Not long ago, she had been like fresh, tender tofu, but was now like one that had sat for days, dry and hard. Her pores were dry and rough, the back of her head was overgrown with white hair. When the columns of water poured over her, I looked down and saw her toes were too long, her thighs stocky, her belly bulging like a dangling sandbag, the bottom of which grew thick from gravity. Her areolas were blackish. There was a certain desire in her flesh. It wasn't lust, but the desire of the organs and flesh trying to break free from the restrictions of the mind, and wildly get loose. But the overly strained relationship between them made her dry and hard.

Her hips were corpulent and sagging. This was the goddess who I had endlessly imagined. She left me and went to the room to receive a phone call and said to the phone: "I haven't moved back, I'm looking after the store." When she came out she was already dressed.

"Do you want to eat anything?" she said.

"Mm."

"Let's eat out?"

"Mm."

"I get something for you?"

"Mm."

"There are some dumplings at home. I'll cook dumplings for you."

"Mm."

"Say something."

"Mm," I said. "I'm not that hungry."

18

Not until dinner did Lili drag her out. *I'd rather starve. I live in yours, and I eat yours.* She sat down and picked up the chopsticks, tips pointing at herself. I said eat something, and she picked up some leaves from the plate. "Go ahead, have some meat. Eat more," Lili said loudly, but she didn't even dare to pick up the leaves. In the end, we got a pile of food for her.

She was very tense and was afraid she would miss some question. Whether we asked in a dozen or dozens of words, a question or several questions, she just mm'd, like a sponge, using her cold uneasiness to swallow down any gesture of our kindness. I became unwilling to speak, also unwilling to watch TV. Whenever I entered the living room, she would stand up, put the remote control on the tea table, and walk back to her room. Sometimes when it was too late to stand up, she would shrink and make herself smaller on the sofa. After I walked away, she wouldn't change the channel I'd been watching, not even if I didn't come back for an hour. I felt like I was living in a hotel. Behavior dignified, atmosphere stiff, impossible to walk around half-naked or sleep while watching TV, legs on the tea table. There wasn't a single piece of tea debris on the floor, which Spring cleaned over and over. The sink was wiped as clean as shiny silverware.

"I should pay for the meals." She said that once.

"Now you are treating me like a stranger," Lili said.

"You see I always eat."

"Don't be a stranger with me."

Sometimes Lili went to her room to have a chat with her. "She smokes occasionally and writes a journal sometimes," Lili said. They'd lost the feeling they had back in school. The relationship, built upon crude loyalty, became cold and formal. Under the table lamp lay the platform shoes, the uppers cracked but wiped clean. Spring said this was probably her only possession.

One day, when the hardworking girl was painstakingly mopping a grease spot on the floor, she accidently knocked over a wineglass. It was one of the few wineglasses Lili had carefully selected and bought. I'd placed it on the tea table in preparation to drink the wine after I replied to an e-mail. Now it was plunging to the floor. Spring dropped the mop, turned and kneeled down, attempting to catch it. Her movement was so swift but she didn't manage to prevent it from breaking into pieces.

"You're okay, right?" I said.

"Sorry."

"I'm asking if you're okay." I looked at the broken glass under her knees.

"I'm okay, sorry."

She stood up, something streaming from her eyes, but she looked down, subduing that emotion. She was grateful for the magnanimity only a relative could give, but she quickly persuaded herself that was just an extravagant hope, it was merely the distant sympathy of a master of the house or the generosity a man should have. She did not dare to look at me for days. In retrospect that was probably another seed of her affection, because in time she became restless and made attempts to test if the relationship existed. For example she began to wear makeup, putting on lipstick one day, earrings the next day, changing her hairstyle the day after. Also, beneath a typical, dull department store uniform, she would wear a colorful shirt or a low-cut T-shirt. Sometimes she wore red high heels. Every day a garment representing her lustful desire would appear on her, just like a gay man, who, once on the street, lets people find certain clues outside his normal clothes and manners. The clue being just what he wanted to reveal to his sweetheart.

She got ill.

She thought this would bring sympathy, didn't know it only increased my resentment. *Um-ah, um-ah, um-ah.* She moaned discreetly and slowly as if calling me. I wasn't moved. After Lili came home, in order to show it wasn't a performance, she started to moan more wildly. In the end I began to suspect she might really be severely sick.

"What's the matter with you?" we asked.

"I'm dying," she wailed, tears rolling. "See, there's no color in my face."

"Drink some hot water, I'll get it for you now," I said.

"Um-ah, I'm dying."

"How about we get you to the hospital?" Lili said.

She shook her head and cried. When we left she went on moaning.

She was probably singing of her endless solitude, I thought. There seemed to be an eternal stream in the room, flowing through the cupboards, TV, cardboard boxes, and every bumpy, uneven thing, filling the entire space, making us irritated to the point of committing suicide or murder. The sound of this indistinct, peasant fakery drove Lili from our own house.

On her birthday she got some money and bought whisky, Wuliangye baijiu, Peking roast duck, and many other luxurious foods only available to high society. *I'm treating you, not just living here like a parasite.* Her face glowed with dignity. She invited us to drink like crazy. We were no good at drinking and got drunk very fast, acting like a family for the first time. She moved over, knees bent, and sat straddling my lap. Lili froze for a moment, then crawled over, and tipped my jaw up with her finger.

"What should I call you?" Spring said.

"Brother-in-law," Lili said.

"Okay, let me ask you a question, brother-in-law. Can me and Lili be your wives together? You agree, Lili?"

"I agree, I agree completely," Lili said.

"You see, Lili has already agreed. Say something, brother-in-law."

Sitting on my lap, she leaned closer to me, I kept struggling. She took a gulp and got down. She walked off, then suddenly turned around. She paused for a moment, then pointed at my hardened crotch and laughed more and more hysterically like a propeller. Then out of breath she told an old story. Lili must have heard it, but she still egged her on. With great effort she controlled herself, and said: "He said he hadn't done it for a long time and hoped I could forgive him; I said I forgive you; he said, If you forgive me it's all right; I started to take off my clothes; he wanted to stop me; I said, what's the matter; he said you already forgave me, I really haven't done it for a long time. I said, it's all right; after I took off my clothes, I let him take off his. He pointed down there, it was all wet, he'd already come." When she was done talking she burst into ear-splitting laughter. Lili accidently spat out her drink, which ignited another round of laughter. It was like our bodies had been strapped with explosives, if any of us held out a hand and pointed, said "I beg you to forgive me," we would start laughing one after another. From then on I realized laughing was a horrible thing. Our shadows were swaying on the wall, every organ trembling. We couldn't break away from the torture of laughing and were about to laugh ourselves to death. I stopped first, Lili followed, only Spring was still making an effort. I felt disgusted. There was nothing at all to laugh about. In the end her awkward laughter exploded like a few lone firecrackers in the wilderness.

Two days after that, Lili went back to visit her sick mother and Spring came back drunk at dusk. She was no longer her former self. She wore high heels, a low-cut T-shirt, a red miniskirt, and swayed like a tree in a storm. Under the creamy light, her lips, smeared with heavy lipstick, were slightly open, giving off an animal smell. When I emerged from the bathroom, she reached out a hand and put it between my legs. I stopped. She put her hand against the inner part of my thigh and moved it up slowly. My penis was as hard as a steel rod. My legs were trembling, and I felt guilty. Before the tip of her tongue reached my ear, I pushed her away.

"Don't do that," I said.

She wasn't convinced and continued to grab me shamelessly. I grabbed the hand and said: "Enough, I said enough." She was humiliated and angry. To make her understand that I wouldn't tell Lili, I said: "It's all right, it doesn't matter, it's normal, happens when we drink."

When I was walking back toward my room, I heard her say: "Fine."

19

She dragged her suitcase and came up from the staircase. She didn't take the elevator. The pulleys touched the steps and gave off nasty scraping sounds. Before she reached the door of the house, she stopped. *I'm not sure if it's here*. Behind the wall was my creative plan. The completed tasks were crossed out in red pen, the ongoing ones marked in blue. Lili pasted slips of paper with all kinds of emojis drawn around phrases like: *I love Qingqing, Cheer up, Qingqing*. I was 15 years older than Lili. Spring stood at the door and started to dial Lili's phone number.

"I'm thinking about inviting a classmate to live with us for a little while," Lili said last week.

I felt unhappy, and Lili just held me, acting spoiled. The guest had come now. Lili opened the door and burst into a birdlike cheer. The person wasn't her classmate anymore. Tortured by time, Lili hardly recognized her. She was covered with dust, looking miserable with a stiff, ingratiating smile. She bowed to me, then ignoring our suggestion, took off her shoes and walked into our house. She wasn't sure how long she would be allowed to stay. When she bent over, her two breasts bounced down. As the master of the house I walked to the door and carried her luggage in.

20

The city moat flowed slowly. Probably because I felt the water was flowing, there was a rushing sound. In fact there was just silence, wind blowing ripples on the water. During the day, it was dirty yellow, foaming, carrying the leftovers, dead cats, and dead dogs discarded by the residents who lived along it. Then it was evening, the river pitch-black, but there was always a spot where ripples glowed in the reflected streetlight. The foam was still visible. There was going to be a heavy rain at midnight or tomorrow morning.

It was just her and me.

We faced the distance, which was like a deep well, not speaking a word. Time after time, I held up the bottle. Mimicking me, she drank as well. My life was ruined by that unnecessary phone call. I just made one call. She was in the middle of something at the time, and beside her stood a jealous man. Later she told me: "You're the only one in the world who asks how I am, on the phone you said, 'Yeah, that's it. Just called to ask.'

"Being with someone else won't get rid of my love for you, you know?" she stressed. Caught deep in such a dreadful fact, I was numb all over, and just talked nonsense on the phone. "I can't, I just can't get rid of my love for you," she said. I said: "Get to bed, it's getting late." She would probably cool off after sleeping.

The next day she made more than a hundred phone calls from the phone booth. "Enough, I said it's fucking enough." I swung my arm as if there was some animal stuck to it. I almost stomped my phone flat, but then I picked it up and reassembled it. I was afraid to hear it ring but had to rely on the frequent ringing to tell myself: *At least she's still alive.* "What are you really up to?" I said. She cried, on and on. After I hung up, she would call again. She was crazy. Then I did exactly what she had done. Over and over, I called, and once she picked up the phone I hung up, until she didn't pick up. I thought she might go and die. "Fine," I said to myself.

An hour later she called from another phone booth and said: "I just miss you being good to me."

"I don't want to be good to you."

"I know, I'm not entitled to ask you to be."

"Sorry."

After a long silence, she said: "It's okay." Like a thief sliding down a fragile rope to the upstairs, I was about to land safely. I said: "Promise me you'll live right." She let me hear a disheartened breath and said: "I'll be fine, thank you."

After hanging up the phone, I was overwhelmed by a flood of guilt. This was probably the most precious, most unsullyable feeling, the feeling glowed with the forgiveness, generosity, and sympathy of shared suffering. But shortly afterward she called again and said: "I still want to see you."

"We already broke up."

"Just see you once, the last time."

"Can you just stop?"

"I can't even see you one last time? I can't even see you after we broke up?

"No."

"I'm begging you."

"I'm begging you too."

I hung up. We just repeated the previous desperation and exasperation game. In the end, I said: "Fine, let's meet at seven at the moat." She wasn't gleeful and wasn't dejected, just coldly said all right. She just wanted to make it happen. I left a note for Lili: *Going to play cards, don't wait up. I love you.* I bought a twelve-pack of Budweiser and a bottle of DDVP. *This is me sending my corpse to you.* I walked really fast.

She was already there. She tried to stand up, but seeing my furious look, sat back down. Her hair was unkempt, her expression bitter, her face streaked with tears. She tried to touch my hand, but was brushed away by me. I said: "This is beer, understand? This is DDVP, understand?" She nodded, horrified. I said: "You asked me to come, right? I came, what do you want?" She bowed her head. "What is it?" I shouted. She reached her hands out, regarded me pitifully. "Hug me," she said. I turned, disgusted. She dug out a balled-up tissue and said: "Do you know what this is?" I glanced at it. "This is your semen," she said. Must be hard and yellow now.

"Take it to the public security bureau and sue me for rape," I said.

"It's not that."

"Show it to Lili."

"Not that either."

"Then what are you doing?"

"We once became one."

"This kind of trick disgusts me." I stood up. "Anything else?"

"I've thought about it a lot, I still love you."

I knew this would happen. I shook the DDVP and said: "I'm going to die now." She shook her head violently. *I don't want you to do this. I just want you to love me.* "I'll let you watch me die," I said.

She stumbled over and grabbed my legs. I couldn't pull them free no matter what. Her tears smeared my pants. I thought if there was someone in heaven, the person could definitely look mercifully upon the loneliness and bitterness in my eyes and could definitely see my legs tied to the ground. "Don't drink it," she said, sobbing. I dragged her to the bench, put down the DDVP, grabbed a bottle of beer, and opened the cap with my teeth."

"How many bottles can you drink?" I asked sarcastically.

"Five."

"Fine." There were 12 bottles. I threw two in the river. "Five for you and five for me."

"Okay."

"We'll drink all our worries away."

"Okay."

"Sit down, let's drink."

When we both got to the fourth bottle, I opened the last two bottles with my teeth. "These are the last bottles." I poured half a beer out of each bottle and poured in DDVP. The disgusting smell wafted into my nostrils. I started to feel sad and said: "There's only one solution."

"What solution?"

"Not to wish to be born on the same day, but to die on the same day."

She only froze with horror for a moment.

"I can't be with you, only down there." I shook my tears and snot. "I can't, Spring, you know?"

She forced a smile. It was probably a smile mocking herself, or a bitter smile at that fate, or a happy smile for this more or less passable ending. She grabbed the fourth bottle and gulped. "Dying is just like that, just a moment's thing." I drank much more gradually. "There might be pain, but only for three or four seconds."

"Like getting punched, we pass out and never wake up," I continued.

"Sorry."

"For what?" she answered after a while.

"I couldn't take care of you when we were alive."

"I don't blame you."

"When we're down there, I will treat you better."

"Mm, I'll be 10 times better to you."

"I hate this world."

"Me too."

"I can go there alone."

"Let me go there alone." Her tears couldn't be held back anymore.

"Us together," I said. "Come here, let me hug you."

I opened my arms. She stumbled over and sat straddling me. We held each other tight. Her body kept twitching. Now and then I grabbed the bottle and took a gulp. She did the same. Tears all over my face, I said: "I actually don't love you, but I feel affection for you. I'll take good care of you down there, all right?" She cried. I said: "Don't cry."

"Mm," she said solemnly.

"After this bottle, let's go."

"Mm."

"You go first."

"Mm."

"You first."

"Mm."

"I'll be right behind."

She hugged me again and again and kissed me again and again. I shook my head, looking overcome by grief, full of hatred for society. She finished the fourth bottle and grabbed the fifth one. The color of the bottle was amber, just like DDVP. She took a sip and bent over vomiting but still took two more gulps to make sure she had taken in some pesticide. I held up the fifth bottle. She took a look at me then, holding her head, and stumbled away. Several times she almost fell down. Soon she was foaming at the mouth and seemed to lose her vision, reached out her arms to feel the way. I put down the bottle. She swayed toward the river and tottered up the floodwall. She once turned and looked at a tree, maybe she thought it was me. At the very end she whined and plunged into the cold river.

I gazed at the road, the slope and the apartment block in the distance; my house lights were already on. She sank to the bottom. I thought I would need to push her down, but she jumped in herself. I got the fifth bottle that was mine and all the empty bottles I'd drank and threw them in the river one by one, then I sat down on the bench, a shiver running down my spine. She sank to the bottom. The river was pitch-black, the distance like a deep well, the world silent as a pocket. She sank to the bottom. Then I heard a faint slapping sound like the sound of footsteps climbing up a wooden staircase in the distance. I jumped to my feet and ran over, saw Spring's hands reach the concrete of the floodwall and shake. She was covered with grass and filth, dripping with water. She didn't even have the strength to lift her head, heavy breath spurting out. Because of the pain, she kept changing hands. I was ready to stomp on those violently shaking hands, but in the end stopped halfway. Why take the trouble? Sure enough she soon couldn't hold on any longer and fell back in the river.

BACH

Overture (1)

Many people's first job is their last job, sometimes even the last job of their entire family. This lines up Chinese people's view of job stability. For this stability Ba Like's father jumped off the roof.

Ba Like was told at the memorial service that he could come back from the remote countryside, take his father's place as a teacher.

– You know the *Songs of Chu*?

– Then how much do you know about functions?

– Know any foreign languages?

– How about paramecium?

Ba Like could answer none of these questions, so the head of the education department said: All right, go teach physical education.

That was 1975, black man Arthur Ashe defeated white man Jimmy Connors, winning men's singles at Wimbledon, Qian Zhongshu completed the first draft of *Limited Views*, while Mikhail Sergeyevich Gorbachev, sitting member of the Central Committee of the Soviet Communist Party, was slowly advancing toward the center of power.

Ba Like, 29 years old, blew the whistle, made the kids sprint on the cinder track. He couldn't squeeze the timer yet, just randomly reported the results. He thought that the world has only one quota, and because he had it, the other one had to stay on in the village, speaking useless Mandarin.

2

In 1991, the Chairman of the Presidium of the Supreme Soviet, Gorbachev, announced his resignation, the Soviet Union came to an end; in 1993, Arthur Ashe died of AIDS, only 49 years old; in 1998, Qian Zhongshu passed away, age 88.

Ba Like was still a PE teacher in one of the city's primary schools. He got to school punctually, poured himself a bottle of tea, carried the tea to the track, taught his students the crouching start position, and left school punctually. At home he had a mother with mobility issues. He cooked for her, washed clothes, read newspapers, helped her to the bathroom.

These things were sometimes done by Woman. Woman cooked, washed clothes, read newspapers, helped his mother to the bathroom.

The first time he saw Woman in the park, he smelled something like face cream. Later, on their wedding night, he once saw her warm pink panties. But in the end they didn't bear children.

Ten years after the marriage, Woman proposed divorce. He gave it some thought, agreed. He wanted to give the modest family property to her, she also wanted to give it to him. They went to the civil affairs bureau, went through the formalities, then walked home together, kept living. Living like aged elder brother and aged younger sister.

3

Ba Like didn't smoke, didn't drink, didn't play cards, didn't even watch TV. He just left home every Saturday at 5 a.m., got on the first number 216 bus, came to the foot of Mount Qingshan, then started climbing. At nightfall he walked down the mountain, caught the last number 216 bus, and went back home. He got home at 8 p.m.; the rice in the rice cooker was just cooked, the bowls and chopsticks were laid out. He washed his hands, sat down, served food to Mother, then scooped mouthfuls of rice himself and ate while Woman sat by his side, and the light bulb hung still between their heads.

– How is it on the mountain?

women asked him.

– The fruit are out (or the fruit aren't out yet), he would answer.

Sometimes he wanted to say, after he crossed the first rope bridge, even walking on the hard, blue rock, he could still feel the whole earth shaking as if there was an earthquake. Or, when he went through the dark, thick woods to the exit, sunshine injected his failing body like hot blood, filled him with strength. He didn't say these things, he said, The fruit are out (or the fruit aren't out yet).

– I like eating these things, Woman said.

Done with eating, done with the dish-washing, showering, and paper-reading procedures, Ba Like fell asleep early. The lights in his home were turned off. Then the lights in the 50 or 60 homes on the street were turned off. Finally, all the lights in the world were turned off. Darkness was like a smooth birth canal leading to death.

4

At 5 a.m. on November 3, 2007, sixty-one-year-old Ba Like, as on every previous Saturday, left home. He was wearing black track pants, a black T-shirt, and carried a backpack. In the backpack there were rice balls, a tea bottle, a flashlight, a machete, some paper, a pen, and a coat to keep the cold out. Woman rolled onto her side, went on sleeping, her biological clock to ring one hour later. She would get up to buy food, come back and wash it, then make a simple breakfast, help Ba Like's mother eat.

– Remember to bring back some wild hawthorn berries, she told Ba Like the previous night.

Ba Like gripped his mobile phone, got on the number 216 bus. The bus window was dusty, the seat was cold, the driver scrunched up, teeth chattering, asked: That's all you're wearing?

– I'm used to it, Ba Like answered, smiling, like a young man responding to one of his boss's concerns. The driver glanced at Ba Like. His face was rosy, skin white, biceps and pecs standing out in his T-shirt; his belly, unlike other old men's, was neither bulging nor shriveled. In fact she had seen him many times, but she still clicked her tongue in admiration. Ba Like didn't shift, just politely sat, watched the darkness slowly disperse like molecules. The gradually arriving light pierced through one parasol tree after another, poured onto the paved road.

5

At 8 p.m., the temperature control switch of the rice cooker automatically switched off, Woman brought out cooked dishes, helped Ba Like's mother out of bed. The door was locked; they didn't hear footsteps on the stairs.

– Like still not back? Ba Like's mother asked.

– No, still not back. Woman glanced at the clock on the wall. A minute had passed.

– Always comes back, Woman said, then picked up food for Ba Like's mother. The old woman rolled up her sleeve, pressed her index finger on her wrist, a small dent was left on the shriveled skin.

– Look, it doesn't go back.

– Eat.

– Look, it doesn't go back, I'm so old.

– Eat.

After the meal Woman helped Ba Like's mother to the bathroom, then to the bed. Ba Like's mother said: What's the time?

– It's nine.

– Why is Like still not back?

– Yeah, why isn't he back? I'm going to make a phone call.

Coming back after the call, Woman said: Phone's off. Perhaps out of power, the bus broke down, or he didn't catch the bus.

– Does he know people at the base of the mountain?

– He does.

– Then he has a place to stay.

Woman washed the dishes, went back to the bedroom, did a bit of needlework, pushed the window open, had a look, found there were some stars in the sky. She thought, it should be him worrying about them, not them worrying about him. She yawned and went to bed.

6

At 6 a.m. on November 4, Woman woke up punctually, found emptiness beside her. She pulled the bedroom door open, saw on the table, on the sofa, on the floor no trace of anyone back, then opened the front door. The stairs were empty too. She called, the phone was off. Woman brushed her teeth, washed her face, rubbed some Dabao SOD cream on her face, then took a shopping basket and calmly went out. From total savings of eighty thousand yuan, she withdrew 24 yuan, which was used to buy pork, vegetables, lotus roots, and eggs. When she came back, there still wasn't any sign of Ba Like in the house. She went to wash rice, cook congee, make pickles. By the time the smell of the congee wafted out, it was already half past seven.

Ba Like's mother called a few times. She went over.

– Like back?

– Not yet.

– What's wrong with that man?

– Guess he should be back in half an hour.

The two women started to eat congee while they waited. Light came through the glass window; the house was getting hot. Ba Like's mother, anxious and worried, shouted: When he's back, I'll definitely break his dog legs. I mean it, definitely break his dog legs. Woman didn't respond, didn't wash the dishes either, she leaned back on the sofa knitting, knitting stitch by stitch. The clock on the wall moved notch by notch. Ba Like's mother mumbled a few words, quietly lay down on the bed.

When the clock struck 10, Woman tried in vain to knit a few more stitches, but her hands had no strength. Standing up, her legs had no strength either. She moved to the telephone, dialed again and again. The phone was off. Woman then moved to Ba Like's mother's room, found she was crying secretly. Woman reached out a hand, she grabbed her hand, like Ba Like was hiding in her hand.

– My son, you come back, hurry back.

– I'm going to the police, Woman said angrily. When Woman went out the door, she ran right into a neighbor, and called the neighbor in to take care of things. As Woman walked on the street, her two legs got stronger step after step, her breath intensified as she walked. But once she got to the police station, her whole body gave out. The police tried to help her but couldn't help her up.

– What's wrong?

– My man's missing.

7

As Woman walked back her two legs were strong again and even trotted up the stairs. But after the door was pushed open, Ba Like's mother sat in the middle of the room crying like all hell. The neighbor said: It's all right, it's all right, even with only one star in the sky, Mister Ba could find his way. Women glanced at the clock on the wall. It was 12 noon. All kinds of possibilities rushed like monsters into her head.

– Eaten by wolves.

– Fell off a cliff and died.

– Struck dead by a falling rock.

– Fell into a hunter's trap and bled to death.

– Frozen to death.

– Robbed and killed by mountain people passing.

– Slipped, rolled down the mountain, hit a tree, died.

– Killed himself.

He couldn't possibly kill himself, he had a mother, had a job. Once he retired, before the school could say rehire, he went skipping back. She went to search inside the nightstand, found six bankbooks, four bank cards, not one missing.

She walked out, stared numbly at the open door. Under the door there was a narrow long black shadow. When the crying, which had stopped, started again, she got annoyed and angry, said: Stop crying, stop crying, then dialed the number of the police station. The police station said, Already contacted Qingshan Villagers' Committee, didn't find any signs of Ba Like going down the mountain, will investigate further. Woman put down the phone, didn't know what to do, began slapping the sofa, threw her body in tears. The neighbor panicked, went out looking for help. A while later a bunch of neighbors poured in (including kids holding rubber balls). They looked anxiously at the two unsteady women, picturing that missing sixty-one-year-old kid. One of them, who had comforted them for a long time, suddenly patted his head, went home and came back with a telephone book. There was a number in the book, the number of the outdoor search-and-rescue team.

– This is more effective than the police, he said.

Foreshadowing

8

Wallace wasn't his real name. Ever since he watched a DVD called *Braveheart*, his real name disappeared.

Every city had some mysterious people voluntarily getting together, like those who feed pigeons, those who sing rock, those who do outdoor search and rescue – they have their own languages, titles, and dignity, do things Don Quixote would probably do. They would never have an office, scorning places of business hung with signs and people in uniforms.

Wallace was the captain of the outdoor search-and-rescue team. On the evening of November 4, he read the map, then read it again, cautiously drew a few circles, then took off his suit jacket, tie, shirt, leather belt, suit pants, and alligator-skin shoes, walked naked to the mirror, smeared his face with oil paint specific to Native Americans, then put on ripped-knee, light-colored camouflage and leather military shoes, put on sunglasses and an American soldiers' beret. He fiddled with the hat several times, to make a cluster of white crew-cut hair peek out from its edge. That's how he wore the hat and shoes as he slipped into bed and fell asleep.

At 5 a.m. on November 5, before the alarm clock rang, Wallace sprang out of bed. He threw the army backpack into the jeep whose muffler was removed, drove it onto the street, onto the concrete road and the paved road, toward Qingshan Village in the dark. There he had smoked nearly half a pack of cigarettes before his 16 comrades had arrived one after another.

At first the sun was weak. He set his watch, tipped up his high nose to make his determined lips show completely. Like a general he said: Target, a teacher named Ba Like, in black T-shirt, black track pants; height 1.80 meters, weight 80 kilograms; square face, scar between eyebrows; area, Mount Qingshan's minor peak, Mount Heshang; strategy, troops divide along four routes, climb the mountain siege-style. Begin.

Mount Heshang was 863 meters above the sea level. Telecom, through mobile positioning, confirmed that Ba Like's mobile phone showed a signal in this area, at 10 a.m. on November 3. Wallace emphasized this was the only available clue. He figured searching this area only required about four to five hours, but being out of practice a long time caused them to make this error of assumption. As the fog spurted out layer upon layer like exhaust fumes, they could only see the tips of their feet, the original extensive search in sunny conditions turned into step-by-step measuring. Then due to constantly getting lost, the search-and-rescue team got all tangled up.

By the time the fog was gradually replaced by a curtain of darkness, they finally gave up their conviction to complete the task in one go.

– How are we getting back?

– Walk toward the center of gravity, Wallace said in the walkie-talkie, sad and disappointed.

9

At 9 a.m. on November 6, the sunlight was splendid. Mount Heshang in the distance was like an awkward bald head, swaying among the mountains covered in red leaves. The team members before Wallace now numbered 38. It took them several hours to gather at the peak of the mountain. What they saw, besides rocks, were other rocks. Wallace ordered them to recheck the potential paths. They checked all the way to the base of the mountain, didn't find any items, odors, or footprints, but found Mount Heshang to be the origin of the world, its zigzagging visible paths and invisible paths winding down, a dozen of them which led to Rome, Tokyo, New York, every corner of the world.

They stopped under an abandoned lime cave to smoke and saw three search-and-rescue dogs drag their handlers, dashing up the mountain.

10

At 9 a.m. on November 7, the sky was overcast, 50 people stood before Wallace. According to the previous night's plan, they advanced toward Mount Qingshan's major peak 1,841 meters above sea level. Once past Mount Heshang, light rain started falling to the dusty earth like dew pearls unintentionally dropping from leaves before growing denser needle upon needle. The mountain paths gradually got wet and slippery. Wallace looked at the yellow mud at the tip of his shoes, extremely anxious, grabbed the walkie-talkie, and shouted: Now all we have to do is race against time, the later it gets, the more damage the rain will do to the scene. Thinking again, he added: Be careful, be sure to use sticks and branches to look ahead.

But still there were people slipping into bushes.

At 1 p.m. a team member on his way up walked to the side of the path to pee. His front leg, brushing a bush, suddenly lost its footing, and he immediately fell backward. Not until he got up and prodded with a branch did he realize it was hollow underneath. He lifted a rock, threw it in and heard a rustle, then the sound was gone. Then from the bottom of the mountain came a clashing echo.

— I can't climb any more, I nearly lost my life.

— Whoever wants to go down, go down now, Wallace said angrily to the walkie-talkie, then added: Brothers from outside, attention please, this year the city's rain was significantly higher, vegetation grew very well, in addition to covering the paths, they also cover deep ditches and cliffs you can't see, please do be careful. But panic like a virus had already spread. The peeing team member went down first, and his companions followed him down. Then those of unknown origin considered it and went down too. Those still climbing turned, saw so many people going down, thought the plan had changed, and followed them. Wallace, like a betrayed chief, went up alone for a while. Once the rain got heavier, he was forced to retreat.

Back in Qingshan Village, he watched his comrades pack, his face iron-gray, not a word was spoken. At that moment, an old woman walked up pushing a wheelchair, in the wheelchair sat an older woman, who was Ba Like's mother. Ba Like's mother gazed keenly at Wallace, wherever Wallace went, there her gaze fell. Wallace got flustered being watched and walked up to her. She, hand trembling, dug a plastic bag out of her bag, then from the plastic bag dug out some cash bundled by a rubber band.

– Chief, this is four hundred yuan I saved, two hundred for you, two hundred for your men.

– Grandma, please don't.

A warm current went through Wallace's spine. Then he said again: Grandma, please don't.

11

At 9 a.m. on November 8, the rain, which had stopped the previous night, again started to fall constantly. The team members before Wallace again numbered 38. He turned, pointed at the main peak of Mount Qingshan shrouded in mist, said: That is the target, there will be no other target.

– He's old, might not climb a mountain so high, a team member interrupted.

– No, you probably know someone once asked the English mountaineer Mallory, Why do you put so much effort into mountaineering?

Wallace turned again, pointed at the main peak 1,841 meters above the sea level, said: Because it's there.

That day there were still people who slipped on the way, and there were people who discovered hidden cliffs with sticks, but there were no longer people backing down. Wallace walked and walked, several times seemed to see Ba Like run out of the curtain of rain. Upon closer inspection, it was just the white rain gleaming. He couldn't tell if it was hope or despair. Hungry, he leaned against a tree root, gobbled down some bread. He picked up the walkie-talkie and said: One day a mosquito and a mantis secretly watched a woman take a shower. The mosquito said proudly, Look, 10 years ago I gave her two bites on the chest, now they're swollen so big. The mantis wasn't impressed.

– Why wasn't mantis impressed? came a few noisy responses on the walkie-talkie.

– The mantis said, That's nothing, 10 years ago I made a slice between her legs, it still bleeds every month.

At 3 p.m. the signal of the walkie-talkie got weak, but after intermittent clacks a piece of accurate information came: Incomplete shoeprint found.

– You're sure it wasn't left by one of us?

– No, this is a pair of walking shoes, the back is printed with four letters, I'll spell it to you, A-N-T-A.

– ANTA, Wallace said.

The shoeprint they found only had a rear sole. A person on the scene took a photo with their mobile phone, walked to a slope, found service, and sent it back to the station at the bottom of the mountain. The station then contacted a netizen in the rear, the netizen then contacted Ba Like's woman. Ba Like's woman found the box for that pair of shoes, fed the shoe style and size back to the netizen. The netizen, based on the information, looked online for a picture of the shoe sole, and sent the picture to the station. People at the station compared the two pictures. The grain, the size, the hollows, completely matched.

– So the footprint points in the direction Ba Like went. He went toward the mountain peak, Wallace said excitedly.

But the endless rain suddenly poured down. In addition, the sky was getting dark very quickly, the visibility was very low. People could only leave sufficient marks where the shoeprint was found and hurry down the mountain. At the bottom of the mountain, many journalists had come. A villager said: There are people getting to the top of Mount Everest, but the road to the top of Mount Qingshan is rough, for years nobody got up there.

12

At 9 a.m. on November 9, the rain continued. Before Wallace stood 197 people. He said: Now manpower is everything, we will collaborate with the fire department. But the bad environment forced the dragnet-style search to end when it was only halfway done, and there seemed no way forward. Wallace came back, got online, saw Ba Like's former students praying. Words like 'friendly', 'smiled all the time', and 'optimistic' were repeatedly used. He was moved. Then he saw another say Ba Like was funny in class, and back then, to have more of his class, they talked about failing it together. Wallace thought, Is that possible? Then he wondered whether if he died he would die missed like this by others.

13

At 9 a.m. on November 10, the weather cleared up. White clouds hung over Mount Qingshan, Mount Qingshan leaned against the vast blue sky. Before Wallace stood four hundred-some team members, volunteers, and journalists. He waved his hand, called out: What is a human being's limit? Some say seven days, some say forty-nine days, some say eighty-one days. We believe it's seven days. Today is the last day, see him if he's alive, see the body if he's dead.

Team members got to the area searched the day before, used machetes to chop brambles and branches, proceeding slowly. Frustrated and desperate, Wallace saw, with the telescope, a long, narrow paper slip hanging from a branch in the other direction. He wandered over, saw the slip had been torn manually, its small, sharp side pointing in a direction. On the paper were two red, Song-style characters: *affiliated primary*.

– Come here, he called out. Very soon, Wallace saw the traces of a bush being chopped, then more and more traces turned up.

– Mister Ba is a smart man, he chose to clear a path through the weak point of the mountain.

Wallace ordered everyone to clear ahead, make it wide. Another paper slip appeared. Then another. More and more paper slips, like torches, blazed ahead, blazed all the way to an open grassy slope. Near the grassy slope there was a tree, under the tree was stacked hay, on the hay was a paper slip wrapped in a plastic bag. The slip read: *Ba Like from the Affiliated Primary School of the Normal College climbed here on November 3, exhausted, lost. Will stay here one night, plan to go down the mountain tomorrow in the direction pointed by the slip at the crossroads, thank you helpers.* Wallace read it out loud, hot tears filled his eyes. Looking closer, by the haystack were leftover wild hawthorn berry pits, human excrement, and crumpled toilet paper. Wallace shouted: Not an average man, you can see he still knew to wipe his ass, the characters he wrote are bold and powerful. They continued looking, then around the grassy slope saw four hard-to-see paths. The one to the north had the last paper slip.

– My God, he went in that direction.

Wallace dropped to his knees facing north. There, mountain joined mountain for dozens of kilometers.

14

At 10 a.m. on November 11, Wallace stood on the police car's running board, took the police loudspeaker. Before his eyes was one head after another, nearly two thousand heads. The two thousand heads like breaking waves came pouring in row after row, pouring in then finally landing. At the entrance to the village there were still many cars busy backing out. At the intersection there were still many cars driving slowly onto the dirt road. Because too many people came, on the usually deserted Xiangqing Road, several rear-end accidents had happened since early morning. The jam lasted for an hour. Wallace looked down at the pairs of eyes looking up, his blood boiling hot, almost unable to believe the voice in the loudspeaker was his.

– Move out, he shouted.

The huge search-and-rescue team, led by search-and-rescue dogs – mighty, dust-flying – drove through the roads, drove past Mount Heshang, drove to the main peak of Mount Qingshan, dispersed north at the grassy slope found before, and carried out a carpet search. Because the weather was sunny, some well-trained people started to use ropes and tools to go down some cliffs to search. At 2 p.m. Wallace's mobile phone received a text: *According to a technology company's GSM positioning, Ba Like's mobile phone briefly showed signal at 7 p.m., November 3, at the train station.*

– What the hell is this?

Wallace looked at the crowd spreading all over the mountain, couldn't believe it. He held the phone, walked around, finally got to a place with two signal bars, and called back.

– What the hell is this?

– They said that.

– Did they make a mistake, ask them again.

A few minutes later, a text was sent to his phone, with this line: *They said, We are not responsible for potential tracking errors.*

– What a shitty company.

Wallace seemed overwhelmed, sat on a rock to sort out his thoughts. Ba Like left a message *Will stay here for one night*, so the message was left around nightfall. He was at the grassy slope at the time. Only if he had wings could he fly to the train station. Even if Ba Like left the message in the afternoon, and was able to race to the train station in time, as a sensible person, he should have destroyed the call-for-help scene he'd set, so as not to mislead anyone. Besides, the paper slip clearly pointed north, but the train station was clearly in the south. Perhaps he remembered the date wrong, miswrote the fourth as the third, but that only meant that on the fourth he was on the grassy slope. He ran to the train station, then ran back up the mountain? Crazy.

He called Ba Like's family. – Did Mister Ba come home?

– No. Something new on the mountain?

– No.

Wallace smoked a cigarette, watching one mountain touching the next mountain's arm, the next mountain touching the next mountain's arm, as they wound and stretched farther and farther.

– Do you still trust Mister Ba? he asked himself. Having asked, he looked at Ba Like's picture in the newspaper. Ba Like was smiling kindly at him.

At 3:30 p.m., Wallace, advancing in a daze, suddenly smelled a strange smell. Smelled again then it was gone. He pinched his nose, took a rest, walked seven or eight meters in each direction, and finally located it accurately. It was a putrid smell. He used a branch to poke around, couldn't see anything right away, called others to help poke, finally found a cliff under a spot thickly covered by branches and leaves. The smell floated right up from below.

As Wallace tied a rope around his waist, his heart raced. People staying above put him down. Halfway down, he looked, but only saw the white tips of rocks. After landing, he looked around, saw only empty stone walls. No ants, no maggots, no scavenging birds, nothing, but the smell was clearly there. Wallace dragged the rope, walked around anxiously. At last, amid the fog of putrid odor, he found a hidden crevice on a rock. Using a twig to poke aside grass and leaves by the crevice, he saw something that would humiliate him all his life: a hawk's nest.

15

November 12: the number of people doing search and rescue was down to 500.

November 13: the number of people doing search and rescue was down to 400.

November 14: the number of people doing search and rescue was down to 300.

November 13: the number of people doing search and rescue was down to 200. The city's TV station broadcast a feature program called *In Search of Mister Ba*, one chapter a day. At the beginning of each chapter a hand firmly gripping a postmark would stamp the date on the TV screen, stamping until it gripped the audience's hearts. Wallace saw his expression in front of the camera was composed. Wallace said, There are only three scenarios for Mister Ba's death: the first is starvation, but the fruit is out now on the mountain, Ba Like wouldn't have just sat and waited to die; the second is he was eaten by a wolf, but searching so far we still haven't seen bloodstains, we all know a fight between man and beast leaves a lot of bloodstains; the third is he fell from a cliff, but the main cliffs, bluffs, and deep ditches have all been visited and marked. Now we can only keep searching the remaining unexplored cliffs, bluffs, and deep ditches. This is the only way. Wallace smoked, watching his strange, bragging self on the screen.

November 16: the number of people doing search and rescue was down to 100. *In Search of Mister Ba* was replayed by the narrative shows on CCTV and 15 satellite TV stations. As Wallace pulled the rope, a comrade handed him a phone, it was a Japanese TV station making a long-distance connection. He already had some experience, and understood procedure. Deep in the conversation, he suddenly heard a scream echoing through the valley: a nylon rope suddenly broke, a volunteer fell off a cliff. Wallace said quickly: We are very busy. Threw the phone to a comrade, and hurried over. At the bottom of the cliff an overly confident volunteer was stiffening his body, moaning, his pelvis broken. Professional firemen raced three hours to the rescue, sent the injured man to the hospital. Wallace took off his sunglasses on camera, revealing the tired redness around his eyes, and said: I don't approve of unprofessional team members continuing to climb the mountain for search and rescue.

November 17: the number of people doing search and rescue was down to 50. A comrade reported the news that withered female clothes were found in a new area, and not far off a male skeleton was found. Wallace was excited for a while, but the conclusion was clear: large-bodied Ba Like could be ruled out. Wallace dragged his legs home and turned on the TV. The TV was rerunning the interview with Ba Like's mother, who was crying in front of the camera, saying, I'm 84 years old this year, you are all good young men, I could never pay back your kindness, you've had accidents, I don't know how to thank you.

November 18: the number of people doing search and rescue was down to 30. Wallace read a newspaper saying Ba Like's woman, at her lawyer's suggestion, went to the public security bureau to file a case, proposing 'suspected foul play'. The reasons were twofold: 1) the body and female clothes found on the mountain did not rule out that a killer was hiding on the mountain; 2) the technology company's positioning, which showed Ba Like's mobile phone had appeared once at the train station, did not rule out that a killer fled there with the victim's mobile phone. The public security bureau said they were considering accepting the proposal. Wallace thought maybe the women had lost heart.

November 19: the number of people doing search and rescue was down to 20.

November 20: the number of people doing search and rescue was down to 15.

November 21: the number of people doing search and rescue was down to 10.

November 22: the number of people doing search and rescue was down to 5.

November 23: the number of people doing search and rescue was down to 3.

November 24: the number of people doing search and rescue was down to 2.

November 25: the number of people doing search and rescue was down to 1. Wallace walked up the mountain alone. His body felt like firewood tied by a slip of paper that could scatter all over the ground at any moment. He said to himself, Just walk as far as possible. Walking to a slope, he glanced at the mountains, saw his own smallness, and planted a red flag. After the sky was completely dark, Wallace walked down the mountain alone. He bought a packet of cigarettes at a corner shop, smoked a few, then started the Japanese-made jeep. After getting on the paved road, Wallace stared at the ground flowing like a river, while his head tried to sort out the events of the past few days, but wherever he went, he got stuck, knew he was about to sleep, and slept. He slept for a long time, then was awakened by a bang, saw the car had hit a huge tree. He felt sharp pain in the ribs near his chest like he was dying. He wearily thought there wouldn't be three hundred, five hundred, or one thousand people looking for him. He wasn't the foundation of things, or, he wasn't the fundamental thing.

November 26: Mount Qingshan was empty.

Climax

16

So things went. The Affiliated Primary School of the Normal College once discussed holding a memorial service. One teacher said a memorial service didn't sound good; they should call it a remembrance service. Another teacher said that didn't sound good either. Someone from the principal's office went to Ba Like's woman, delicately told her the idea, Woman stood numbly for a long time, gently shook her head, said: Not really dead, not really alive.

Not really dead, not really alive, better dead. Dead would mean a clear conclusion like 'on the first time the spirit was boosted, the second it declined, the third was exhausted', reason lost. Like many days later you know you were cursed by someone, want to settle accounts, but the reason is lost. Woman put on gloves, stepped one foot firmly on the pedal, pushed the bike, and trotted a few steps, another foot flew over the seat and straddled it. She started to go to work.

So things went. People automatically counted missing people as dead people, automatically counted Ba Like's woman as a widow, automatically counted Ba Like's mother as a white-haired person seeing off a black-haired person, thought no human sorrow could match this. A family with the surname Ba was now left with two women with other surnames. People found many opportunities to express their condolences.

February 6, 2008, Lunar New Year's Eve: first a bunch of people from the school came in carrying gifts big and small, covered the sofa, then neighbors came in carrying wrapped dumplings, covered the room.

– Please go, Ba Like's mother said.

But everyone had no intention of going.

– Then eat the peanuts I fried.

Ba Like's woman scooped handful after handful for them. In the room at that moment were the passionate voices of Zhu Jun and Zhou Tao. In the kitchen was the sizzling sound of dumplings being fried. Outside the window was the sound of fireworks shooting up into the sky. In the distance was the sound of the huge clock striking. Amid these sounds was the sound of a key being inserted into the door and turned. People didn't notice it. Then a white-bearded, white-haired, sunken-eyed, worn-faced, bony old man, supported by a walking stick, stooped over like a baby shrimp, drifted in. Under the gaze of stunned eyes, he dropped a greasy bag, walked to the tea table, kneeled down, grabbed peanuts and candies with dirty hands. He chewed the candy paper too, spit out peanut shells. Strong bad breath wafted out of his mouth, a pair of greasy track pants trailing.

Ba Like's woman fainted right away. Ba Like's mother picked up the walking stick, cried as she prodded him, prodded three or four times and said, teeth clenched: See if I don't break your dog legs. The crowd, as if suddenly seeing a secret that shouldn't be seen, got awkward, all rushing to help Ba Like's woman. They pressed above her lip, the flesh between her thumb and forefinger. Then Ba Like's woman, like a baby being born, cried out. People said: Good he's back, good he's back. But took a few steps to sneak away. They walked in the wind, walked in the snow, as if tricked, unable to laugh or cry. They sent texts to people they knew: *Mister Ba is back.*

– Back?

– Back!

17

Where exactly did Mister Ba go? This question remained unanswered. At first people thought the shame to speak it out had to do with an old man's dignity, after a sensitive period he would say it himself, but he just remained silent. Later people believed the secret was at least known to Woman, but Woman said: I said if you don't tell me, I'll die. Guess what he did? He rolled his eyes.

He rolled his eyes, looked at Woman like a stranger, as if he'd lived for a long time in a wolf's den, his heart gone wild. So began an invisible war. People (including his woman and mother) tried to seize that secret, but Ba Like, seeing it as a height from which he could not retreat further, defended it firmly, guarded it with his life. Sometimes walking on the street, even when people didn't talk, he would say, annoyed: Don't ask, what's there to ask?

– Mister Ba, you should at least give an explanation to the search-and-rescue team members who fell crippled or were struck dead, right? Not that I'm gossiping, the police station even filed a case.

Bold neighbors pointed behind his back. Ba Like stood still for a moment, angrily walked away.

The consequence of the deadlock was that Ba Like became a lonely soul, people (including his woman and mother) believed he had broken the basic trust between them. But Ba Like seemed to be happy to take on this identity. No need to go to school, he started combing his white hair, put on clean, neat clothes and leather shoes, wandered around the city like a gentleman. People said he liked standing outside the glass window of the hair and beauty salon, hands fiddling with his loose hair. This story increased Woman's suspicion, because although Ba Like still hadn't touched the six bankbooks or the four bank cards, the school pension no longer came. Ba Like had it withheld.

– What are you doing with the money? Woman asked.

– Is it your business?

– Of course it's my business, Mom is your mom, not mine. You don't support her, so I support her?

– Haven't you saved up seventy or eighty thousand?

Though long used to such a cold voice and cold tone, Woman still couldn't bear it. Tears pouring down, she didn't speak and like years before walked angrily to the bedroom to pack up, ready to leave. She packed for 10 or so minutes, packed nothing more than the evidence of the thirty-year life together, bits and pieces of it appearing before her eyes, and again she started sobbing. Ahead was the uncontrollably dark night. She wasn't young anymore, even the 'divorce' countermove had long vanished. Thinking of this, the word death flashed in her mind. She thought it was okay to die. Then Ba Like went in, dug out a pile of RMB from his briefcase, said: Count. Suddenly Woman, from the middle of the sea, grabbed the edge of a boat, licked her finger and counted one by one, counted and did a sum in her head. Not a cent was missing.

– I called the school, will send it to you from now on, Ba Like said.

– I'll leave you some, come, here.

Woman drew out three hundred-yuan notes, gave them to him. He hesitated, reached a hand, took them. Later Woman blamed herself for being generous, but back then being generous seemed to be the only way. Ba Like stood in front of her like a sad, bankrupt man; that money had been earned by him.

After Ba Like walked a hundred meters, Woman quietly followed. Ba Like didn't walk as briskly as when he was fit, Woman walked and got closer, even had to force herself to slow down. Ba Like looked straight ahead, past the bank, supermarket, telecom office; past the sidewalk, crosswalk, tactile paving; past the movie theater, restaurant, bathhouse; past the Chinese chess stall, Yangge group, busking spot; past the hair and beauty salon. At the entrance of the hair and beauty salon sat a prostitute wearing platform shoes and pig-blood-red lipstick. She crossed her white legs, squeezed her arms hard, squeezing out cleavage, deliberately or undeliberately said, Wanna play? Ba Like looked straight ahead, walked past, then about one kilometer ahead, turned, went back along the previous route, looking straight ahead, past the hair and beauty salon, busking spot, restaurant, and supermarket and walked back home.

The eighth time Woman followed, she lost interest. She didn't catch up but went to the Agricultural Bank and waited in line. About an hour later it was her turn, she inserted the bankbook in, said: Today is the 15th, I wonder if my salary was sent to my account. The teller put the bankbook into the printing machine. After it came out, it showed Ba Like's pension for the month was paid, not a cent less. Life is like that, people can become hard to believe, money cannot.

18

On July 15, 2008, many old people went to the bank to wait in line to see if their salary had been paid. Ba Like, as usual, walked on the street, walked on with no destination.

When he walked to an intersection, he waited patiently for the red light to turn green. It was still early, about three or four in the afternoon. A sprinkler truck came sliding like a crab, sprinkled water on bicycle tires. Ba Like moved back up the stairs, watched it slide to the right. The green light was already flickering, but he was in no hurry. After crossing the intersection, he squatted on the stairs outside the department store, watching people play chess. There were the two same old heads, which got together to play mysterious games like kids. He watched a moment, walked away, then stopped at the entrance of a hotel. In the open area of the parking lot outside the entrance, a bunch of servers in Song dynasty costume stood straight in three rows. The manager in a suit called out: Welcome. They called out: Welcome. Then bowed together. The manager called out again: Please come back soon. They called out: Please come back soon. Then bowed together. Faces serious.

Walking to a newsstand, he picked up an evening paper, leafed through it, through four or five pages. A head poked out from the inside: Buy? He gave the paper a shake, put it back, like it wasn't worth buying. Walking to a home appliance store, he saw twenty-odd color TV sets stacked up like boxes. Each TV set was playing the scene of Fan Wei limping away. *Thanks*. People watching nearby all laughed, Ba Like let his two arms hang, numbly watching. By the time a wall of TV sets turned to snowflakes at the same time, he was still standing there alone as if waiting for something. He took a look at his watch, finally went to walk again.

He looked straight ahead, past the hair and beauty salon. As he passed, a prostitute wearing platform shoes and pig-blood-red lipstick crossed her white legs, squeezed her arms hard, squeezed out cleavage, disdainfully said: Want to play? He looked straight ahead, walked past. Ten minutes later he walked back. The prostitute crossed her legs again, then rose, pulled the chair. The cleavage, like it had two eyes, blinked at him. He was like any other newcomer, palms sweating, looking inside in surrender. Inside sat five or six similar prostitutes, they dug toward the entrance like piglets. Blond, green, purple false eyelashes fluttered together as if saying: Come eat me, come eat me. They reached out their hands to grab Ba Like's stiff arms, pulled him in.

He pointed at the woman smoking by herself in the far end. She hadn't looked out at all. There were oohs and ahs around. He blushed. The woman flicked her cigarette ash into an ashtray, turned – a numb oval face, crow's-feet, and wrinkles had left their marks. She sat but seemed to look down at Ba Like.

– Me?

She gave a smile, her teeth weren't white. The smile suddenly, very impolitely stopped. Ba Like evaded her gaze, nodded quickly. She stood up, brushed her black miniskirt, grabbed a roll of toilet paper from the dressing table, stuffed it into her bag, then said: Let's go. Ba Like was like a donkey, head bowed as he followed her.

19

— How old are you now?

Walking to an empty alley, Ba Like's heartbeat steadied a bit as he spoke. The heels clanking ahead stopped, then started clanking again.

— Twenty-five.

— Where are you from?

— Sichuan.

— Where in Sichuan?

— You guys always do these pointless things.

Ba Like felt embarrassed, after a moment he went on: I don't think you look like you're from Sichuan.

— You tell me, boss. Say where I'm from, and I'm from there.

— I think you're from Jiangxi.

The footsteps ahead stopped, then started again.

— Where in Jiangxi? You guess.

— Ruichang County.

Girl turned, looked Ba Like up and down, eyes showing vicious scorn. Then the scornful glow became resentful fury.

— Sorry, no business today.

— Girl, you misunderstood, I didn't come for that.

— Then what'd you come for?

— I just want to talk with you.

— You're pretty old, don't be like those college students. Aren't you going to tell me to get married soon, go get a decent job? And tell me you love me, will wait for me?

Ba Like was extremely embarrassed. The moment Girl turned to walk off by herself, his tears suddenly came in a trickle. Girl never saw a man that old with snot hanging on the tip of the nose, gave him a few sidelong glances, then stopped.

— All right, whatever you want to say, say it.

— Let me buy you a meal.

Girl didn't respond.

— Let me buy you a meal.

Girl bit her lips, gave it a thought, looked around the alley, said: All right, all right, that donkey burger shop then.

20

They walked into the narrow donkey burger shop. The table was greasy. The shopkeeper, in a dirty apron, eyed them suspiciously. Ba Like tried to clear up the obvious misunderstanding, but Girl wore her professional expression, looking at Ba Like coldly and disdainfully. The shopkeeper walked away with a fake smile.

– I know who you are, Girl said. Took out a cigarette from her bag, sharply clicked the lighter, focused on the first smoke ring. Before that Ba Like had been an emotional lion, now it seemed unnecessary to hide. He moved his lips, ready to speak.

– Go on. Girl flicked the cigarette ash to the ground, eyes looking directly at him.

– The journey back here from there was 1,350 kilometers in total, past 25 cities in total. Before Spring Festival there were no vegetables in the vegetable fields by the roads, only frozen soil, but a lot of people were getting married. I had one wedding meal in each city. I'd walk straight into the hotel, pretending to have business.

– The Spring Festival Gala had been performed. The husband's side thought I was the guest from the wife's side, the wife's side thought I was the guest from the husband's side, slipping in an empty red envelope was enough.

– I didn't do that, I went in pretending to have business. I didn't know where to settle down, so I went to the bathroom, washed my face, came out refreshed, knew which table had single guests, sat there, ate, ate everything. The bride and groom came to toast, I went to the bathroom again. I burped in the bathroom, and tears came down.

– Why?

– Because I didn't know anyone.

– Go on.

– I ate, thinking there wouldn't be a next meal, but I had a meal in each city. At first it went well, then my clothes got stinky, a waiter reached out a white glove to stop me. I said I had business, they said what business. I couldn't say, so they kicked me out. But northerners seemed kinder than southerners. The bums went to the entrance of the wedding banquet rattling clappers, singing, singing until people inside came out, poured leftover fish in their plastic bags. I followed behind them, they said: Not one of us. But those women still poured me a portion. I got it and ran.

– Eat some. Girl's head leaned back slightly, keeping the pressure on Ba Like.

– I'm not hungry. When I didn't have enough I went digging in trash cans, at first I knew it stunk. Later I didn't know. When my body was still clean, I got up the railway embankment from far away, walked toward the train station, walked to the platform. I couldn't get on the express train, the express train has people punching tickets at the doors. I followed a bunch of migrant workers squeezing on the slow train. I always thought I could ride for a few stations, but they always spotted me quickly, pushed me off the train at the next station. As it got closer and closer to here, fewer and fewer migrant workers got on the train, I couldn't squeeze in. I could only walk along the railway. I saw there were stones, lunch boxes, crap, and dead babies on the rails.

Girl put out a half-smoked cigarette, yawned.

– You never went through a time when you didn't have a single cent, huh? Ba Like asked fawningly. Girl shook her head. At that moment a young couple walked into the small shop. The man was tall, gripping a BMW key in his hand, the woman was pretty, an expensive necklace around her white, tender neck. Both faces took on the gladness of upper-class people who visit for adventure. Girl, sitting in front of Ba Like, had already shifted her gaze to the food, but couldn't help but steal a glance at the wife. The glance spotted the hard-to-see scar behind her ear. Girl sneered quietly.

– Go on, she said.

– I spent nearly three months coming back here, but only one day and one night going there. I rode the cheapest, slowest train, only spent one day and one night. I transferred to a minibus, and only spent an afternoon. One day, one night, and one afternoon I was there.

21

– I could have gone there earlier.

Ba Like looked at Girl desperately, Girl was looking up at the lizard crawling on the ceiling. They didn't talk, the lizard didn't make a sound crawling on the ceiling. Ba Like picked up the seaweed egg soup, took a slurp, the sound was loud. Girl heard it, sat up straight and said: Right, why didn't you go earlier?

– Saying it out loud feels a little better.

– Go on, I'm listening.

– I could have gone there earlier but postponed it for 32 years.

– Why postpone it?

– Because there was a portrait at home. I saw the face on the portrait was handsome, elegant, with good features. But I heard mother say, when the corpse was carried back, the head was cracked, blood kept dripping, dripping all the way home, followed all the way home by ants. If I came home a little late from work, my mother would sit there silent, sulk. I said why? She pointed at the portrait, said, If you want to go, it's okay, see your dad before you go. So I sat with her through that dark time like sitting in a bottomless well, sitting for 32 years.

– Go on.

– If I had left, my father would have jumped for nothing. He jumped, I shouldn't have gone back to the city, I ended up going back to the city.

– Should have, shouldn't have, I've been hearing this since I was little, hearing every day, tired of hearing it.

Ba Like suddenly felt upset, blew his nose, went on: My mother said to me, pinch my leg, it's worse every day, if you go, I'll have no one to rely on, will have to crawl on the street, beg for food. Other people walk with legs, several inches each step, I'd walk with my belly, I'd get run over by a car and die. Later, as if to make the prison solid, her legs were completely ruined. Eventually the walking stick couldn't support her. She said you can't look after me on your own, you have to have a woman, so I got a woman. It was like I knew nothing. Out of the blue I got a slip of paper telling me to go to the park, so I went to the park.

– Twenty yuan total. The shopkeeper, seeing Girl crook her finger, came to collect the money.

– Let me let me, Ba Like said quickly. The owner glanced at him, thought of course he should pay, so gave the money back to Girl. Girl didn't speak. Ba Like handed over a hundred-yuan bill, said, Add a pot of tea, dessert or something.

– I'm not leaving, Girl said.

– Good. In the park I met the woman covered in the smell of face cream, my future wife. I rushed to agree, but what would I have done if I didn't agree? The fundamental issue was the portrait, the woman was just another factor. Since I couldn't break away from my father, marrying a woman I didn't like was only natural. If I didn't marry this one, then I'd have to marry that one...either way I had to marry. On the wedding day my face was pale, was very ill. Everyone looked like they had gotten married, faces rosy, colored paper stuck in their hair. They thought there couldn't be a better-matched couple, they threw me on the bed like throwing a bound animal. They closed the door hard, then locked it from the outside. They giggled outside. I looked at my woman, smiled awkwardly, let her hand stroke my head, felt like a child being held by a strange woman, like a person jumping into water to commit suicide, step by step walking into a deep lake, drowning.

– And then?

Girl played with a new Nokia, the couple nearby looked curiously in their direction.

– Later I became an amateur mountaineer. When the teachers from the school first invited me, I didn't say yes. Then they came where I lived to invite me, I still didn't say yes. My mom and wife said, Go, remember to be back at eight for dinner. Colleagues took me to the mountain like escorts. My feet were free the moment they stepped out of the house,

I could feel their lightness and joy. But when I had almost arrived, I became desperate again, because I saw clearly that after arriving I still had to go back, obediently go back to that forty-square-meter prison.

Girl put down the phone, arms folded, looking at him.

– The fresh air was false, the lush trees were false, the murmuring brooks were also false. They weren't air, trees, or brooks, they were a steel fence. I sat on the mountain, around me was just the steel fence. I thought I was close to some kind of miracle, in fact I'd just fooled myself. I was just allowed out for some air. I was out for some air, but the thick rope and thick shackles were still on my body. However far I walked, I walked in vain, my mother just needed to pull gently, and I had to obediently go back.

– Chen Shimei would say the same, Girl teased.

– Right, Chen Shimei would say the same, Chen Shimei would find excuses.

– Why did you go there in the end?

– Because I heard Bach on the mountain.

– Bach?

– Right, Johann Sebastian Bach, the father of western music.

– Right, I think I remember, that person always taught me, said this Bach was ignored until long after his death, later honored as the father.

– Right. If it weren't for a young man named Casals who bought a new cello and wanted to practice, and went to all the music stores looking for scores, his great *Suites for Solo Cello* would have lain dormant forever.

Ba Like paused, said: I remembered I was also named Casals, but lived here a full 32 years.

He went on: When I went back to the city to take my father's place, people from the education department asked me, Do you know the *Songs of Chu*? How much do you know about functions? Know any foreign languages? How about parameciums? I shook my head, sweat broke out on my forehead. They said, All right, go teach physical education. I should have told them, I know Beethoven, Mozart, Tchaikovsky, and Bach, but I got nervous for a moment, and became a PE teacher for 32 years.

From outside came the sound of the BMW starting up. Girl turned her head. When the luxurious silver car slid by, Girl showed an overwhelmed look. She was jealous.

22

– You said you heard Bach on the mountain. Girl said, turning her head back.

– Right, heard it the last time I climbed the mountain, which was also the first time I climbed the mountain alone. Because the colleague I had an appointment with was sick. I got on the bus alone, watched the darkness slowly disperse like molecules, the gradually arriving light pierce through one parasol tree after another, pour on the paved road. Suddenly I sensed a greater freedom than before. I got off the bus, stretched out my arms, the soles of my feet felt the stones and the heat of the ground. I walked alone toward the mountain, without a destination, without worry, just walked up foolishly. Arriving at Mount Heshang, I suddenly shivered. I turned off my mobile phone. I thought I should have one day like that, nobody knowing me, nobody able to find me, just enjoying this world quietly and alone.

– And then?

– Then I cut through brambles, full of spirit, walked to Mount Qingshan's main peak 1,841 meters above the sea level. Before then all my companions said that was an impossible thing, but with just one look I pointed out the weak point of the mountain and easily cut a path through with the machete. At the end there was a grassy slope, over the grassy slope there were four paths to the east, south, west, and north, I simply took the one to the east, climbed a hundred meters, got to the main peak. There the unimpeded wind blew over, blew through my T-shirt. Clean air pushed into my lungs as if giving my internal organs a bath. I looked at the usually terrifying mountains standing shoulder to shoulder, nestled together, and shouted: Huimin.

Girl was suddenly startled.

– After I shouted, the name started to travel across the mountains, as if it could travel to Bazhou, Huangchuan, Macheng, travel all the way to Jiangxi Province. But then I saw clearly that it hit a mountain not far off, was extinguished. I sat there, disappointed and unspeakably sad. I thought I couldn't get there. But as I sat dully, packing up, ready to go home, suddenly a wind came. Red leaves, grass and branches all over the mountains started to dance like waves of wheat rolling past. I stood up, immediately heard the poem I would never hear again in my life: *Suites for Solo Cello* by Bach. My ears were filled with the sound of *feng-feng-feng*, *feng-feng-feng*.

Girl stared at Ba Like. Ba Like gestured rapturously.

– I leaned against a tree, tears covering my face, heard the sound of cello all over the mountains. The sound of cello passed through me like tides layer upon layer, then left layer upon layer, until they were completely gone. As if they never came. I felt alone. I stood on the mountain alone. I started to feel restless, I didn't, as it says in the textbooks, gain a pure heart, become broadminded and generous ever after. I started to feel restless, walked back and forth like a lion. I shouted: Fuck you. Fuck you, Father. Fuck you, Mother. Fuck you, Woman who divorced but still lives with me. Fuck you.

– Are you all right? Girl said holding the teacup.

– I cursed enough, released enough, leaned against the tree, gasping, then laughed out loud. I didn't know why I was so happy, so free of hatred. I walked down the mountain according to my own will, walked to a grassy slope, put together a haystack, ate a few wild hawthorn berries, took a dump, then took out paper and pen, left a slip on the haystack saying I got lost here, would stay for one night and tomorrow go down the mountain along the path to the north. But.

– But what? Girl saw Ba Like chuckle at her.

– But I walked south, that was the way I had taken climbing up the mountain. I took out a piece of blank letter paper, tore it in slips. I put the slips at the entrance to the grassy slope and on the branches by the path, telling them I went north, but I went south. I disappeared under their noses, I disappeared, I once thought there was no hope at all, but that day I found the wings to fly. I flew away, used a just excuse to fly away from their prison.

– So you went to the south?

– Yes, I walked eagerly down Mount Qingshan, down Mount Heshang. At the bottom of the mountain, I saw there were villagers in the distance, so retreated to the woods, headed west. I went across invisible rivers, passed the line of sight of the village, walked to a distant road, waited for a bus there. When the number 216 bus came, I turned, squatted down, told myself not to make mistakes. I got on another bus, then transferred to another bus in the city, rode it back home. Of course I didn't go home, I walked to a building under construction, walked to the third floor, tore open a cement sack, threw out the broken bricks, dug out a plastic bag inside. Inside the plastic bag was a Rural-Urban Bank card, I took the card to an ATM, withdrew the seven-hundred-yuan paper-grading fee. I took the seven hundred yuan, took a taxi to the train station, bought a train ticket to your Jiangxi, your Ruichang. I remember I was the first to go through the ticket check. I walked fast to the car, found a seat, sat down. I saw some people silently get on, dragging luggage, silently stuff the luggage into the luggage rack, then silently get off the train to smoke. I wondered why it still hadn't left, why it still hadn't left, so I turned on the phone to check the time, saw it was 7 p.m., November 3, 2017. I figured the train would leave in 10 minutes, but it might be late. I nervously looked out the window, looked at people running on the platform, as if they were coming for me, coming to catch me. I was afraid they were being followed by a white-haired woman and a freckled woman. I was afraid. When the conductor rudely closed the train door, I felt at ease. I thought you might as well be a bit ruder. As I listened curiously to the Henan dialect, Shandong dialect, Hubei dialect, the conductor's odd Mandarin, and your Jiangxi dialect in the car, warmth grew in my body layer upon layer. I thought I was a traveler, a traveler after all. My traveler's heart jumped like a young man's, like a young man, I almost stood up, shouting: Huimin, I'm coming.

The words suddenly stopped. Like the crest of a wave pausing midair.

After a long while, Girl flicked the long cigarette ash onto the plate. She looked at Ba Like, Ba Like was sitting sadly.

– You came, you only spent one day, one night, and one afternoon. But that Huimin was dead, Girl said mercilessly.

23

– Why don't I speak for you now, Girl said.

Ba Like lifted his eyes, looked at her pleadingly, like a dog shut outside, anticipating, afraid the club will fall again. But horrible truth came out of Girl's mouth once again.

– Let me speak, You came gloriously to our Jiangxi Province, Ruichang County, Leshan Tree Farm, Guangming Village. Look, this is my ID, Guangming Village. You came to Guangming Village, only saw a grave, didn't you? The characters on the grave were carved wrong, weren't they? Hui as in Anhui was carved like wei as in weixiao.

– Right, right.

– We peasants can't read, it's normal to carve things wrong, unlike you city people. She could read, but she died, couldn't know her name was carved wrong. Good she died, just died a bit terribly, drank pesticide, didn't die, then used a belt to hang herself. We looked for two days and two nights, didn't find her, ready to quit, but the dog barked, the dog barked, ran toward the mountain peak. We followed it up, saw a black shadow hanging on a tree. We used the torch to light it, lit her eyeballs, bulging and cracked, tongue hanging out long as a chopstick. We were shocked, my dad was shocked too, but still my dad climbed up the tree, let her down, then carried her home. My dad just said one sentence on the way: She stood high, saw far.

Ba Like bowed his head. Girl said: Every day she waited for you to come, you didn't come. When she was dead, you came. Ba Like's shoulders started to tremble over the table.

– Every day she waited for you to come. She got a big chest at home, padlocked it. Put a small chest inside the big chest, padlocked that too.

She opened the padlock of the big chest three times a day, then opened the padlock of the small chest three times a day to see the black-and-white photos inside. If we walked up she'd immediately put the pictures away, lock the two locks. After she died we pried the chests open, finally got to see what they looked like.

Ba Like lifted his head, eyes anxious and eager.

– Yes, square face, parted hair, brows just like yours now, there was a scar. How'd you get the scar?

– From fighting.

– A fight in our village, huh?

– Yeah.

– She said it a hundred times. Said it to everyone after she went crazy. She said she slept alone on the tree farm, dared not turn on the light in the evening, dared not turn off the light either, always rustling outside the window. She went looking for you in Guangming Village. You brought 20 educated youths to the tree farm, said nothing, just smashed the cafeteria to smithereens. You took her away like a guardian spirit, took her toward Guangming Village. Halfway through, two or three hundred workers and local villagers gathered at the tree farm with hoes, cleavers, and axes and caught up, surrounded, and beat you. You were beat into a jumping, flying mess, crying and calling for Daddy and Mommy, running all over. Then she said you were already lying facedown on the ground but suddenly broke free, rose, and shouted: You're tough, huh? Beat me to death, today I'd like to see how you spell death. Your head was bleeding, nose was bleeding, corners of your mouth were bleeding, face and clothes were covered with blood. You scared them like a ghost, those two, three hundred people froze, looked at you. She said you suddenly snatched a cleaver from someone, aimed the cleaver at your shoulder, chopped wildly. After a few chops, some people started laughing, because you used the back of the knife on yourself. You took a look, turned the edge around and gave your forehead a chop.

– Yeah.

– You only did one chop, the 20 educated youths and two or three hundred hostile people all hurried to stop you. You jumped around like you were having a seizure. All they could do was wrap you up. You jumped a few times and said: Okay. Nobody knew what it meant. You said okay again. They let you go. Then she said you pointed at the two or three hundred people and shouted: You guys pretending to be gangsters or what? Someone hiding said: What if we are? Then you grabbed a hoe, sprinted over to fight, and another scuffle started. At that point in the story she was very happy, said you beat them up by yourself, you won.

– We didn't win, Secretary came and fired a shot in the air. Secretary said: Whoever is a warrior in the camp of Chairman Mao's Proletarian Cultural Revolution put your weapons down and come here. So everyone quickly went over. Secretary said: Promise me, not even internal contradictions among the people matter. I shook hands with the Secretary of the Tree Farm Youth League branch and said, Right, not even internal contradictions among the people matter.

– After this she said: Little Ke would give his life for me, he'll definitely come to get me.

Ba Like seemed to take another blow.

– Do you remember our village had a supply-and-marketing co-op branch?

– I remember after the fight Huimin was placed in Guangming Village, stood behind the counter there.

– Right, she stood behind the counter there. During the Cultural Revolution, at the town level there were supply-and-marketing co-operatives, at the village level there were supply-and-marketing co-operative branches, but why did a broken village need a co-operative branch? So much candy and cloth laid out, but who would buy them? She just clung to it. Later when the town issued a document saying the village-level branches were being closed, she wrote a report for the authorities. The authorities didn't approve it, so she met with higher authorities. The meeting came to nothing. People came to collect the signs and official seal. She clung to the ground rolling around. A person her age who liked to be clean and pretty, just rolled on the ground like a cat or a dog. They said, Fine the sign you can keep. She was still rolling, so they said, Fine, you can keep the official seal too. Then she got up. Do you know why she would keep the sign? To tell people coming to buy things I'm still with the state, I'm not like you, right? As long as she stood on that pitch-black, shiny cement ground, touching that pitch-black, shiny counter, she felt like she was different from them. Couldn't she just feed pigs, couldn't she just haul manure? She couldn't even sell a few packs of cigarettes a day but had to keep up the front – whose money she was wasting? My dad's. My dad would go up the mountain, only able to chop down three trees. A tree made three clubs. Three days of chopping was enough for 27 clubs. Took them to Mojia to sell, sold them for less than 20 yuan. The clubs were carefully carved, the money hard-earned, but it wasn't enough for her to stock up once. She didn't carry what people wanted to buy, only western stuff, who would buy that?

Ba Like's head pressed to the table like a criminal's, shaking from side to side. Then the manager walked out of the kitchen, walked to the entrance, stretched, and squatted down to smoke and look at the legs of the girls coming and going.

– She just stood behind the counter, stood until white hair peeked out from the black, stood till it all went white like a spirit fox. When it was dark she didn't turn off the shop light, why? Because she was afraid you wouldn't be able to find her in the dark if you came. She waited there, reluctant to go, sometimes waited until all the lights in the village were off. You know what my dad said? My dad said, You'd better go look, go look in the city, I won't stop you. What did he do wrong? My dad didn't insist on marrying her, she wanted to get married out of spite. She waited, she waited but you didn't come, instead a bunch of relatives from the city came. She was happy for a long time when she got the letter, asked my dad to go hunting 10 days in advance, asked my dad to buy food three days in advance: rabbit, wild boar, wild chicken, even prepared things city people usually don't eat, but those relatives put their visit off a week. The food all got spoiled. They ate their fill, drank their fill, drove the car away and never came back. When they left, nothing could stop her from running after the car for a long time, her mental illness breaking out again. Before that she liked to hold me and say, When little Ke comes, I will go with him, I will take you along. From that day on she liked to pinch my arms. I was little, the pinch made my arm purple. She imitated the words of the relatives to me, Wow, a daughter. She blamed herself for having me. She had me, so Little Ke wouldn't come for her.

– How old are you now?

– Didn't I tell you twenty-five?

– Twenty-five, so your mom was thirty-six when she had you.

– Gotta have kids, being thirty-six with no kids isn't right.

Ba Like looked out the door, sad and terrified. The shopkeeper stood up, said to a passerby out of sight: Come later, still have two customers. Ba Like said: How about I take you to a teahouse?

– Don't go too far. Say it all here, say it all and we're done.

– All right.

– Do you know how scared I was before? The moment I saw the crazy lady coming back from the supply and marketing co-op branch, I ran from the entrance to home, then from home to the base of the mountain out back, found a root cellar there, lifted up the board, squeezed down. The root cellar had a rotten smell. Mice saw me come in, didn't know where to run to. I got scared, started to cry, but I didn't dare cry out loud. I hid in the pitch-black root cellar, counting time second by second, counting to 1,000, 10,000, counting till I figured the crazy lady had left, then dared to come out. I was afraid she would pinch me, beat me. I had to wait until my dad came back from the fields, then I could go back home gripping his clothes.

– She beat you often?

– She always stood in the supply and marketing co-op branch thinking crazy. When she thought I was the cause of her problems, she ran back looking for me. Always like that. I really didn't want to learn Mandarin from her, really didn't care she was a city person before. I just hoped she would die soon. Speaking of her death, we looked for two days and two nights, looked everywhere, just didn't think of the mountaintop. We should have thought of it long before, because she always blabbed about how you two once ran off to the mountain peak, played cello to the mountains. Played some Bach song. She said when she played, the red leaves, grass, and branches started to dance like waves of wheat rolling past. She said you stole a big drum from the tree farm, drilled two holes in the middle of the drum, then looked everywhere for string and thread, slowly put the cello together. She said you tuned it for a month. She said there couldn't be anyone else like you in the world, using such simple materials to make such a precise cello. She stood behind the counter looking at it, came back home holding it, sometimes fell asleep holding it. She held it, saying, Little Ke will come back, he made such a good cello.

As the shopkeeper went back to the kitchen, he glanced sideways at Ba Like, who had tears swirling in his eyes. The shopkeeper glanced again.

– When she died my first thought was to throw the cello away. But my dad stopped me, said after all it's your mom's. I let my dad handle it. Now the cello's still lying next to the pee bucket.

– Sorry.

– So tell me, shouldn't you be responsible for this? The crazy lady said every day, she shouldn't have come, she followed you here. You shouldn't have gone back to the city, but you went back. Tell me, since you brought her there, why didn't you take her with you?

– Because there was only one quota back then.

– She said, she shouldn't have come, in 69 you graduated, had to go to the countryside. It wasn't her turn yet, but because she couldn't leave you, she voluntarily applied to go with you. She was a woman too, was fooled by you. You men are all shit.

– Sorry.

– What's the point of saying sorry?

– Sorry.

Ba Like started to bang his forehead on the table again and again, the shopkeeper couldn't look on any longer, walked up, and said, What's wrong? what's wrong? But Ba Like cried louder and louder, completely unable to stop.

– Sorry, he tried to say to Girl.

At that moment, there seemed to be something like pity brushing Girl's pale face, but in the end her thin lips pressed downward.

– Sorry for what? she said.

– I'm sorry for you and your mother.

– Hah, you can be sorry for her, nothing to be sorry for me about. I'm not your child. If I were your child, you could be sorry for me, but I'm not your child. Forget it, can't fix it, thank you for paying the bill.

Girl sneered, stood up, slung the bag over her shoulder, and walked away without looking back. The shopkeeper behind said loudly, Lili, come back soon. Ba Like turned his head, looked despondent. He saw the descendant of Guangming Village who carried the last traces of Qin Huimin in black shorts as she disappeared. The knock of her heels stomped his heart knock after knock.

Her father was more generous than her but kept him from crying. Her father didn't say anything to him, didn't blame him or beat him up, instead invited him to eat rabbit, wild boar, and wild chicken. Afterward he took him to the grave. Her father said: Huimin, I waited for Little Ke for you, and he came. Little Ke's still so young.

24

One day, three or four months later, at 5 a.m., sixty-two-year-old Ba Like left home. He was wearing black track pants and a black T-shirt and carried a backpack. In the backpack were rice balls, a tea bottle, a flashlight, a machete, letter paper, a pen, and a coat to keep out the cold.

If he disappeared this time, very few people would look for him – just look a little then forget it. Woman and Mother would grieve awhile of course, but because of the previous experience, would be much calmer. But at 8 p.m., just when the temperature switch of the rice cooker automatically switched off, his key was inserted in the door. Because he turned sideways to open the door, the backpack fell to the ground, and wild hawthorn berries leaped out of it, jumping down the stairs.

HUMAN SCUM

Zhaoyu was a younger guy in my town. Of all the young people living on the market street in our town, he was the buffest. I don't think it would be an exaggeration to describe him as an iron man with the back of a tiger and waist of a bear. He liked playing basketball. When he made a drive to the basket, his shoulders heaved up and down like a calf's, knocking over everyone in his way. Sometimes the water would stop running, so he'd go to the water supply station a kilometer off and carry back two large barrels of water without breaking a sweat, like he was on a stroll. When knitting together the neighbors asked his mom, Aunt Wu of Nanyi, how she raised a son so strong, even though nobody was richer than anybody else. "There was no trick to it," she said. "I just fed him eggs, milk, and apples every day. I bought as much as he could eat and let him eat it."

Once when I was back in town, Aunt Wu came to me, telling me that Zhaoyu was going to Beijing, so I was, of course, expected to keep an eye on the little guy. That was the reason for our ceremonial meeting a few months later at a bar near Workers' Gymnasium. Inside some sappy songs played (a woman sounding nonchalant like she was being forced to sing: Today you are already lovers... Love can't be split in two... Can't love and can't hate...). Some of the others really made you cry.

During the meeting, despite his best efforts, Zhaoyu couldn't help pick his iPhone up from the table, look down, and play with it. He was so experienced, so fluid with it, sometimes even showing the scorn belonging only to longtime users. But I bet it wasn't until the day before that he had a smartphone like that. As soon as he got to Beijing he must have immediately bought that new model with the money Aunt

Wu had given him, forgetting about her repeated warnings to spend it slowly, and thrown his father's Nokia 8210 in the trash.

There he was sitting in front of me, legs spread, pants stretched tight around his bulging quads. His upper body was clothed only in a white suit jacket, unbuttoned, his pecs and nipples appearing and disappearing, his abs and belly button always exposed. I could hardly look away.

Zhaoyu's eyes that day were very bright, and his face didn't show the slightest creases. He was brimming with vitality as if he'd just had a long, deep sleep. The whole afternoon at the bar he talked to me in a grown-up voice and seemed eager to try anything I suggested. I understood his feelings about the first breakaway from parental control. I had been like that, like a bird just released from its cage setting out for the city with a feeling of liberation. I remember when I had just arrived I ceremonially stretched out my arms and shouted, "Ahhh." In Balzac's *Old Goriot* the provincial Rastignac says with the same fire, "Paris, now let us fight."

That day the nineteen-year-old Zhaoyu leaped to his feet. On the terrace, facing all of Beijing, he raised his arms and shouted in English, "Come on, come on." After coming down, as if answering my doubts and expressing his determination, he said: "Got no skills but still have two balls, right?"

I also remember I asked him about his nutrition at that meeting. I asked how much he could eat in a day. He said if just apples he could eat half of one of those plastic fertilizer bags. Some years later – ah yes, time flew – because I couldn't register with Union Medical's outpatient department, I paid out of pocket to see a doctor at its international medical department. I never thought I'd see my old acquaintance Zhaoyu on the entrance ramp. He was dressed in a hospital gown, carefully moving step by step on an after-meal stroll.

I recalled that Zhaoyu had a frame as stocky as a weightlifter's. Whatever he wore was supposed to stretch tightly on him, but when I saw him that day his clothes seemed unusually loose. The ruddiness on his cheeks was gone for good. His face was pale white with some black around his eyes, purple on his lips. Strangest of all, his eyebrows glistened with frost. "I always think the air conditioners are on inside, but they aren't," he said, shivering.

I couldn't hide my shock one bit, so after we sat in one of the rows of chairs in the lounge I asked, "What happened? You look awful."

"I knew you'd say that, just like everyone else," I heard him respond angrily. "If you can't give me a hand, don't put me down. Do I really need you to tell me I look awful, like you're the only one who can see? Do I really need you to break that news? I guess you'd also like to tell me I look like I'm dying, huh? I'm begging all of you, if you don't know what to say, don't talk. You know what, I got up this morning, feeling I couldn't possibly get worse, completely wrecked. Do you know how long it took me to convince myself that feeling was wrong, unfounded? Then you come and tell me it wasn't wrong at all, it's the truth. So what should I think, huh? Tell me. You completely ruined my day."

I think my dear readers can certainly imagine the shock I felt then. I sat stiff, face scorching hot. When I heard him say sorry, I said sorry too, multiple times. I saw it was a lesson for me. I said: "Then what should I say?"

"You should have said, 'Wow, you look amazing today'," he said. Then he told me he got his bed because the man ahead of him died earlier than projected. At the time the man's doctor, leafing through his test report, gently said, "How'd it get so bad, wow." After the doctor spoke, the patient was finished.

This meeting of ours hadn't gone on long before it was ended by a rushing woman in green. She walked up to Zhaoyu, took off her sunglasses, kneeled, hugged his legs, and, eyes shut, pressed her ear on his knee. "Oh, baby, baby, my poor little baby." I heard her confide a wave of emotions in a hoarse voice, hugging his legs closer.

When she'd had enough she finally asked: "Drink the milk and the ginseng water? Get the nutrient injection?" The woman's age was an enigma to me. Her face was completely frozen like she was wearing a Halloween mask. When she stood up to leave I caught sight of a bunch of silver mixed in her hair.

More years passed, and I had my last meeting with Zhaoyu while he was alive. The location was a small apartment of only a few dozen square meters on Dawang Road. The walls, ceiling, window frames, and floors were all painted scarlet. The bedsheets, duvet cover, and pillowcases on the mattress and the tablecloth covering the rectangular dining table were off-white. There was nothing else. It made you feel like the apartment was only for lovers, a warm cave.

Zhaoyu sucked oxygen, lying in bed, breath still in his lungs. The oxygen machine made a burbling sound. "You're so stupid, so stupid." Aunt Wu futilely rubbed snake oil on her son's body (where he was lying a layer of dry skin like oatmeal had fallen off) as she spoke. Then she said to me: "Look, he's like a ghost now." Then one of Zhaoyu's eyes was already blind, starkly exposed, bloodshot, terrifying. The other one wasn't much better, could only faintly detect light. His hair and eyebrows had fallen out completely. There was no sign that hair had ever grown on his brow. His upper lip was covered in ulcers. A few remaining teeth stood like dilapidated gravestones, barely erect in his gums.

He was as scrawny as a human being could possibly be. When Aunt Wu lifted his top I only saw skin wrapping a protruding skeleton. "That detestable, hateful, horrible woman ran away after paying the rent for the month, leaving my son here alone. She just ran away to avoid punishment," Aunt Wu said. She went on: "And you. You're like a brother. I asked you to take care of this little guy. Is this how you take care of someone?"

Her blame was reasonable. I knew nothing about what Zhaoyu had done over the years in Beijing. To that day his hand still rested on a textbook, so I knew he hadn't stopped classes at his private university. Other than that, I guessed he probably provided sexual services to rich women in his spare time. But later, from his fragmented accounts, I learned that wasn't the case. And it was from his accounts that I got a glimpse into how much the world had changed.

When Aunt Wu and I turned over his body, I found a wound the size of a ventilation tube on his waist. That was how modern women and men had physical relations, not through the sex organs but through a round wound. Vitality departs from the young man's wound and travels all the way through a tube to the aging woman, rejuvenating the latter.

Several weeks later in a plastic surgery hospital in Bawangfen I soon got a look at the Speed King 206 Anti-Aging Machine. There was nothing mysterious about it. The main part (including a motor and a filter) was about as grand as a cement mixer. On either side was a 560-millimiter-wide transparent brown rubber tube. One tube was inserted into the donor (Tube A) and the other into the recipient (Tube B). During the transmission, the filter mainly functioned to remove stale gases, stale liquids, stale blood, pus, and other bodily waste. Thus, when the machine was in operation Tube A became murky while Tube B remained transparent throughout.

"There is nothing to hide or to be ashamed of. The surgery is not only scientifically proven (it is theoretically based on three articles the Wei Fuli team of Singapore published in *The New England Journal of Medicine*), but also completely legal," said Dr. Wu Jialin, a graduate of Tongji Medical School. "It actually reflects the very essence of a liberal market economy. That is, everything can be traded as long as it is traded voluntarily – everything, including human health and organs. To comply with the conditions in our country – not just in our country but almost the whole world – we currently only accept voluntary donations. Our hospital will perform surgery only after the donor and the recipient have given written consent. Whether there is any monetary exchange between them in private is their own business."

"How damaging can surgery be to the donor?" I asked.

"Not very. Say, if the value of a person's vitality is 100, one surgery could lead to a loss of 10 per cent, with 90 still left. And it's not impossible to recover the lost 10 per cent with sufficient nutrition and exercise," he said.

Dr Wu's statements lined up with what Zhaoyu had told me. There was no discernable damage after the first surgery. The following day he went to Dongdan to play basketball. But because of the wound he just practiced by himself, not daring to compete full on. The second and third surgeries showed no signs of damage. But as the transmissions accumulated and hit a certain threshold, he found that if he just gave his pecs a gentle poke it made a dent like an iron sheet that didn't go back. And even walking a few hundred meters exhausted him.

That was when he started to panic. "Because she begged me, time after time. You saw that yourself. She'd fall to her knees and shuffle over on her knees to hug my legs, crying and begging. If I didn't say yes, she'd get hysterical, tearing off pillowcases, pulling out the feathers, scattering them everywhere. She'd smash the TV, then the glasses. And get on the windowsill and threaten to jump off the building." This was his answer when I asked him why he didn't reject her cruel demands. "I didn't ask for it," the young man added.

"If she was paying it would have made sense to do it so many times. Not a penny," Aunt Wu said.

Then that mummy of a body let out a sigh, which sounded full of disapproval for his rural-born mother. He was sighing to say to me, "Look at her. She doesn't understand anything."

"Why then?" I asked.

"Love," he said.

"How much older than you is she?" I asked.

"Don't know," he said.

"Even older than me. I think she's more than 10 years older than me," Aunt Wu said, stomping.

"She doesn't look that old," he said.

Later when Aunt Wu was out buying food, Zhaoyu burst into tears. He said he'd seen her (her real name was Chen Lixia) scoop up hair dye like mud and spread it on her privates. So he figured even her pubic hair was white. "Once a surgery was over, she'd stand up and snatch the mirror they were always too slow in handing her to examine herself. Then, it's hard to believe, but in the time of a class period she became a completely different person. Her skin which had been as rough as old tree bark, shone, oozing fragrant sweat. Her white hair turned lush black. Her droopy eyelids got taut, eyes big and bright. Her waist got thinner, legs more slender. She looked 18."

"'Is it real? Is your mirror real?' she'd ask every time. After getting an affirmative answer, she bit her lower lip, trying to contain her glee. But she couldn't contain it. So she just let herself go and broke into rude laughter. Then she made for the cloakroom, put on the girly garments that were waiting as she made phone calls, and left in a rush. She wanted to get back to her circle of celebrities – their events, parties, and TV appearances.

"Before leaving, she'd glance at me sideways with the vanity and pride of a beautiful woman. Usually that same evening I'd see her on TV, talking with that ageless male host with a two-character name. He'd hold her hand like he was her best friend and say politely, 'Miss Mary, you look younger again. Where has Miss Mary been on vacation all this time we haven't seen her?'" Zhaoyu said.

"Really, because her beauty was fading, she was hiding again. Usually she hid here," Zhaoyu went on. "Each time, the aging came sooner and sooner, faster and faster, more and more fully. At first a surgery could keep her young for two months, then a month and half, then one month, then 20 days, then 10 days. And she was even older than she was before the surgery. And gave off a stench like a corpse. Lots of times I heard her sighing in a dark corner. She didn't eat or drink. Sometimes when she had to pass me to use the toilet I could see in the light leaking from the open door, her messy hair and the tears trickling down her rough, bumpy face.

"Sometimes she'd scream and vent her anger at me. I figured she was blaming me for giving her less and less pure vitality. But was it really my fault? I did what I could. I gave all I had. I couldn't give any more, couldn't constantly give her the vitality of a young nineteen-year-old. I was already totally drained. Not my fault. Then it would all start again. She'd come back and beg me. Sometimes she'd beg me right after she'd vented at me. First she'd be kicking me with her high heels, next she'd be holding me and begging me to help her again. Obviously she thought she'd get me no matter what. And she did. As soon as I agreed, a car outside would start up. We'd go right to that hospital."

"How did you meet?" I asked.

"We met online, then met at a bar the same day. I'd never seen such a beautiful woman, such a well-dressed woman. My heart kept pounding. When she started to talk, I gave myself over to her completely like a dog," he said.

I went to that plastic surgery hospital after Zhaoyu had been cremated. His corpse reminded me of the human food in ancient books. Not long after his death, 'self-media' reported the discovery of several desiccated male corpses in an abandoned warehouse on the outskirts of Beijing 'scattered about like mannequins', which are suspected to be related to anti-aging surgery. But we all know you can't believe all self-media. In response to my question Dr. Wu said multiple surgeries between the same recipient and donor would certainly lead to the surgery's diminished effectiveness. He joked that aging – humanity's most dogged enemy – may have developed a resistance to it.

FAT DUCK

for Cai Bojing

Anyone who'd been along the river came away with an impression of Little Big Zhang – when giving out his business card he'd say, "Call me Manager Zhang Liuling please" – and his overly serious demeanor. His complexion was pale when he was young (he must have been very proud of it at the time), but now it was sallow and nearly transparent. His face was narrow and long and flanked by a pair of long, easily pullable ears. Because his upper lip covered by a brown mustache was always downturned and shut (the teeth inside seemed to be grinding a sesame seed), and he had the hooked nose of a Caucasian and a bald head, his face appeared even longer. Under his prominent brow bones hid a pair of eagle eyes. They always fixed on you unblinking, unwavering, and made you nervous. Even in summer, he wore two tops. Inside was a shirt, white-collar, buttoned-up, stuffy. Outside was a knee-length trench coat. He reminded people of a monk, a judge, or an undercover policeman. The grim air he exuded gave people chills.

Being around him was like being around a dark forest that blotted out the sun.

Some kids who were typically unruly and reckless shut up around him and gripped their parents' hands or the hems of their clothes. Really anyone who knew him a little knew he was useless. He was born to a peasant family with 10 brothers. Of the 10 he was the only one who was taught at a private school, then studied at a teacher training school, and managed to live in the city. Later he started a wholesale office paper business that worked with several schools. Despite his wisdom, he couldn't figure out what allowed him to surpass his own brothers, so he kept all of his past temperaments and allowed certain elements to flourish. He was like a man who had accidentally made a full recovery with no idea which medicine had cured him, so he used all the ones he'd taken indiscriminately. Reticence was one of those medicines. And by observing others he found that taking on a posture of not speaking created an inscrutable self. People were intimidated by him. Sometimes he shoved his hands into his trench coat pockets and got the false sense he was a powerful man who could arbitrarily dictate the actions of others.

★   ★   ★

Really the only people he could control were his family members (he didn't control them exactly but coordinated them according to the circumstances and their characters – like never having two roosters in the same cage to peck each other bald, he kept his mother and wife apart most of the time, so the two could treat each other respectfully for a few days).

Another example: his wife and son, being his primary kin, lived with him in a two-bedroom apartment with a mortgage by the river in the Shuimu Development. His son studied in Jiujiang Foreign Language School 37 kilometers away and came back to Ruichang on the weekends. His wife was a rural resident and illiterate. This made her see herself as a sinner and not dare to voice her opinions (especially when she thought that, because of her, her two children were born rural residents and laughed at by their classmates...Little Big Zhang bought them urban residency later). She willingly served her husband. Apart from household chores, she was responsible for transporting goods on a rickshaw from the warehouse to where clients designated. Sometimes she used a pushcart with two wheels.

His mother and daughter, like his secondary kin, lived in Jigong Ridge north of the city in a condo, which Little Big Zhang bought with the money he borrowed when he first came to the city and which still had no running water. About two thirds of the houses there were vacant, so untiled blood-red bricks were exposed (the yellow mud that filled the gaps between the bricks had long since cracked) like a body that had been skinned. The facades of some houses weren't fitted with window frames let alone windows, some randomly covered by bright striped polyethylene. Some just let their insides be exposed, rusty steel bars like weeds coming from the ground and through the walls, while the inner walls were pitch-black from squatters cooking. After night fell, those who took the shortcut to or from the train station got an eerie feeling when facing those buildings as if they were facing buildings abandoned after a bombardment.

People called Little Big Zhang's mother Grandma Zhang, though back in the countryside, she was called Aunt Huojin. Since she came to the city she had to be called the city way. People called her daughter-in-law Aunt Zhang, so they called her Grandma Zhang. Grandma Zhang had given birth to 10 sons in total. In that sense her constitution was exceptional. Ever since she became widowed, she had lots of time she didn't know what to do with, so she came to her seventh son, Little Big Zhang, to the city (those in the family who came after the sixth were called Little Big Zhang; it required some familiarity to distinguish them, which I won't explain now) to lead the city life her ancestors never had. She acted first and reported afterward. After she came to Jigong Ridge, she sat waiting outside the locked house, dripping with sweat, until her son came and let out a long sigh. "Fine, you live here with Ruijuan and cook for her," her son said.

So Little Big Zhang sent his daughter Ruijuan who had been living with him to live with her grandma. Afterward, once or twice a month, in order to pick up boxes of printer and copy paper he went to the condo, which doubled as a warehouse, and gave his mother and daughter some money. Ruijuan was always restless and shy in front of him. Sometimes, though he said nothing, she'd hurry off, squat down at some distance, back to him, sobbing. Little Big Zhang had sloped shoulders (why else would he wear a trench coat with shoulder pads?), but back then his daughter was broad-backed and thick-waisted. When she started to cry it was like a big loaf of bread was crying. A few times Little Big Zhang felt sympathy for this strange, distant blood relation of his and wanted to go over and encourage her, for example by patting her shoulder and saying: "Who's this beautiful little girl?" But some deeply ingrained thing held him back. I guess even if his daughter fell off a bottomless cliff in a runaway carriage he wouldn't move an inch, just painfully and silently gape. Every time he jumped off his Jinbei pickup, his sturdy mother would totter over and, right in front of the girl, tell on her. Hearing all the exaggeration, he couldn't help but despise her. He would teach his daughter – her face red, seemingly about to cry – a lesson, unaware that as soon as he left, she would beam with joy, bouncing up and down like a pony to meet her friends who had been waiting a long time. One day his daughter's main teacher at the Number Two Primary School came to him and revealed the shocking secret that his daughter was a problem student with a less than 50 per cent attendance rate, and she had been absent again that day. They found her around Railway Dam. She was standing on a railway track, holding hands with Liang Lianda from the class next door. Facing a coal train approaching in the distance, they sang loudly.

The green grass on the riverbanks,
stretches to where the sea begins.
The road to the sea never ends,
Nor does my love for you.

They ran in opposite directions. As a result, Little Big Zhang handed over full custody of his daughter to his mother: that country shrew seemed to have been waiting a long time. *That's right*, she thought. *It's right to give her to me. There's no one I can't tame.* The old woman gazed down at her son, fully confident.

★　　★　　★

Time flew. After that horrible thing happened, and the deceased Zhang Ruijuan had long been cremated (rumor had it that she remained prone when being pushed into the incinerator; the worker skillfully pierced her corpse with a sharp knife, then lifted up the diesel barrel and shook diesel out over the body), people still remembered her as the little girl chased home by her grandma: the latter holding a tailless whip like a cattle salesman, whipping the former's bottom every few steps. After each whipping, the former would shudder and straighten up, face contorted in agony. The whippings didn't ease as the girl showed greater compliance. For at least four years residents of Jigong Ridge were used to hearing the reoccurring whippings at noon or dusk near and far. By its sound, they could conjure up the arc the whip made in the air. Whipping wasn't easy for the old woman. I mean there were times she almost let herself succumb to laziness and fatigue and give it up. But the sense of responsibility to discipline the vile child for her son made her steel herself once more. Sometimes people could hear that the whipping really came from the old woman's vicious desire or sometimes from her intention to get revenge for the girl's past offenses (before Little Big Zhang clarified her custody situation, the granddaughter always saw herself as city-born and scorned the country folk who stubbornly argued with her). But sometimes they could hear nothing more than the whipping itself like it was an old custom people had to follow (such as human beings whipping animals or landlords whipping serfs working in the fields). Like rain. When the rainy season came, the rain would go on for 10 days or so. People had no idea why it rained or why it stopped raining. So when the sound of whipping suddenly stopped, people panicked (of course it was a rather unimportant type of panic). Some walked out to see why the whip stopped falling on the girl. "I need some water," the old woman said. She wasn't answering their question, just being an illiterate peasant living in the city, explaining her actions to the locals. When she'd drunk enough she capped the plastic bottle, slung its strap over her shoulder, and started to chase her granddaughter home. Sometimes being the grandma, she pulled the girl's ear – that pullable ear the girl inherited from her father – all the way home. Blood dripped on the ground. The girl titled her head, gripped the old woman's arm, and let out a heartbreaking scream: "Aunt, Aunt, my aunt." (That was the only time she used dialect to call her mom *Aunt*. Most of the time she was reserved with her. She couldn't bring herself to call her *Mom* in Mandarin, or *Aunt* in dialect because doing this amounted to revealing her ugly and shocking origins to the public.)"You're going to rip your granddaughter's ear off," people would sometimes stop their knitting, concerned, and warn her.

"It won't come off," Grandma Zhang would say.

"See. She's clinging to me like a monkey."

Once Ruijuan was home Grandma Zhang would go in and latch the door. Sometimes people saw her leave alone and pull the black bolt outside then go play mahjong (she only played poker in the countryside but learned to play mahjong in the city by watching only two rounds). From inside the house came the girl's desperate shrills. Grandma Zhang was an eccentric and meticulous disciplinarian. To show her determination, she went to the parking lot just to ask the driver to fetch the stiff broom tainted by the blood of her 10 children from the countryside. Before it was used to wash pots, clean the stove, and sweep dust. Some summer days, on the dining table lay a green mesh cover to keep flies away and beside it the tightly woven broom. It had given her 10 sons, and later her granddaughter, lashes all over their bodies, streaks and streaks of lashes like they'd been raked. Sometimes she used a club to strike the girl's shin again and again. People often heard the old woman's eager, irritable teaching:

"You have to admit you were wrong today – if you don't admit you were wrong, you can't eat – can't leave this spot – just keep standing – stand till tomorrow morning – you hear – you hear, long ears – I'm telling you to admit you were wrong – don't act pathetic – don't call your aunt – you and your aunt are the same – hurry and say you were wrong – you hear – don't trick me with that language I can't understand – speak the language I know – okay – don't talk like a mosquito – don't try to get away with mumbling – what are you saying – louder – I can't hear – you damn kid, I can't hear, I can't…"After being punished, sometimes Ruijuan was furious and threw herself on the bed (and slept), sometimes she was forced to pump water. Ashamed and resentful, she pumped the handle five or six times then realized she had done it wrong and she took a big scoop of water from the tank and poured it on the mossy pump walls. When the water got through the rubber cap she immediately pumped the handle. That way, the water would be pumped up from deep underground. Completing this process required mental focus, so only after Ruijuan finished this work, and saw the glistening water splashing down the water tank, would she go on with her crying. Other times the girl seemed possessed, madly running and finding her grandma as if she hadn't seen her for a long time, lying prone on the ground, and shouting sorrowfully:

"Grandma, I was wrong. I know I was wrong."

She gripped her grandma's calves with both hands, lips trembling, mouth wide open, panting. Sometimes she'd start coughing and so have to pound her chest fast. Shamelessly, she let herself roll on the ground until she was covered in dust. Thus was her horrifying repentance. Then as if receiving a voucher, she left the house, looked herself over in the shiny window of the parked car on the side of the road, shook off the traces of humiliation, found good friends standing by the manmade lake, and began chatting. In front of her parents and grandma, she was cautious, didn't talk much. Often you couldn't make out half of what she said. But around classmates her age she was surprisingly loud. Vulgar sayings and swear words only the boys used to ridicule the female sex poured out of her mouth. *Fat Duck always said, Your mom's cunt*, those classmates would later remember her. *Or fuck your aunt's old cunt*. They always gathered around, three or four of them, scrupulously gossiping about the affairs of people around them like hyenas in a cult ritual. This always made me feel bad. I remember in Ruichang City (a county-level city, which I called Ruichang County in my previous novels but readers from my hometown sent me letters requesting me to correct the mistake: please keep in mind that Ruichang is a city, don't degrade us) when I was living there I always came across such throngs of people. Sometimes they even brought their babies with them. For three or four hours, they'd huddle around, cover their mouths, talk without restraint. Day after day, still there. Year after year, still there. Decade after decade, their hair turning gray, still there. That was their daily ritual, a way to defend themselves against the desolation of life.

★   ★   ★

One day Zhang Ruijuan graduated from middle school. The other students were 16, she was 17. She didn't go to school to check her scores, and Little Big Zhang couldn't be bothered to ask (wasn't it already decided, how good could it be), but her head teacher was restless (like a naughty child who can't leave an unlit firecracker on the ground). She called Little Big Zhang: "Your daughter scored 126."

"126?"

"Yes, 126 total."

"It doesn't matter if she scored 126 as long as her little brother can score 621." Later, recounting this story to others, Little Big Zhang, once and only once, showed his humorous side. It seemed he had been waiting for the day to rent his daughter a shop close to Jigong Ridge, on Qiuzhi Road facing Number One Middle School, a shop with a sign reading *Advertisement Design Center,* doing typing and copying work. "You can type, can't you?" he asked. "I can," his daughter said. That year, his mother, Grandma Zhang, found that if she poked her swollen calf, the indentation would stay for a long time, so she did it in his face. "I can't work anymore," she spoke the line long-prepared in her heart. City folks were already retired at her age, free of all duties. They only had to open their mouths to be fed and hold out their hands to be dressed, and enjoyed the support of their children. In order to get similar treatment, she spent the first six years in the city cooking for Ruijuan (though she only cooked once a day and they ate leftovers for breakfast and dinner). She believed she had done enough. No matter what it was her turn to lead a leisurely life like the song that says: 'You're too tired, time to have a rest'. She widened her eyes, which easily got teary and red in the wind, and shut her lips. She had her counter ready in her head as she gazed at her seventh and weakest son. The latter closed his eyes and considered it a moment, then made a decision even God might praise:

"For now on Ruijuan will cook for you."

From then on, every day at eleven thirty young Ruijuan would get on the electric scooter she bought on installment from the store next to the printing shop, and rush back to Jigong Ridge to cook for Grandma. Meanwhile, the latter would be holding her belt, complaining as she walked around the neighborhood. "I peed blood again this morning, peed this much," she'd say, making gestures to justify giving up kitchen service. People, including Aunt Liang, Aunt Ai, Aunt Wen, and Aunt Chen, said afterward that the illness which kept her from oil smoke came from her wish. Grandma Zhang didn't want to cook anymore, so her body made the illness to exempt her from cooking. (Doctor Zou Huoquan, who ran a clinic near the train station, said: "Old woman, you'd better take it easy."). Before, so as to be more comfortable, save some effort, she would just make a quick meal, offhandedly give it to her granddaughter, offhandedly have it herself. Now she found her granddaughter treated her that way too. Sometimes she'd finish eating and her granddaughter would snatch the stainless bowl, put detergent on it, rub it in the bucket of dirty water then rinse it in the bucket of clean water – in 20 seconds everything was pretty much finished. When the old woman, forgetful of her past meanness, banged the table and reproached her, the girl would remind her, sometimes even of the exact day. "Besides, you and I eat the same," Granddaughter said. This was exactly what the old woman had once said to the girl. Things seemed to have achieved an equilibrium with the beauty of geometric symmetry (like Borges said in 'The Immortal': *Because of his past or future virtues, every man is worthy of all goodness, but also of all perversity, because of his infamy in the past or future.*)

When Grandma Zhang implied her granddaughter's behavior to Little Big Zhang, she received only the other's bitter remarks.

In the end what Grandma Zhang could do was watch the clock (or ask the time from Old Wang, a retired hydroelectric worker who listened to the radio) to see if her granddaughter had come back to cook on time or not. Being punctual was something she could have a clear conscience about. Though a bad cook, there had never been a day she didn't cook on time. Around noon she got agitated, thinking her granddaughter wouldn't came back on time and that she would be neglected or mistreated by the girl (which she had said would happen sooner or later in complaints to neighbors). It had never occurred to her that her granddaughter, seeing cooking as a burden, wanted to have it done as early as possible so she could return more quickly to her own, youthful world. In her own world she talked about her grandma like this: "Bad teeth, can't chew nothing, and don't know when she'll die, she had so many kids, had 10, all sons, unbelievable, a woman with 10 sons." She also talked about other things, for example, the closeout sale of Camel Outdoors lasted 10 years; Yishion began to sell menswear and its staff just left the air conditioners on despite the large space; whether Propitious Phoenix had copied Auspicious Phoenix; Digital Telecom also selling gray market goods; and the pharmacy trying to recruit trustworthy night-shift workers but paying too little. But there weren't many things worth talking about, only five or six each quarter. Then one day, Ruijuan herself became a hot topic.

A locksmith with a long dick became Ruijuan's first love. Anyone who knew thought it was a scam. The poor girl who was just out of school had no idea of the abyss she faced. The man was collecting women. So far his collection included the deaf-mute at the foundry, the spinster with an artificial limb who worked as an accountant on the distant tree farm, and other half-alive women like Ruijuan herself whose skin was ashen from malnutrition. Some said that for years he'd been sending women to Guangdong to work as prostitutes.

"What do you like about me?" Ruijuan asked him one day. What she disliked the most about herself was her eyes, which were too wide-set, almost without eyelashes and eyebrows. Everyone said that while answering this question the man's eyes rolled rapidly. He was thinking in front of her.

"There are good things about you," he said.

"What are they?" she asked.

"Well, there are good things. Don't worry about it. You just need to know I like you," he said.

People thought Ruijuan would have left a man so short on words, but their relationship lasted a very long time. Sometimes he told her bullshit like, "You're the bone of my bones and flesh of my flesh." When the words seemed insufficient to express his loyalty, he would gave her things hard to come by in the little city, like a Coach bag and a pair of leather ECCO shoes. When she first received that coral-red, litchi-skinned handbag, she carried it for 24 hours, refusing to let go, unable to resist walking around to show it off. That was the year I went back to Ruichang and saw her. I was heading southward on Qiuzhi Road to Central Hospital to see my father. She was coming in the opposite direction, up the ramp I was going down. She was eating one grain at a time, her body incredibly thin. The exposed ribs around her chest reminded me of a grill, each bar clearly distinguished. Her skeleton was big, bones from the genes of the shabby working class, which must have done a lot of work and taken a lot of beatings. She wore a pair of six-centimeter platform shoes and an above-the-knee dress bluer than the day's sky (which was so blue it was almost unsettling). The dress was so startlingly blue that I couldn't help but turn several times to look. In the hours of afternoon slumber, she was walking on the glaring street alone and sweating as she exhibited. I saw dense blue sweat trickling down between her legs like blue menstrual blood.

Later in Ikea I saw – I have no idea why I mention this – an extendable dining table with the following description: *The extendable dining table has one spare leaf, seats four to six people, and can be adjusted as needed. When not in use, the spare leaf can be let down under the table, ready at hand.* I stood there, unable to help but stroke it, then knelt down to insert the spare leaf. Meanwhile I felt a sense of shame and resentment, was eager to leave with my wife. I told her I would never buy a product like that. If it weren't for that I never would have realized I only owned under 50 square meters of living space. Later, I also saw things like drop-leaf tables and foldable chairs. They seemed to have eyes that looked at me scornfully (sometimes in a slightly fancy restaurant or clothing shop, I also felt condescended to by sophisticated attendants). I have no idea how this was related to seeing Zhang Ruijuan on Qiuzhi Road, nor why I talked about it when talking about Zhang Ruijuan. I guess the dining table, which became as spacious and luxurious as the tables of the rich when the spare leaf was inserted, and the flamboyantly colorful dress even a supermodel from Paris wouldn't dare wear revealed shabbiness one cannot stand. When she held the parasol, stepped on the muddy bricks, and one step after another climbed the stairs leading to Number One Middle school, I felt my gnawing at my heart. A few days later, after I left my hometown, I heard this girl I saw was dead. It seemed somehow related to a strange curse.

★   ★   ★

One morning the sanitation worker Li Shili found Zhang Ruijuan's body on a four-feet-wide cement path off Railway Dam. The rail tracks, shiny from the grinding of wheels, were still dripping with water. The deceased's hair was soaked through and parted into several strands, her skin horrifyingly white and covered in goose bumps, her fingers and palms soaked in water were slack and thus so shriveled skin was about to come off. The body lay prone, facing south, seemingly trampled prior to death, the mouth and nose submerged in a small puddle a cow could drink in a gulp, and bubbles came out the nose. One hand holding the garbage grabber, the other holding the strap of the windproof dustpan, Li Shili stood vacantly in the falling drizzle. Then as if suddenly remembering something, she hurried to the nearby early market, gesturing her discovery to the vendors dumping vegetables in their stalls before finally making herself clear.

Then came the spooky probable cause of death. After hearing Ruijuan had died, Aunt Wen, one of the residents of Jigong Ridge who had resolved to hide some things, who was known for her integrity, strained to hold the doorframe but was still unable to prevent herself from collapsing. When she came to from a brief stupor, there were three things:

– the unquestionable existence of the netherworld (she thought of her sister who had gone missing 38 years ago)

– the selfishness, tyranny, narrow-mindedness, and ignorance of human beings

– God's complete indifference

she kept crying for. She was horrified. But it was the hatred toward one person and the sympathy for the other that made her tremble. Then she summoned courage and disclosed what Grandma Zhang and Ruijuan had told her before their deaths. This caused a great stir in the little city. Many people, including government officials, who were sworn atheists and had been accustomed to think in an atheistic way, participated in the discussion and dissemination of the story. Even when there was nothing more to discuss, they were not willing to leave, just lingered and kept sighing.

First Grandma Zhang, who lived on 43 City-Country Commerce Street in Jigong Ridge, went out at noon the day before. The weather was awful and gloomy, the rain seemed to be approaching yet distant, only wind chased fallen leaves about. The old woman wore a brown outfit like a monk's robe whose neck exposed the red cotton-padded jacket inside. A hairnet wrapped around her iron-gray hair. Her face was as skinny as her son's and was covered with tired wrinkles. Stooped, she held a dragon-head walking stick as she went down the street. She showed people the metal clock in her left arm which she'd just taken down from the wall of her house. "I can't read, even if I could, I can't see clearly. Tell me, is it one thirty?" she asked.

"It is, Grandma," somebody answered.

"Look at your watch. Is it one thirty?" the old woman asked again.

"It's one thirty."

Then tears poured out of her bloodshot eyes as if a rock stopping them had been removed. "Poor me. Nobody came back to cook for me yet." She pulled out a decades-old handkerchief. She wiped tears, shaking and explaining her tragic situation. Soon people crowded around to watch. She seemed to think they were qualified to witness, whether quantitatively or qualitatively, and some other day they would attest to her sorrow and outrage that day. So she leaned her walking stick against an electric pole and threw the clock on the ground. It was dented.

"Come to my house to eat, Grandma Zhang," somebody said.

"Eat and go to my death? Eat at your house. My house isn't empty."

She picked up the walking stick, knocked the end against the ground, and walked off in anger. Then as she walked she kept wailing, "Does anyone really care? Don't you all really just want this old woman to starve to death? Nobody starved to death when the Nationalist Party was in charge. Now someone will."

In fact, prior to this, at home, she'd thrown everything on the ground. You could say it was on purpose and could say it was by accident – at first it was by accident, but she had a chance to stop and instead indulged in the consequences. After breaking a porcelain bowl came the recklessness of one murder means death and so do 10 murders, or tearing the imperial cloth means death and so does killing the prince...teacups: four, porcelain bowls: four, porcelain plates: four, black-and-white Kunlun TV (really basically only the cathode tube was left): one, Hong Deng radio: one, iron wok: one, red thermos with "囍" printed on it: one, porcelain teapot painted with pine trees: one, a mirror: one, a flower pot: one, a flower vase: one, and a bottle of Hero carbon ink were broken. There was no way to break the water dispenser, so she pushed it over. Same with the chest of drawers. All her granddaughter's clothes that could be ripped were ripped. The shoes were thrown into the water tank. Actually this fire had started three days ago and never extinguished. Like fire buried under ash, with a good stir it spreads. Three days prior Granddaughter came home at eleven fifty. Two days prior it was twelve fifteen. One day prior, at one in the afternoon. When she saw Granddaughter come back, Grandma Zhang muttered: "So you still know you need to come home. Why not come back even later, do you still care about this grandma, you really made a waste of all the time I spent looking after you for six years, six years, why don't you just put rat poison in my food and kill me, poison me to death and get even?" Ruijuan just tossed her a cold, baffled look, not explaining, not responding. She left after cooking like hired help, without a word. This day, Grandma Zhang started expecting Ruijuan at eleven thirty, thought the girl should be back at twelve, if not twelve then twelve thirty. But at twelve thirty she still wasn't back. Grandma Zhang thought, when you're back at one see how I rip off your ears, how I use my dragon-head walking stick to break your dog legs. But at one she was still not back. The old woman went out a few times, all she found was vacant, boundless air and the smell of food cooking in other houses. What made her fly into a rage was when she asked Aunt Chen at the grocery store to call her granddaughter (she found five cents, but Aunt Chen pushed it back, saying she couldn't accept money from her). Expecting a big scolding over the phone, the latter didn't answer. She didn't answer then turned it off. Grandma Zhang then smashed everything she could smash.

Grandma Zhang left the clock, walked down Guilin Road, passed People's Park and the old prison all the way to Number One Middle. From there, she turned east onto Yanpen Road. After walking almost two kilometers, someone reminded her, and she turned back, then walked down Qiuzhi Road where her granddaughter was. Store by store, she asked, "Have you seen my granddaughter, my granddaughter is named Ruijuan," (somebody said her granddaughter had left at 10 and not come back) until she got to her granddaughter's store. The door was open. A white printer inside was plugged in, still humming. The old woman raised her walking stick and struck the cover, then the paper tray. The owner of the store next door, Chen Li, rushed in, grabbed the walking stick, and said: "Don't break it, the thing cost more than 10,000 yuan." The old woman wouldn't listen. She said, "What do you care if I break my granddaughter's stuff? You want to be nosy I'll go break the stuff in your store." That Chen Li defended herself, "If your granddaughter hadn't asked me to look after her store I wouldn't. Since she trusted me I have to be responsible, if you want to break stuff you can wait for her to get back." They each gripped one end of the walking stick, shoving it left, shoving it right, on and on. Then the old woman almost knocked the young one over. So the young one said: "Grandma, I really don't want to say this but with this energy you could have cooked the meal and washed the dishes by now. You don't have to make things difficult for your granddaughter. It's not like you can't do it." The old woman gaped, pointing at the girl, unable to speak. Then an acquaintance came to mediate. Seeing there was a mediator, the old woman said toughly to the girl: "What's your name, tell me." The girl wanted to say, My name is none of your fucking business. Just fuck off so I can attend to my store. The words almost slipped out of her mouth, but she gritted her teeth. That was when Grandma Zhang started to cough. She forgot how she got home, just remembered coughing all the way home. "See, I coughed up blood," she said to Aunt Wen, her only visitor, and folded the bloodstained handkerchief in half to preserve the evidence. A while later, she unfolded it again to look at the red bloodstain one more time. Then she shut her eyes and squeezed out a pool of tears. "I'm so pathetic," she cried, gripping Aunt Wen's hand. "Pathetic."

The old woman passed away at five in the afternoon. Aunt Wen (to this day she regrets visiting the Zhang home, the old woman wasn't without children. Then, when Grandma Zhang had just returned to Jigong Ridge with a handful of dried grass from the park, she tried to set the house on fire with it, but her hands kept shaking and the matches kept breaking. A failed attempt. Seeing Grandma Zhang vent her childlike anger in such an extreme way, people called Little Big Zhang. Little Big Zhang said: "Let her, let her do whatever she wants to do, she has that kind of temper." So everyone left except Aunt Wen who couldn't face her own indifference. Holding a bowl of rice soaked with shredded meat soup, she avoided the broken porcelain and glass on her way to the second floor of the Zhang home) said she saw astonishment in Grandma Zhang's eyes, the kind of astonishment she'd seen on a child's face years before. The child kept jumping wildly on the roof of a hut in a brick factory. People warned him but it was no use. Then the roof, made of asbestos or linoleum, split open. He fell through like a heavy stove. Very heavy. Grandma Zhang sank into intense, resounding wails. Aunt Wen opened her lips and teeth with the spoon, forcing the food into her mouth, which had sworn never to accept food from anybody, the few calories from little food immediately being burned away by more manic wailing. "Go away. Go away. Pease leave. Just let me die," she wailed feverishly, until she saw Death standing before her. Then her crying became real crying, and she seemed to become softer.

She recalled to Aunt Wen the things she regretted most and told herself to take a pill, she'd feel a bit better if she took a pill. Then she must have remembered who caused all this (how could she censure herself, think she was in the wrong) and grabbed Aunt Wen's collar to sit up, starting to curse angrily.

Done cursing, she used a vicious tone to tell Aunt Wen: "You'll see."

"Okay, I'll see," Aunt Wen said.

That's how the old woman died.

★   ★   ★

Ruijuan went home for the wake. Her waist-length hair cut by half, her lips smeared with dark-red lipstick – wild, dangerous, aggressive yet aggrieved. It seemed she wanted to change her look to please others and wanted completely to ruin herself. Her eyes were cloudy. Two hours after her grandma had died, her phone was still off. The news of her death got to her by word of mouth. They said in Jigong Ridge a fierce old woman had been killed by her own anger.

When she got back, the first rain had wet the spent firecrackers. The doorway was being lit temporarily by a light bulb. Above the door green letters read: voice and image remain clear. Her uncles, who wore muddy black rain boots, sat hunched in the hall on the first floor, smoking silently. Halfway through a cigarette, one of them tore open a new pack and handed each person another one. "Still got one," they said, taking it and putting it behind their ears. When Ruijuan entered, they raised their heads at once, took a look at their city-born niece, then bowed their heads. The look in their eyes was as elusive as an animal's. She wanted to greet them then decided not to. (When they brought back their mother's urn from the funeral parlor two days later, they each spat at it, some even blew their noses on it. They hailed a little pickup to take the urn back home. But halfway, still burning with anger, they threw their mother's ashes in a dirty pond.) From the second floor came the fake cries of Ruijuan's mother: "My mom, my mom, my mom, how could you leave us to go first, Mom?" How fake was it? It was fake to the point that the crying and the person could separate: the person could go pee and come back while the crying still soared beside the corpse.

Ruijuan's father, Little Big Zhang, waited on the second-floor landing, smoking a cigarette. Due to the smog, he squinted one eye. He obviously didn't smoke. He tried to pry open a perfectly glued-shut box, phone between shoulder and ear. He watched Ruijuan coming up while attending to the third hour-plus-long issue on the phone (first, he asked his son, Ruijuan's younger brother, Ruijiang, not to come because exams are soon, studying is more important. Second, the cremation, it's all right if the funeral parlor doesn't want to send a car, we'll take the body back to the countryside and bury it, don't say we're breaking the law. And transporting the remains was supposed to be the responsibility of the funeral parlor. We'll pay, but they still refuse, I don't understand what they're thinking. Third, demolition, if you're demolishing my house, you can do it however you want, I 100 per cent agree. The problem is the houses are up against each other, the houses on either side share walls, I can make my own decision, but I can't make a decision for the neighbors. I said that yesterday, and the day before, hoping you would understand, this has nothing to do with me being a Party member or teacher of the people). It was the first time he watched his daughter coming toward him like this. He couldn't see her face, nose, eyes, or neck, just the top of her head slowly moving up the stairs. Her newly cut hair looked like a ponytail palm, puffing up on top and hanging down around her head. He saw in her hair a slight quiver (because she was in awe of him) and a few premature white strands. *I'm not the only one with white hair. My daughter has it too,* he thought sorrowfully. As she was coming up, he hardened his tone and spoke each word clearly:

"You did a good job."

He saw his daughter lurch and cry out loud. "Stop crying," he added. Then, to his wife who had ceased crying (his loyal and ignorant servant), he said, "I'm going home. I may come back. I may not. Call me if something happens." As a decent man, before leaving, he thanked Aunt Wen again for staying there. "There's nothing to thank me for," the latter said as she was walking his grieving wife to the back room to rest.

Ruijuan was left alone with the body. She picked up a black gauze strip from the straw basket, pinned it to her sleeve, and quietly moved toward the body covered by a shroud. Back when she studied at Number Two Middle School, during recess, she and her classmates would run wildly to Railway Dam to see the corpses crushed by trains casually covered by straw mats. It was human nature to be curious about death. She was being curious now, though she seemed to have gone through so many things that day and was psychologically drained. The old woman's eyes rolled up. The nostrils and mouth were wide open. A few remaining teeth were sticking out randomly like stones. She looked like someone come to a halt in a snore about to swallow down the air left in their mouth. Her female friends who went to a sermon later said: "God said to Israel that Joseph would be on his death bed and close his eyes with his own hands. But Grandma Zhang died with her eyes open."

Then Ruijuan started to cry. Her crying was filled with the imitation of other grown-ups. She punched the edge of the bed, loudly blamed herself for not cooking for her grandma, which had led to her death ("It can't be, it can't be, it can't be this way?" she asked herself). She also blamed herself for not coming to her grandma's deathbed in time. Thus she took responsibility upon herself but not for a second did she believe it was the truth. Later, probably at the thought of her own unhappiness and frustration, the young woman let herself go and indulged in wailing by the body. When the crying became overly excited, she stomped. Aunt Wen hurried over, patted her back, and said: "Enough, enough. Crying like that is enough. Don't hurt your body." But she was still wailing, "My grandma, my grandma". A few times her eyes rolled up in her head, and she almost passed out. Aunt Wen took care of her until she came back to this rational and normal world. The traces of tears were still on her face, but she was completely sober. She was sober yet puzzled. Like a confused pupil she asked Aunt Wen: "I wonder why my grandma said this. It seems I just heard her say: If I die, I'll definitely take you." Aunt Wen suddenly stood up, almost out of reflex, her face deathly pale. Half an hour later she was at her own home. Looking in the mirror, she found her face still deathly pale, without the slightest blush. Then, at the thought of what Ruijuan had said to her, she could still feel the chill in her body. Because when the old woman was about to die, she heard her say the same thing, word for word:

"If I die, I'll definitely take her."

To prove she meant it, the old woman gripped Aunt Wen's hand and said again: "You'll see, you'll see when I take her."

★   ★   ★

Some people remembered, around midnight in Liuhu Bar, seeing young Zhang Ruijuan wearing a black gauze strip. Grandma's death gave her an excuse to drink. She always said, "You know, my grandma died, the grandma who raised me died." As she spoke she shed tears. Hard rain fell all night like the Bible says: *That same day were all the fountains of the great deep broken up, and the windows of heaven were opened.* Early the following morning, the sanitation worker Li Shili found Ruijuan lying prone in a puddle, already dead. Later Li Shili returned to the scene. When two hired hands turned the body over at the instruction of the forensic scientist, everyone shouted – there was a deep hole in the body's white waist from the body being pressed against a pointed rock, pressing the whole night. After Li Shili returned to the scene, she nervously looked at the shiny ring the dead wore on her right middle finger. She struggled a long time with herself about whether to remove it or not.

The forensic scientist denied that it was a murder or that the body had been moved there. "If she drowned herself, how could it be possible in such a small puddle?" Little Big Zhang asked. "You just never saw this before," said Little Yuan, the forensic scientist. Little Yuan had graduated from a five-year bachelor's program at Gan'nan Medical School, a highly educated person whose words people tended to trust. In the end, Little Big Zhang picked up his daughter's wet body. Her eyes were like the eyes of a dead chicken, slightly closed but a slit. Her extremely thin deer legs hung loosely. She was so scrawny, so totally different from the chubby little girl she once was. She had gotten her weight down to less than 80 pounds. When Little Big Zhang first heard the news, he started running, but no matter how he tried he couldn't get going. Walking was too slow, so he skipped, he skipped all the way. As soon as he saw his own daughter, he couldn't help but let the tears fall.

PREDATOR

1

I appeared at the entrance to the Research and Analysis Center like an invisible man. My footsteps were among the footsteps of a crowd of returning travelers. The one in the lead was dragging a suitcase, the fixed wheels rolling on the cobblestones, from north to south, rolling through the lane. After five o'clock, every few minutes a large part of the sky turned black. All of them were grandly dressed like yaks, to keep out the famous damp cold of their hometown. I quietly stopped at the entrance to the Research and Analysis Center. Only it still had business. Mr. Fish and a shrunken-neck woman sat by a heater, turning their palms up and down to get warm. "Right right right," they very genially responded to each other's words.

The reason he was called Fish was because his head looked like a fish head. Because of his bimaxillary protrusion deformity (buckteeth) and nasal bone concavity, his lips protruded more than any part of his head. When the mouth was almost closed, between his lower lip and chin there was an obvious bulge of soft tissue. On either side of his upper lip there were long strands of hair, similar to a carp's.

 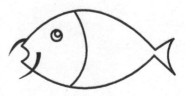

The streamlined structure of a fish allows it to swim fast and long in the water. Mr. Fish craned his neck like a turtle almost all year round, which made the head, and the lips and teeth at the front of the head, dissociated from his body, which also seemed to show an evolutionary force. Ever since the door of light was forever closed, he had been filled with the desire to pry and confide. He was so keen to get information from the outside, so keen to communicate with the outside, he always turned his head to listen, always asked questions, laughed, and flattered. To receive his visitors, he bought two long benches, each could seat four people (although to some customers, fortune-telling was supposed to be a private matter). When I quietly walked in, the woman in an eggplant-purple down coat quietly turned her head and looked toward me. I was followed by a woman in a light-yellow wool coat. The timing was quite good. The newcomer thought I was inside, the one inside thought I came in with the newcomer. I sat down at almost the same time as the newcomer. She sat on the bench on the south side, sat by the woman who had come earlier, Mr. Fish gently adjusted the space heater, allowing the newcomer to be blessed with the warm light too. The round reflection sheet gave out a dazzling shine, like a sunflower, always facing a newcomer. I sat on the bench on the east side. The newcomer gave me a slightly uneasy glance. *I don't know him, he doesn't know me*, I thought she was thinking. She turned her head back, told Mr. Fish the eight characters of her birth time, which was not improper. I did my best to steady my breath. I really was blatantly hiding three feet from him, could even smell the foul smell baked in his crotch.

He started rambling. Just like the one I had seen before at the north entrance of the street (East Street), only without an erhu in hand. Before, those blind men would sit in a row at the foot of the wall, basking in the sun, waiting for customers. Now they all rent a storefront near the south entrance, set up their own business. Mr. Fish's was called Yuan Tiangang Research and Analysis Center. Inside was just an electrometer, a hanging scale, a water dispenser, and a table clock which rang in spasms when it was almost time. The north wind blew through the lane, blew into the room, I was a bit drowsy. He was simply babbling. I turned my head to have a look. The street looked lonelier, colder, the girl selling socks across the street stamped like a crane. Took a long time to stamp once – keeping the leg lifted, then finding the chance to stamp again. When I turned back, I was startled to see his entire face facing me. I almost stood up. His two useless, wax-white eyeballs were staring at me, head shaking slightly. I was horrified by the sheer hollowness in that pair of eyes, right in the hollowness great resentment hid: I hoped no one would secretly show up beside me, make fun of me, really hoped not. They stayed looking at me. I tried to convince myself and to convince him that this was just the overreaction the blind always had, they often, feeling extremely confident, attacked aimlessly. But I didn't make a sound at all. I held my breath, waited for him to slowly settle down. Then just as I was about to settle down as well – he got relaxed, went on talking with the woman in wool coat – he suddenly turned his head again, gave me an extremely strange, even biting smile. My face went completely red, though he couldn't see anything.

I'd underestimated the vigilance of a lord in protecting his land, also underestimated a blind man's unusual sense ability. Perhaps even the shadow of a bicyclist gliding by like a swallow could startle him (my philosophy lecturer from the normal college had repeatedly preached that 'shadow has mass' – 'existence is mass, like shadow, light'. But I believed that a sharp blind man could certainly sense the fleeting coolness, capture the subtle variations of air current), and besides, I came with a body full of smells. The smells from a long-distance trip hid deep in my hair, coat, and gloves, couldn't be shaken off. When they spoke, they faced him, but the one or two times they faced me (especially when coming to crucial points), were enough to convince him: there was a person, a young man embodying atheism who made them uneasy. He did sit there day and night, his sense of smell, sense of hearing, sense of touch had been cut square, like a fence planted in the area he rented. I'd heard before that some magical blind men have stronger abilities than ordinary people in sensing the course of events.

They can, just by hearing a passerby stop his clanking footsteps a dozen meters away, determine that there is a hesitant stranger behind them. They turn, before the other greets them, and greet them.

We often forget this point.

Mr. Fish went on with his shameless speech. For him, he just needed to open his pocket, and the woman in the wool coat, ready to sell herself out with credulity, would jump in herself. Women that age were the easiest targets that fortune-tellers, magicians, and manipulators could get their hands on. I listened carefully only a moment, then got sleepy (there was some kind of funny music to his tone, which paralyzed people's wills, made people sleepy). In my view his performance was actually pretty unprincipled.

★   ★   ★

First,
    he chanted a passage of incantation:
    ....(rhyme).

★   ★   ★

Then,
    commenting on the incantation, he made ambiguous remarks (like "Worse than the best, better than the worst"), considered the other's response, observed the other's expressions, beat about the bush.

★   ★   ★

Third,
    waited for the other to reveal information, as if choosing between A and B.

★   ★   ★

Fourth,

firm judgment. If the other reveals more information, then he'll cut in loudly, making the conclusion his own.

* * *

And repeat.

After calculating the other's age, making judgments everywhere, like a judge pronouncing a list of judgments.

* * *

When Mr. Fish said, "We may as well meet schemes with schemes," I couldn't help but snort. Of course this didn't stop the two women from praising his magic. They always mistook what they said to the other as what the other said to them. Right right right. They responded to him enthusiastically, with such keen enthusiasm and the excitement of complete immersion, like the concubine who heard a faraway aunt would come visit. At that moment, a straggler in the crowd passed the Research and Analysis Center, said to me: "What you staying here for?"

"Staying to listen a bit."

(Sometimes while window shopping, friendly shopkeepers walk up, ask me which one I have my eye on, I casually say: "Just taking a look.")

"Don't be late."

He walked briskly away with the anxiety of missing the bus. The sky was completely dark a few minutes later. The two women rose one after the other. Following them, Mr. Fish rose, smiling wholeheartedly. "It's a twenty-yuan note," the woman in the woolen coat said. Mr. Fish humbly took it, took out five yuan, and gave it to the other. Once they were gone, I seemed to have lost my cover, was about to go too. Then in the light coming from the heater, I saw, on the blind man's face, the awkwardness of not being able to deal with himself after the jabbering, which we ordinary people often experience. *Why was I being so mouthy?* I thought his heart must feel hollow at the moment.

Then the remaining, slightly abashed smile faded forever – like an iron flower folded up cruelly – in its place was an extremely deep, sharp indifference. The play was over, the stage was empty. He felt the Braille on the money, folded it up, slowly jammed it into the hidden pocket of the trousers. Then squeezed the thickness of it. Then stood there, started counting on his fingers. I was about to, as I'd come in, go out silently when I heard him say:

"Is Ai Zhengjia your grandpa?"

My legs shook. In my heart a sense of weightlessness rose like there had been a cushion waiting where it fell every time, but this time the thing was gone. My heart had never been as flustered as it was now. Deep fear took root and sprouted in my body. My grandfather was Ai Zhengjia, my father was Ai Hongsong, my name was Ai Guozhu. I didn't know what was going to happen next. He followed me out, cold and merciless footsteps probing behind me. I walked to the road. "You should—" Hearing him about to go on, I started running. When I ran to the Luohu Parking Lot, I vomited up a mouthful of water. The minibus bound for my birthplace was just then starting. They all said my hair was completely soaked, as if showered by rain. I'd never had a word with him. I had nothing to do with those two women. Nobody had reminded him who I was midway. Equally impossible that someone had reminded him in advance that I would come. That was the first time I ever got close to him. I had been away for 11 years. I was one of the 400,000 or so people taking shelter in this county. I only had a word with an acquaintance (I knew he and him had never talked). So many people, so many fish, how could he nail me in one go? Before he said anything ("You should—"), I ran away, I knew that was how Grandpa had fallen into their trap back then.

Grandpa had once been a cadre in charge of 40.47 square meters of land. As his subordinates righteously examined the itinerant quacks whose eyes and words wavered, he, driven by curiosity, leafed through the seized books. To them his attitude was contemptuous. Just like years later, I, already a middle school student, treated Grandpa who took notes on the hand-copied fortune-telling book, with contempt. I looked sideways at the relative who was lost forever in the wrong, felt loathing and sympathy. Reproaching him always made me unbearably tired. "Don't you know this is just a trick?" I said. To this day I still believe fortune-telling is a magic trick, it goes against honesty. According to an article, the key to magic is to direct the audience's attention away, then use their 'inattentional blindness' to do tricks. The fortune-telling book is a distraction technique, a magician's fairy dust, what's real are the six techniques: observe, probe, attack, fool, praise, sell; it's the crazy stealing of your secrets and privacy. But my grandpa had been immersed in the study of fortune books, unable to extricate himself, till finally, others couldn't stand his pestering, said: "This is just fraud, all the techniques are fraud." Astonished, he said angrily, "Fine if you don't want to tell me, no need to say that." Cut things off himself. Grandpa went insane because of obsession and died of mania. Because of his tragic life and the corresponding changes in our lives (following him, we went from a city household into a rural household), we believed people from the mystical societies had set him up, made painstaking efforts, moved carefully every step, after doing a lot of groundwork, used Zuo Zongtang's warcraft of 'Move slow, fight fast', in one breath, seized Grandpa.

"How could this be a trick?" Grandpa defended himself, embarrassed. "This can't be explained by coincidence."

That day what felt like caterpillars crawling all over me was that very sentence. I had imagined a fortune-teller's hunt and kill, thought it would be like a bullfight, with a long process (entice, pierce, thrust the dart, and so on), confident that I could pull myself away in time. But right in the moment of natural relaxation, he suddenly turned up, nailed me in one go, pierced my neck with the sharp, hooked sword. I couldn't help but shake from its startling precision. When the minibus reached the village where graves seemed to flicker in faint flames, and broke down, I took the suitcase, stumbled out the minibus, turning back every three steps as I headed home. I was afraid Mr. Fish would turn up in cloth shoes behind me (in his world there was neither light nor darkness, perhaps in our darkness he could actually fly). Before closing the door, I looked silently into the empty darkness for a long time, until I was convinced there was nothing. Mother found a dry towel, stuffed it on my soaked back. "So big already, still can't take care of yourself," she said. Her frame was still so short and small, her movements still so rough, powerful. But I knew, on her face, rotting spots like an orange peel's had long appeared.

For a few hours, I fell into a terrible mania. The more I knew its harm — my grandpa, from overthinking, had long suffered from insomnia and often like an uncontrollable tap, spurted food on the bed and eventually died of cerebral hemorrhaging — the more I couldn't help but fall into it. I seemed to be very close to the answer, just had to find the right stem that could poke through the layer of window paper, but in the end got nothing. Why, I sat up in the middle of the dark night, wanting to look for that person in town, grab his neck, demand him to say why. My brain was crammed with tangled iron wires. In the end I fell asleep by giving myself harsh orders. *Do not become a victim of magic*, I said, *Do not.*

Very early in the morning, I found the driver and the cousin who had reminded me the day before to catch the bus early. They both denied knowing Mr. Fish. But just then I thought things couldn't be simpler. As if once the radiance of the sun came to the fields people's minds and rationality recovered, the things and sounds that had been pounding my body the whole night — those bluffing things — didn't exist anymore, and he became an old man, tricks exposed, huddled and shaking in the corner. "One sentence is enough," my uncle Ai Hongren said. He taught math at the village primary school, when it was closed, he transferred to the town's central primary school, then when it was reopened, came back. He searched out the county chronicle published in 1989. On page 446, there was a list of dialect zones in the county:

~~The Official Language Zone of the County Seats: Pencheng, Guilin~~
~~The Official Language Zone of the Villages: The Eight Villages of the Northern District — Wujiao, Baiyang, Liuzhuang, Matou, Nanyang, Xiafan, Henglishan, Huangjin; The Nine Villages of the Western~~

~~District — Gaofeng,~~ Hongxia, ~~Dadeshan,~~ Hongling, Jiuyuan, Fanzhen, Qingshan, Henggang, Emei

The North-western Gan Language Zone: Huayuan, Zhaochen, Hongyi

The South-western Gan Language Zone: Heping, Leyuan, Nanyi

Back then, I walked from north to south through East Street. Those who moved in packs at 5 p.m. could only be the returning travelers. Just like those who went north through the street at 8, 9 a.m. were mostly town-goers. That's why East Street was built up into a marketplace for farmers going to town. For the townspeople (including the villagers and merchants living in Luohu Village on the outskirts of town), they would rather walk another one or two miles than take this shortcut. At the end of East Street, open like a pocket, was the mire-like Luohu Parking Lot. It was responsible for parking buses coming from those villages:

~~The Official Language Zone of the County Seats: Pencheng, Guilin~~

~~The Official Language Zone of the Villages: The Eight Villages of the Northern District — Wujiao, Baiyang, Liuzhuang, Matou, Nanyang, Xiafan, Henglishan, Huangjin; The Nine Villages of the Western District — Gaofeng,~~ Hongxia, ~~Dadeshan,~~ Hongling, Jiuyuan, Fanzhen, Qingshan, Henggang, Emei

~~The North-western Gan Language Zone: Huayuan, Zhaochen, Hongyi~~

~~The South-western Gan Language Zone: Heping, Leyuan, Nanyi~~

The guy said: "What you staying here for?"

I said: "Staying to listen a bit."

This sentence was enough to narrow the range in half. We were a county where talking to each other was difficult. The north-western Gan Language Zone was very much influenced by the Gan dialect spoken in south-east Hubei the south-western Gan Language Zone was influenced by the Gan dialect of the Changjing subgroup, which was entirely different from the Official language. 'Stay here' was a common phrase, whose pronunciations were respectively:

The North-western Gan Language Zone: dē gé biān

The South-western Gan Language Zone: dē gé dá

The Official Language Zone: dē dǎ lǐ

Therefore:

~~The Official Language Zone of the County Seats: Pencheng, Guilin~~

~~The Official Language Zone of the Villages: The Eight Villages of~~
~~the Northern District – Wujiao, Baiyang, Liuzhuang, Matou, Nanyang,~~
~~Xiafan, Henglishan, Huangjin; The Nine Villages of the Western~~
~~District – Gaofeng,~~ Hongxia, ~~Dadeshan,~~ Hongling, Jiuyuan, Fanzhen,
Qingshan, Henggang, Emei

~~The North-western Gan Language Zone: Huayuan, Zhaochen, Hongyi~~
~~The South-western Gan Language Zone: Heping, Leyuan, Nanyi.~~

Even in the Official Language Zone, there were many nuances. Like
for 'doing what', some places said 'do what thing', some places said 'for
what thing'. The 'for what' places can be eliminated:

~~The Official Language Zone of the County Seats: Pencheng, Guilin.~~

~~The Official Language Zone of the Villages: The Eight Villages of~~
~~the Northern District – Wujiao, Baiyang, Liuzhuang, Matou, Nanyang,~~
~~Xiafan, Henglishan, Huangjin; The Nine Villages of the Western~~
~~District – Gaofeng,~~ Hongxia, ~~Dadeshan,~~ Hongling, Jiuyuan, Fanzhen,
~~Qingshan, Henggang, Emei~~

~~The North-western Gan Language Zone: Huayuan,~~
~~Zhaochen, Hongyi~~

~~The South-western Gan Language Zone: Heping, Leyuan, Nanyi~~

In the end there were only four villages left. Among them, Hongxia
and Fanzhen were big villages, with one bus per hour on average, the
last bus departed as late as 8 p.m. Hongling was the place en route to the
other three places. Therefore, the passenger who said "Don't be late" at
5 p.m. could only have come from: Jiuyuan Village.

There were two buses to Jiuyuan:

one went up, after passing Fanzhen and Zhaoao, the route was
Zhuba–Luojia–Xilong–Lifan–Zhongyuan–Shangyuan. The two drivers
were master Zhang Jizhao, apprentice Zhang Jisong; the other went
down, after passing Fanzhen and Zhaoao, the route was Baiyanglong–
Liai–Zhangjiawan–Lifan–Zhongyuan–Shangyuan. The driver was
Ai Xiaomao.

As for the last buses departing from the county seats, Zhang's departed at 17:20 (adjusted for summer, as below). The route was as above, and in the end it returned empty to Zhangjiawan; Ai's bus departed at 17:45, only got to Liai – Ai Xiaomao's and my birthplace – and broke down. "Because this son of mine's very lazy," Ai Hongren said. "He said at this hour there wouldn't be passengers from Zhongyuan and Shangyuan taking his bus, he didn't drive so of course there wouldn't be, whatever he says happens, whatever he wants he does."

Bayanglong had no people. Yuanjialong, tucked away in the depths of the thick woods (which could be reached from Baiyanglong by climbing miles of mountain path), had four or five households before. Then one day, all that was left were four or five abandoned houses. So when Ai Xiaomao started the bus from the county seat in the late afternoon, those who rushed to catch the bus could only be people from Liai. Liai was made up of Lijiawan and Aijiawan. Out of a kind of pride, the Lis, since the year before, had decided to ride Zhang's bus only. The several miles between the village and Zhaao were done by walking – though Ai Hongren had been to every Li household, given out cigarettes to apologize, in the end it didn't change their minds. Whoever rushed to catch the bus at 17:30 could only be: an Ai.

Mr. Fish knew this very well. It was just common knowledge. The common knowledge all the locals knew, the thieves messing around in the parking lot knew, the merchants on East Street knew – they always went out several times at dusk, targeting the passersby rushing to catch the bus, shouting about discounts. Only I who had been away for years didn't know. *You don't have to know.* When Uncle Ai Hongren looked at me, his eyes were full of understanding, also a tentative blame. *In comparison you're the one who's blind.* I was thinking about Mr. Fish. He always sat in the dark Research and Analysis Center, opened all his sensing organs – like a fierce dragon hunting for food in the dark night secretly beating its giant wings – to catch the information coming and going, sometimes this information required no fishing from him, like drizzle it floated into the room, fell naturally upon him. He was interested in transportation, weather, human affairs, public order, policy, conscription, business openings, exams, recruitment, loans, epidemic prevention, funerals, and other local information, was most interested in the information about people: as soon as someone entered the Research and Analysis Center, he could establish their relationship with many other people (women marrying here and there in the hundred-mile area were like flying threads that bound nearly all the local families together. Like Dong Jiahong and Dong Jiayuan's younger sister, Dong Chunmei, who married Zhu Zhizhong, and Zhu Zhifen and Zhu Zhihua's elder brother Zhu Zhiliang; Zhu Zhihua was the manager of the motor repair shop opened by the family of his classmate Wu Xiaoming; Zhu Zhifen was Wu Xiaoming's elder brother's ex-wife; the Wu's fourth daughter Wu Aiwu married Chen Xuping from Henglishan, gave birth to Chen Gang, Chen Yong, Chen Li, Chen Qiang; Chen Yong went to China University of Political Science and Law and after graduation was assigned to the prefecture's intermediate court, married the younger Zhou's only daughter Zhou Haiyan. Everyone was related to everyone else. Everyone was like a descendent of a close relative, had some incestuous debauchery). He always started the gears in his brain, calculating those relationships, late at night, would also lick his fingers, slowly leaf though the ledger in his mind that recorded their entire lives, compare and check. It was a huge ledger. When the weather was fine and clear, he would, as in his youth, roam in the countryside, like a census official, from house to house, knock open the doors of their hearts with a bamboo pole. This ledger was his entire property, he possessed everyone – without the memory of them, he would be like duckweed, going with the tides, getting lost in the land of ignorance, he wouldn't be severed from society by people, but would be exiled from the human world by himself.

In fact we were a pair of memory's giant beasts. We had the same worries. After age 40, we could remember more than one thousand local people and more than 10,000 relationships between them. Mr. Fish was famous in society, also for his three marriages, the start and end of each, was initiated by him.

Aijiawan had 50 or so households in the past. After the living in the city trend, only 30 households remained.

My voice was the voice of a middle-aged man: between 35 and 38. That's what others heard, more or less. There were three people from families who hadn't left Aijiawan: Ai Shijun, Ai Shiquan, Ai Shikun (Ai Guozhu). Due to a car accident a few years ago, Ai Shijun was in a grave. Ai Shiquan first fed free-range chickens in Baiyanglong, then fed free-range pigs. The last was the legendary idiot who gave up public office, went out to work, Ai Guozhu, for 11 years, body carrying the smells of instant noodles, perfume, blended cigarettes, perm solution, and the foul smell of not showering for days. The leather shoes he wore gave off the smell of fresh leather. You could even tell from the strange smell that it was a pair of brown leather shoes.

Aijiawan's three previous generation names were Zheng, Hong, Shi. The Zheng generation had seven people, the Hong generation had 21 people, the Shi generation had nearly 70 people. Like a big tree, branches grew from the knots, the branches flourished, the leaves thrived. *As far as this generation of grandchildren, there were a lot, I'm not sure I can remember clearly, but as for the Zheng generation, I can remember*, Mr. Fish thought, *I could ask him, Is your grandpa Ai Zhengjia?*

2

What made me, after returning to my hometown, pay a special visit to fortune-tellers (I passed nearly 10 fortune-tellers on East Street, saw only Mr. Fish's still had business) is a story. That story gave me a profound understanding of all women on earth. It happened in Laoyangshu Town, a small town 36 kilometers from the city where I worked. Every week I went to the city to work three days, then came back to the town and rested for four days. (Ten years ago, by the old poplar tree, next to the auditorium, there had been a few roadside shops, old tires hanging outside the windows, tap water always spilling out of the red plastic tubs, washing feathers and scales to the ground. A paved road black as the pond water ran to the horizon. Now it has three or four million people. Every day, dozens of planes quietly rise from behind the buildings, their silver-gray bodies leave giant shadows on the ground.) At first, the townspeople, Zhangsan or Lisi, each possessed a fraction of the story, after someone started, they couldn't wait to piece it together into a whole, like weaving a giant and incredible tapestry together. In the end, they all felt that they had absolute private ownership over the story. They said more and more, to the point that the content had long outstripped the original facts, but they still found it far from enough. "This really is a very shocking incident," they said. As if seeing the cloth-like blood once again splash onto the front window of the white truck (the car body, after braking sharply, leaned forward then finally settled back). The driver Anfang was wide-eyed, tongue-tied. He dared not handle it with the wipers or a rag, until the dry air turned the bloodstains into shiny rouge chips, naturally falling off. The half-life of this story's circulation was so long that I, after going in and out of town numerous times, inevitably heard talk of it:

Junfeng's mom,

or, Chen Zonghuo's woman

a fifty-going-on-sixty widow

without any great experience worth mentioning

without even the tiniest scandal or travesty – with just a little self-importance, human beings easily end up with a tacky or splendid tragedy, don't they – she wore

dark-blue or indigo garments (sometimes a robe dyed with ladybug-like dots),

a camouflaged animal like the dead-leaf butterfly or geometer moth, making herself invisible before people's eyes

time slipping away again and again from the walls and the crevices in the walls

Death, like the safest ship, coming slowly

Her – when people finally remembered her because of a certain incident, they had to think a long, long time before scraping together a conclusion

only mission in this world, was constantly worrying about one of her two sons

like a girl at the edge of a cliff, palms together, head bowed, trembling
worrying about the lover walking on the tightrope
Thursday afternoon, after calling him
she felt a flurry of panic

★   ★   ★

It was an overly accurate panic given the logic of the conversation. The woman, from her son's response, sensed the patience the spies would show when passing a sentry, they would light a long cigar, wave their hat, act very co-operatively, as if willing to stay there the whole afternoon. That was a bit unusual. Usually, he would irritably say, "That's it," and hang up. Sometimes, she could tell he had pressed the speaker button, his person walking back and forth, always long after she spoke, after a scary silence, he realized he had an obligation to fulfill, and so answered: "Oh." Once, while waiting for his response, she watched one of the country's rockets take off on TV, after rising, almost still, for a long time, it quietly disappeared into space. He was so reluctant to speak to her. At first they talked over the phone three times a week, then it was down to twice, once. All were calls from her. "Once a week, call at this hour, understand?" he said.

That day, his answers were fluent.

Gentle as the usher in a red robe at the entrance of the foot spa center. Even holding a sort of gentleness tinged with fear.

When the panic came, in most cases it was to prove she was a sensitive, suspicious woman, but once or twice – for example, many days after he smiled strangely, she rolled up his trousers leg, found the leg had swollen to twice its size, covered in black bruises ("If maggots take hold, this person is done for," Chen Zonghuo shouted, carrying him, running madly to the clinic. Meanwhile he tilted his head, eyes tinged with some drunkenness, looking sourly at her running behind in great shock.) – was enough to prove he was a cold-hearted traitor.

Like his two elder brothers who had died young, body here, heart elsewhere. Since his birth, the expression in his eyes was not right. His two elder brothers were killed one after another by the legendary quilt killer (a mysterious respiratory failure occurring in sleep). This made her and Chen Zonghuo more tense. He, like his elder brothers, was silent, as if waiting wholeheartedly for Death to come, as if that was his real father, he was waiting for his real father to take him away. As if the waiting was his career, but she and Chen Zonghuo had delayed him so, so long.

She called again, expected to get his approval.

"Nothing's wrong, why come to see me?" he said.

"I just think something's wrong," she said.

"You think something's wrong, so something's wrong, huh?" he said.

"Yeah," she said.

"Nothing's wrong."

"Something must be wrong."

"Hey, why would I lie to you?"

"Something's wrong."

"I said nothing's wrong, it means nothing's wrong, why would I lie to you?"

"If nothing's wrong, why are you coughing?"

"Coughing's very normal. You cough too."

"You must be keeping something from me."

"Why can't you be reasonable, why would I keep things from you?"

"I'm coming anyway."

"Don't come."

"Don't tell me what to do."

"I'll say it again, nothing's wrong, nothing's wrong, nothing's wrong, nothing's wrong, nothing's wrong, okay? If something was wrong, fine, come, nothing's wrong, so why come?"

"Even if nothing's wrong, can't I come to see you?"

"No."

"I have to come."

"Dammit, old woman, how can you be so annoying?"

"I'm not coming to see you."

"Then to see who?"

"I'm coming to see someone else, I'll see someone else. Be a good person, do good things, bring something to someone else, is that wrong?"

"Fine, go see someone else."

She thought he had hung up, then heard another vicious sentence from the phone. "You are really fucking sick you know. You are really fucking sick." She stood, stunned. Not ruminating on her son humiliating her, but as usual, letting herself argue with herself. The first self was like his stepmother, or the aunt next door, the second self was his real mother. The first self said: *I don't let my son make fun of me.* The second self's face went crimson, putting up with the lengthy reproach from the first self, finally tenaciously saying: *So what, what I would lose going there, wouldn't lose any property, any land.* Thus the woman ended up leaning on the worry flickering nonstop in her heart (perhaps it was the overdose of tea that day that caused the palpations), and that afternoon, with her head held high, headed for Laoyangshu Town a dozen miles away.

"She was like a monkey jumping off the huge, heavy-duty bike," Qiuchen, who ran a noodle restaurant, said. "She said she planned to go back, because she remembered that last time her son said that to her too." The noodle restaurant stood like a sentry at the end of the country road, only a dozen meters from Laoyangshu Town's paved road. It wasn't until two months later that Junfeng's mom would come to this noodle restaurant again. Then she looked extremely hungry, gobbled and gulped, the tip of her nose and forehead sweating. "Are my noodles really that delicious?" Qiuchen said.

"Very delicious," Junfeng's mom said.

Finished eating, she looked straight at the poster pasted on the side of the refrigerator (there Pan Weibo tilted his head to gulp a bottle of coke), sneakily inched the paper napkins to the edge of the table, pulled them into her pants pocket. "A big stack, more than 10,"

Qiuchen said. "She thought I didn't see, or, thought I couldn't see, or, thought I wouldn't say anything even if I saw. She thought right. Then I thought, even now, still knows how to take advantage, then clearly this person's okay."

She held the bike, said to Qiuchen, "Said this last time too, dammit, old woman, how can you be so annoying." The more he said this, the more she wanted to come, but last time she didn't find anything, it was like he had been insulted, cursing at her with extreme anger, telling her to fuck off. So she was hesitating, would this time be like last time. Qiuchen felt like reminding her (like someone itching to say the answer to a riddle, wanting to give a hint to the person about to head in the wrong direction), but, as she was about to touch the other's arm, this female cook stopped. If the other was told…Qiuchen couldn't foresee the risk it would bring, or what risk it wouldn't bring. Nothing was safer than pretending to be the ignorant. Qiuchen cleared her throat, just like God, mercifully watching the other turn around in circles. She looked only as tall as the bike, funny even imagining her getting on it, but when she did get on it, she was so dignified. She glanced at the time and the distance she had gone, then pedaled a few steps, lifted her right leg over the bike frame, steadily rode to town. *Still early*, she seemed to say to Qiuchen, or seemed to say to the little person inside her body, *Almost there, besides, why's this town your town alone?*

On that overly bright afternoon, the townspeople walked out in disappointment. Twenty minutes ago, the police cars drove out of the police station and the transport police division, blared sirens, stopped at several intersections, intercepted cars. Their intercoms kept blasting, as if a fleet was clamoring over, but the rumor only spread a few minutes then stopped: no sort of founding father but a bunch of deputies of the National People's Congress would pass through. The situation was just as expected, after a police car sped by to clear the way (its siren only gave a shriek, very abruptly), a light-brown minibus followed, rambled past. That's all. But they still kept glancing back, until Widow sped down riding her bike.

She flew by in a whizz.

Those who knew Junfeng and her, couldn't help but half raise their hands, move their feet forward, but very quickly were stopped by an invisible boundary of pain (like fishes in an aquarium anxiously jostling against the glass wall, while knowing they couldn't wake up the ignorant travelers walking briskly by in the transparent, underwater tunnel). On Widow's wrinkled face there was neither pain, nor lack of pain, there was just what Chairman Mao called seriousness. She rode the bike with extreme seriousness, rode toward her son's place of work. The bike brushed past the quiet street, too fast for the spokes of the wheels to be seen. For the people it was a helpless kind of pain, difficult to share with the party concerned, could even be called the pain of the philistine. The last time they felt such pain was when they watched a father narrow his eyes, hold a cigarette between his lips, and driven by curiosity, make his way to the bank of the pond (he didn't know why he suddenly got such respect that everyone made way for him. His only son, the dead, like a shaved dog corpse, dripping with water, was lying on the grass, waiting for him).

Since that afternoon, the townspeople, like Qiuchen, just held their useless pain, stood afar, watched her break through to the truth, indulge in the truth, struggle with the truth, and drown in the struggle. The tragedy that happened later was like an awl piercing their hearts. It seemed so unexpected, but it also seemed fated.

Widow was going to hear at the end of this trip:

her son Junfeng, 33, still unmarried, would punctually die three months later.

This was the conclusion reached by two professors (one was a PhD supervisor; the other was a Master's supervisor) after multiple calculations. That day, they got off the medical school's bus like generals, followed by a dozen pretentious students, who from time to time gave the crowd sidelong glances. The director of the local health bureau, like a dog, led the way himself. When they jumped onto the extremely filthy stairs of the township health center, the hems of their robes rippled, their presence was quite something. Because the newcomers were too great in number, three other patients in the ward were kicked out. Junfeng showed brief excitement as the honor to do something for medicine shined in his heart, he knew nothing about medicine, but he knew he was a precious living body. In the future, perhaps he would become a precious dead body, long soaked in formaldehyde (through his entire convalescence, he was lifeless, his body seemed already on the mortuary bed, just waiting for the breath to slowly drain). Equally honored was Doctor Liu, head of radiology at the township health center, it was she who had sharp eyes, discovered this difficult case from a pile of photos. Then in the Tuberculosis Institute (the Tuberculosis Research and Prevention Institute) of the Number Two Municipal Hospital, he did a series of tests (including a sputum culture, an enhanced CT, a CT guided puncture, a bronchoscopy, a bone marrow aspiration, a lymph node biopsy, and more than 70 tubes of blood withdrawal) which confirmed that

it was tuberculosis, but also not

it was pulmonary embolism, but also not

it was pneumoconiosis, but also not

it was interstitial pneumonia, but also not

it was panbronchiolitis, but also not

it was fungal infection, but also not

it was tumor (lung cancer, lymphoma), but also not

it was vasculitis, but also not

it was an IgG4-related disease, but also not

It was a familiar, ambiguous, diagnosable, but not exactly diagnosable, severe disease. It had many similarities, but from somewhere inside, it denied it was a definite disease. Perhaps the medical journals of the future could provide a clear name, provide a solution. But at present, clinicians could only consolingly give the patients an IV of anti-inflammatories, or, to deal with the cough, prescribe some compound methoxyphenamine capsules. Every day it seemed that he was evaporating, irrevocably trimmed down from all sides. Because of their own inability, and in order to save him money, they let him return to the township health center. First the doctors kept it from Junfeng for a month, then he kept it from his family for almost two months – She always gave him reasons to feel shamed (either by wearing blue polyester work clothes printed with the manufacturer's name like 'Xuejin Beer' on the back, or by wearing that pair of wintermelon-green liberation shoes), so he always objected to her coming to town, so as not to harm his identity as a townsperson – Until she, pulled by strong worry, stormed town herself. The two professors took out the CT photo buried under the bed, held it up to the light, pointed to each other, Look, so crowded, huge development from last photo, and still developing. This reminded Junfeng of the frights he experienced the previous few times. When he went to the Tuberculosis Institute's outpatient department for checkups, he waited more than a week for the results of the laboratory tests, when he registered again and came to the doctor, the other said anxiously: "Go to the big hospital, we're a small hospital, this checkup, that checkup, all take a week to get the results, will have you completely delayed." There was another time, in the Number Two Municipal Hospital, the ward doctor looked at the blood test result, stood still for a long time then said, "How'd it get so bad?" That day sweat poured out from Junfeng's soaked hair, his whole body seemed to have sweated a layer of thick hot mud. But also from that day on, he had little regard for life and death. Like indulging in games, he indulged in waiting for death. He regained his detached nature, detached from things, and detached from himself. He put on earphones, lay for a long time, listened to a song with a tragic melody but no lyrics, as if his pending, soon-to-be-effective death, as the song replayed, attained some kind of divinity. Until the uncontainable cough knocked him over again. He always ordered himself to hold back the cough, hold back, but like a gambler gambled everything away and began to see red, he was always defeated by that unbearable, extreme itch.

He had cut meat for almost every family in the town. In the supermarket, he wore a white robe, in charge of the meat counter (unlike the soft white robe in the hospital, the fabric of this white robe was very thick, seemed to have been converted from a tablecloth, and often pilled). People liked coming to him, because they need only

arrive for him to know which cut they wanted, then according to
their liking, diced, cubed, or sliced it. Meat was grouped as tenderloin,
butt, belly bacon, and so on, more than 20 kinds, priced differently,
but whether a customer wanted a certain price, or wanted a certain
weight, he could always get it precise in one cut, the error so small it
was negligible. Later people thought, perhaps it was to avoid too much
communication with people that he studied it over and over again, cut
so precisely. This was a young man who gave a light cough from time
to time, and didn't like talking. His tragedy came about on a morning,
when he coughed while cutting a piece of pork, the cleaver stopped
midair, from his throat a blackish red blood clot flew out – big as a
plum, or big as a big cherry. He watched it fly to the pork: a clear
rising then falling, but also a seemingly nonexistent, merely delusional
arc. He stared stunned at the stuff he had coughed out, as if figuring
out whether it was the pork's or his. He even reached an index finger
out to touch it. And smelled it. He didn't show uneasiness, instead
using a piece of paper to list the foods he had eaten over the past two
days, to check if there was watermelon, tomato, strawberry, wolfberry,
or other material that could easily cause confusion. It wasn't until he
came out of the township health center that he began to feel a bit
worried. He told the apprentice, Little Qi, he found it a bit unreal.
"As if the world has nothing to do with me," he said. That day, the
sunshine was very strong, because of the waves of heat, everything was
changing shapes, at noon, the security guard hid in a shady place, the
pancake seller sweated like rain, the cars on the road flowed, bustled,
while he and Little Qi held a chest X-ray which gave doctors difficulty
choosing words.

An hour after taking the chest X-ray, he got the result.

Doctor Liu asked the intern to call him in: "Chen Junfeng, is Chen
Junfeng's family here?"

"Here," Junfeng said.

"You're Chen Junfeng's family."

"I am," Junfeng said. "I am him."

"Come here."

This meant he was getting some kind of special treatment. Other people got their photo, went to see the outpatient doctor, but he was called in by the radiologist to be examined. Many of Doctor Liu's words were only half-said. She said she still needed to discuss things with the outpatient doctor. The outpatient doctor told him he better to go to the Tuberculosis Institute to check for tuberculosis, and go to a grade-A hospital to check for signs of a malignant lesion. Back then he didn't know what malignant lesion meant. He went unhurriedly to the Tuberculosis Institute, got registered. As if he could choose his own disease. He chose tuberculosis, but the kind female doctor in the Tuberculosis Institute sent him away.

The professors approved the former doctors' method. This made the doctors following them there from the Number Two Municipal Hospital and everyone in the township health center relieved, they were basking in the joy of getting approval, becoming noticeably more talkative. On that same day, their Mandarin level and the provincial nature of their behaviors, because of the authorities from Beijing, were clearly exposed before their fellow countrymen. But they would still discuss this event for a long time. Not everyone could receive approval from Professor Xu and Professor Gao, especially Professor Gao – he graduated from Harvard Medical School. As to whether to do the video-assisted thoracoscopic surgery, and the more invasive open-heart surgery on the patient, they wavered, watched time pass quietly and resolutely in their wavering. Today, the two professors are very certain that their decision to give up was right. If surgery had been done, the patient's life would have ended more quickly, even if larger pulmonary tissue had been taken out in the surgery, it's not likely that they could have come to a better conclusion than the previous one. Nothing would help. There was no way. The professors jammed their hands into their pockets, like they couldn't make a bear crawl out of barbed wire, or make a camel go through the eye of a needle.

The professors asked every student who followed them there, certified or uncertified, to walk up, and perform auscultation on Junfeng's stark-naked back where the clothes had already been rolled up. Breath in, breath out, breath in, breath out, okay. Every one of them felt a bit sorry, held the head of the stethoscope, tried to grasp the classic symptoms their supervisors had mentioned this strange disease would show. They signaled with glances to the classmates who had experienced it, *Right, that's right.* The ceremony went on for a long time, only Junfeng alone had reasons to immerse himself in the terrible disease. But even he got bored. In the end, as if to deal with the boredom of being in the middle of something and also unable to speak, he asked: "Doctor, could you tell me how to treat my disease?" The two professors, as if seeing a frog in the laboratory tray speak, exchanged a look. In the end the one who had been expressionless answered: "What do you need us to do?"

Junfeng didn't speak any more.

After all comers heard the incredible moist crackles (including the director of the health bureau who had graduated from the agricultural college), as if to make up for their regrets, the two professors found pen and paper, and checking with a stack of blood test slips and CT photos, started to make rough calculations. They argued in low voices now and then, scribbled on the paper (sometimes, one of them would stare long at the other, as if waiting for the other's opinion, but was really doing his best to think). It was like they were solving a math problem we had all encountered in primary school: Suppose there is an inlet pipe inside the swimming pool, which can fill the empty pool in eight hours, and there is an outlet pipe at the bottom of the pool, which can drain a full pool of water in six hours, with the condition that half of the pool water is left, how long does it take for the water to drain completely? One hundred days, they gave the conclusion with two horizontal lines drawn underneath to the doctors of the health center, margin of error: ± 2. After they were gone, the entire health center fell into unbearable loneliness – a great event that rarely happened once in fifty, even a hundred years (although the center had been founded less than five years before): the very top talents in the field, international authorities, nationally renowned doctors who had probably treated central leaders, came to visit. Then, without meals or group photos, they left (the only thing the health center could keep was the piece of paper they left behind, the paper wasn't full of equations or coordinates as imagined, but a few lines of Russian). Now, the concrete ground is still smooth, shady, gives out the fishy smell of being mopped. The one-meter high green paint around the bottom of the walls is already old, even time is old.

When some of the townspeople noticed Junfeng's mom again, she was already running back. Presumably she had heard about her son's news in the supermarket, the bike already discarded. She ran back to the health center she had just passed. She was among a bunch of raging motorcycles, electric cars, and electric trikes, like striding in deep water, laboriously running forward. Her body leaned forward, two arms raised in front of her chest, swaying left and right. We rarely saw women nearly 60 running, That day when she started running, we knew she was no better than a cripple with one leg longer and one leg shorter. Her two legs never left the ground at the same time, her whole person seemed to writhe left and right, writhe forward. Her face looked so aggrieved. "Son son son." Near the health center, she gave sad cry after sad cry. "Son son son son son son son." This time the son didn't push her away, just let her throw herself at him, tear at the quilt cover. He looked blankly at the ceiling, gave sighs that could no longer be hidden. The long sighs, like balloons being pricked, brimming with blame for her, and brimming with blame for his fate.

This pain seemed to take root in her ever since.

Whenever people, or say, whenever she thought she was a bit more normal, the pain would, like the ferocious Monkey King with sharp nails, grip her viscera tightly. She rubbed her hair, stumbled to the wall corner, crouched there, dodged left and right – as if there was a young worker kicking her again and again from the outside. She took one from the left, took one from the right, took a kick again and again. She bared her teeth, opened her mouth, wanted to cry but no tears came out, her face contorted, as if catching a chill shivered for a long time. People were frightened by this horrible rustle, this unshakable pain. It wasn't until 10 minutes later when she gave low calls of ohs and ahs, that it started to show signs of retreat. "If I had seen through your tricks early, you goddamned fool, this tragedy could have been avoided," she scolded her son, announcing with an attitude of certainty, that she would be in charge of him now, but the latter looked at her with contempt. Like there was obviously a lock nobody could open, but everyone took it for granted that they and they alone could open it. All went to try. Sometimes she would stand dully before the window of the corridor, staring at the endless white smog emitted by the big chimney in the distance, saying to herself, *I really should die, hearing the news late, my son is dying, but I am still alive, I really should die.* Every time she went to pester the doctors and nurses at the health center – when she said to them, "Don't look at me like I don't have money, I do, I have two houses" – it would always bring on a new round of pain. She gripped their sleeves or pants hems, begged them to save this son, which only brought on their repeated emphasis of when they estimated he would die. Two months later, it was they, those angels who had spoken coldly but still fairly polite, and got her water from the water dispenser, pinned her down roughly on one of the health center's front doors, and using the ceiling light, jabbed a tube thick as a finger into her throat, jabbed it straight down, let water push into her stomach. The water, from the corners of her mouth, from the mouth of the tube, from the doctor's hands in rubber gloves, flowed down endlessly, down her body, down the worm-eaten lines and crevices in the door panel and the stairs, flowed toward the black soil burned the previous night, still lingering with some burned scent. She lay on her side on the shiny door panel, exposing her belly button and bare feet with the shoes and socks scraped off, like a boar fallen into a coma from injury, under everyone's eyes, twitching horribly.

"This is a hopeless thing," they said after she begged. Suggested she'd better take her son home.

"Can't give any medicine?" she asked.

"Already gave all the medicine that could be given."

They also wanted to say, under the present circumstance, any medicine would not only delay the patient's recovery, but might activate hidden lesions, hormones for example. This was what the professors had said. But figuring she wouldn't understand, they didn't say this.

When her thirty-one-year old daughter Dongmei and twenty-nine-year-old son Zhifeng came late, she vented all her anger at them. Of these children, she loved the strange Junfeng the most, such partiality had been open, had been voiced again and again, as if she was afraid Dongmei and Zhifeng wouldn't remember. *I just want to be good to him, just be good to him.* Such unfair treatment continued from their childhood to the present. Dongmei and Zhifeng felt they were their elder brother's slaves, helpers, and servants. They knew full well that defense was useless, but couldn't do without mumbling a few words. One said, "Put the child in the nursery, can't just leave him outside, and let him be, huh?" (Zhifeng's suburban wife echoed, "Right right.") One said with hidden bitterness, "Look, I'm really sick too, yesterday I vomited all over the floor." Since Chen Zonghuo died of cerebral hemorrhage, Dongmei had fallen ill. The illness was real and unreal, neither what Dongmei herself exaggerated (she said the veins in her brain tangled together, tangled more and more tightly, like shoelaces being tied), nor a complete farce as other people thought (checkups showed her blood pressure was really a little too high). Dongmei is still alive today, but life is like a huge burden, oppressing her with extreme cruelty – People had never seen a person whose fear of death came so early, so deeply, so meticulously and so long-lastingly. She shook all the time. After her blood relatives died one after another, she inherited their legacy: the seed of cerebral hemorrhage, the seed of rapid weight loss and acute mental illness. The punishments that had blossomed and borne fruit in her relatives, the seemingly inescapable misfortune, were nearing her inch by inch. She had never felt so close to her relatives as she did now. She thought she would definitely, in their way, before everyone else, die extremely shamefully, die in the shit from sphincter incontinence. "My body is full of these genes," she told neighbors. They were tired of this pleading and pestering day after day. Fundamentally speaking, she had hypochondria. In the history of her suspicion, only once was she completely right: she suspected she had hypochondria. But then she denied it: "How is it possible, what happens in my body are real reactions, I feel out of breath." She always stopped halfway, shaking, felt the world and passersby were like islands splitting, rapidly receding under her feet – "I am so lonely," she started to cry – until Death, which had been riding on her neck, gripping her throat, drifted away with a ferocious see-you-later smile.

"People your age, so many sick, everywhere in the hospital, don't you see?" That day, Mother frightened Daughter to warn her about not coming in time. Then she said, teeth clenched: "Would be great if you had a stroke early, you don't care about your big brother, your big brother got this fatal disease all because of your laziness and negligence."

As in childhood, Dongmei started crying – in Chen Zonghuo's words, started crying very poorly, just let her cry, nobody should pay attention to her. She would stay in a corner, cry unhurriedly (like those finicky people who spend an hour or so eating a bowl of noodles in a restaurant), until the tears dried and became salt stains. She'd sit there a long time, in a trance, already forgetting why she cried, or even the fact that she had cried, then stand up, walk to her family, respond to everyone's words, flatter everyone. Like she was still the person very important to them – But that day, crying wasn't a cleanse, an escape, or a game she played with herself, that day, Mother's words stomped on the roots of her life. Mother's words swept away her last bit of hope, made the boat of her mind shake fatally: "Don't you see, people sick like you are so many, I'm talking to you, don't you see."

Faced with such harsh abuse, Zhifeng just threw his mother a glance. *Is it fun to talk like this?* He walked into the ward, hands behind his back.

"Zhifeng, you came." Junfeng tried to sit up, but due to lack of strength, slid down again.

"Yeah, brother." Zhifeng helped him up.

"Sit," Junfeng said.

Zhifeng brushed the bed with gloves, sat down. Half raised his head, looked at the window. Before long, he took out his cell phone, quietly swiped the touch screen. You can't say he treated his older brother coldly, deep in their hearts, there was a tacit intimacy, such intimacy didn't have to be concretized in a hug or words of concern. And you can't say he didn't treat his older brother coldly either. He already had his own family, when a person has his own family, he gets a bit estranged from his original family. We all know, a person's most intimate relation in this world is his partner. Because they can meet naked, make their genitals mesh. Their immoderation and vulgarity in words and behavior (which means boundless freedom between people) have moral approval. Besides, in the big suburban house provided by his wife's older brother, his wife had given birth to one son and one daughter. After Junfeng was asleep, he whispered to his wife, "Look, there's nothing going on here, better go back, go back, make something delicious, I mean –" he raised his voice so his mother could hear "– Better take Brother home, take him home, make something delicious for him."

Widow looked glum, full of pain, looked at the eldest son who had a moment of peace in sleep, tucked in the blanket, took the bag of photos out from under the bed. "Can you take it to find a city doctor, you're a city person, there must be a way," she said to Zhifeng.

"Hard to find."

"Go to your wife's two brothers, they're capable people."

Zhifeng put down the phone, raised his eyelids. He had just given it an understanding smile, like he was talking face to face with his friends on the phone. "You only play on the phone, day and night playing on the phone." She went on, "Play on the phone less, okay, you've only got one older brother."

"I know."

"I didn't ask you to carry him to the city. I just—"

"I know, look, we went to the Tuberculosis Institute, we went to the Municipal Hospital, the best doctors from Beijing came, everyone said no way, what else do you want me to find?"

"Go find other doctors, maybe there are other ways."

"It's already diagnosed, whoever I find it'll still be the same."

"How do you know it'll be the same, after all you're just lazy, just don't want to lift a finger."

"This isn't about whether I'm lazy or not."

"You don't even want to make the slightest effort for your older brother. Are you going to just watch him die?"

"I'm not, I'm just saying this is hopeless, hopeless, so why keep doing it?"

"Why's it hopeless, haven't tried and still say it's hopeless, aren't you ashamed to say that?" She started crying. "Aren't you sorry?"

Zhifeng shook his head hard, Mom was so stubborn, stubborn as a cow, he snatched the bag of photos, walked quickly away, coming back, the result would still be the same, you just have to make me make the useless effort. He registered with an expert at the Number One Municipal Hospital, to see the doctor three days later, the doctor examined the photos, very fascinated, took photos every two squares with his mobile phone. "This needs more research, if you can go borrow the biopsy from the Number Two Hospital, that would be great," he said. After asking the borrowing procedure, Zhifeng said okay, went out, called his mother: "Have to nurse him carefully, they said, there's still a glimmer of hope, depends how you nurse him." He went to his father-in-law's, took care of his son for a while, as Mother required, went to buy a piece of jade and a copper bell cast with the inscription *Om Mani Padme Hum*, then went back to the township health center ("Buy jade for what?" he said. "You're not paying, I'll pay," she said). While his mother-in-law, in the very early morning, went to the temple and burned incense for Junfeng. Dongmei, meanwhile, sat gravely on the edge of the bed every day, like an intelligence agent, softly asking her older brother what reactions he had, what reactions he'd had before, what reactions he had afterward, in order to compare with the signs that had already shown in her own body. "Sometimes, I cough a little," she said. But their mom always asked him pitifully: "Do you want to eat anything, child, whatever you want to eat I'll go buy now." He didn't respond to her. He always stared at the ceiling with his eyeballs popping out. The eyeballs were like half an egg stuck in a chicken's asshole. He could hardly move, except when a violent cough came up, which made him suddenly, almost uncontrollably sit up. Whenever this happened, Widow would rush over, slap his back with her palm to make him cough smoother. Son, cough harder, cough out the phlegm and it'll be better. The intervals between his coughs got shorter and shorter, the time longer and longer. Sometimes the cough, like a repeating crossbow, could not be taken back once fired, sometimes it was like a whimper that made people cry, sometimes it was like the flint on the gas stove which sparked, sometimes crackled, sometimes it was like the wind whipping rapidly in a tunnel, making sand fly, stones roll, sometimes it was like a car laboring up a slope on a rainy day (the wheels spinning rapidly in the ever-deepening ruts they created, struggling in vain), sometimes it was like an iron shovel digging and scraping the concrete road where only ground gravel was left after rain erosion, sometimes it was like a section of burning intestine rolling up, sometimes it was like mercury thrashing in a sealed tube, sometimes it was like a shocking attack in the dark of night, sometimes it was like a hung body dangling in the air, sometimes it was like a solid flogging, whip after whip, sometimes it was like an animal howling (picture a dragon, its tail pinned, lifting its upper body again and again, dripping with blood as it tears itself), sometimes it was like two trains quickly scraping the wreckage of the other, sometimes it was like a flagrant murder. Each time, they felt it wouldn't be until the victim coughed out a small earthworm, a sticky worm, a black lump, or a mouthful of blood red as a red flag that he would stop. Everyone coughed for purpose, there isn't a cough without a purpose, just like there isn't a revolution without a purpose, there isn't love and hate without a purpose. Coughing was a prison you couldn't plead to, only marbles couldn't cough.

"I'm dying." After Junfeng screamed agonizingly the whole afternoon (because of fever, in the early winter, he only wore a blue vest, kept talking crazy talk), and after asking an acquaintance to find a 'photo-reading expert' in Number One Municipal Hospital to check the photos (he said: "Incurable"). Afterward, Widow considered it over and over, deciding to take him home. That day, everyone calmly watched tightly wrapped Junfeng being carried into the car, they had long grown used to the fact that Junfeng had a strange disease, in the way oysters contained sand, they contained this fact in their lives, regarded it as normal, their faces showed relief that things was finally pushing forward ("Care at home may get him cured." This, instead of being a way to console Widow, was what they optimistically thought.) Only Widow was sad, unusually, that she understood clearly; from then on, her son would have one day less for each he lived. She found the vegetable field in the backyard of the health center, and facing a mound of used syringes, had a good cry.

When the car drove to the village, she said to the women coming up to it: "I say he's calling me, whenever he gets anxious, curses me, I know he's calling me." They wanted to comfort her, but didn't know where to start. "His language and ours are just different," she went on. As soon as her eyes closed slightly, a pool of tears poured out. The creamy-white light truck didn't break down, the body, because of the engine's throbbing, was purring, shaking. Zhifeng carried Junfeng down. Widow opened the door of the new house. It was a house built for Junfeng by her orders, done with tiles, aluminum alloy window frames, good paint, and western-style pendant lamps. It was being saved for when Junfeng got married, so she and Chen Zonghuo never came to stay one night, preferring to live instead in the smoky, fiery, old, old-fashioned house. Once in a while, she came to the new house to clean, kneeled on the ground, wiped carefully, as if Junfeng would come back anytime to use it. But it wasn't until he was sick beyond recovery, that he was brought there. As light as a chicken, Zhifeng said to those who told him to be careful. Junfeng drooped his head, eyes like two short clubs moving at will in front of others'. After sitting on the sofa, he pursed his lips tightly for a while, eyelids blinking in panic, forehead breaking out in sweat (as if smeared with a layer of shiny lard), while his entire body struggled in vain. He seemed to be tied up, couldn't move. Ah, perhaps it took a very bright mind to know, it was because he knew he was back in the village, so difficult to get away, but back again, and back forever. Zhifeng pulled out his leather belt, whipped it hard against the red seat of the folding chair, he was completely quiet. Ah, my older brother is light as a chicken now. It was like Zhifeng was introducing a new product. Almost as light as a pillow.

Afterward, Junfeng, as if he was being enslaved or ruled over, refused to talk, eyes calm, dull, and thoughtless as an animal's. He always woke up with no idea where he was, but then was unusually at ease with this confusion. He let shamans wave burning charms before him, let Mother put a jade pendant to expel evil on him, hang bells to expel evil on the windows, let two or three people feed him medicinal liquids from thunder god vines, then let it trickle down from the corners of his mouth. "Coughing is hard for him, hard as the work we do," sometimes Widow said. At that time she was unusually calm. But very quickly she was startled by her carelessness, hurried over to grip his hand, like he would die soon or had already died. When he strained to cough – it took a full 15 minutes, like a middle-aged man standing hunched in the cold field, gripping the cold handles, trying to make the stupid, stubborn walk-behind tractor rattle – and almost burst his windpipe, boundless hatred arose in her heart. *Who on earth has he offended, has he harmed,* he coughed out a mouthful of blood the size of a ping-pong ball, a thread of blood drooled from the corners of his mouth. She reached her shaking hands out to catch the blood that was like black juice. *Who has my son offended, who on earth has our Chen Zonghuo family offended?* The more she thought, the angrier she got, walked toward Chen Zonggong's house at the village entrance. She walked fast, as if she wasn't walking herself, but carried by the flying bird of hatred.

"There is something I have to say today," she said.

"Go ahead," Chen Zonggong who could hardly rise said.

"When burying Zonghuo, digging the grave, why did your son-in-law throw an iron spade into the grave?"

The grave was reserved for me, never thought Zonghuo would die first, Chen Zonggong responded with silence. *My son-in-law was afraid I would die without a place to rest.*

"How can you be so unreasonable."

"I have no idea about what happened back then, I wasn't well either, didn't go."

"You just tell me if it is true."

"It is."

"Wasn't Zonghuo your younger brother?"

"He was, not the closest by blood, but very close."

"The younger brother from the first wife, but still. Be clear today, what's your intention?"

"No intention."

"You harmed my Junfeng so that he was about to die you know."

"I know, Aunt," Chen Zonggong's tears poured down. "I regret it."

"What's the use of regret, my Junfeng is already like this."

"My son-in-law is at work, hasn't gotten home yet, if you want to get back, get back at me."

"Fine, I will."

"I'm going to die soon too."

"Dying soon won't do any good."

"What do you want me to do now, Aunt? If you want to curse, curse me. If you don't, I won't have peace."

After saying this, Chen Zonggong gripped Widow's hands, wiped the blood covering her hands on his white hair and face. "Punish me, I didn't mean to be difficult with Junfeng. If I could trade, I'd trade my life for Junfeng's life now." He started crying with no restraint. "Hurry and find someone to beat me to death."

"Can't beat you to death."

Widow swung her arms, headed back. Cried out loud the whole way. *You tell me who he has offended, who he could offend.* Every time she saw a person she sobbed complaints. One day later, she carried the same hatred to the supermarket in town. She figured it was the supermarket's damp and bacterial work environment that made her son's lungs defenseless, but she gained nothing there. The ground was much cleaner and drier than she imagined, no dirty blood in the seams between the floor tiles, not even a strand of hair in sight. Imagine, in the height of summer, no mosquitos or flies. Little Qi wasn't around. At the exit there were two cash registers. The proprietress, looking ferocious, wearing a red vest, with dark circles around her eyes from anxiety, stood outside the exit, glancing down at every customer's bag. To keep them from losing their tempers, she wore a smile for everyone. *Take care, mind the steps.* At times even made a gesture to help. Those irritated people would deliberately swap the bag back and forth between their two hands, then gave it to whoever was with them, her gaze always following anxiously, until she raised her head, saw they had been watching her, and started to feel embarrassed. You'd better fucking go back running the corner shop. People shook their bags and walked out, hated her for being despicable, and hated themselves for being despicable. *One stolen, 10 fined* said a notice pasted on the wall. It was because there were more and more thefts in the supermarket, or the proprietress thought there would be more and more thefts otherwise. That day, when she heard a poorly dressed country woman had been standing on tiptoe, looking behind the meat counter for a long time – the staff used looks like relay beacons to relay the information to their only master – she walked up briskly, turned the other's shoulders. They looked at each other maliciously, one suspected the other was a thief (otherwise why so sneaky), one suspected that the other wanted to shirk all responsibility.

"You want to buy something?" the proprietress asked.

"Not buying anything," Junfeng's mom said seriously. "Just looking."

She didn't reveal her identity. She thought she'd better go back and discuss this matter with the young people, perhaps Zhifeng could see something in it later. *You just wait.* She headed for the Laoyangshu Town street. After she was gone, the supermarket staff told the proprietress it was Junfeng's mom. That day, the smog very heavy like a bunch of fairies kept blowing smoke from the distance. The ground still had snow on it, a strong smell of chemicals used to make smoked chicken hovered over the entire street. Junfeng's mom parked the bike outside the lottery shop the local villager Reai opened. Reai smoked, had already smoked so much her teeth were black, but was still a trustworthy girl. Reai asked: "Is Junfeng better now?"

"Still the same," she said.

"Is there something to be done?"

"Nothing to be done."

"I mean, when it rained, Junfeng never took an umbrella, just walked out and got wet."

After getting directions, Junfeng's mom walked down Hongguang Lane in the north. There was a line of red-brick, single-story houses and asbestos-roofed woodsheds that filled every bit of available space and occasional pigeon cages and chicken coops. The urine spilling from the public toilet flowed in the middle of the street. Right on this quiet lane (after the lane bent to the east) hid a huge, fantastic, underground market which she, living five or six kilometers away, had never heard of before. When Junfeng's mom walked into the beautiful world made of formal hats, felt hats, Korean-style knit hats, shawls, scarves, silk scarves, wool coats, down jackets, V-neck sweaters, Erdos wool sweaters, shirts, vests, pajamas, thermal underwear, bras, panties, sexy lingerie, lace lingerie, shoulder bags, cross-body bags, handbags, genie pants, sagging pants, leather pants, jeans, skinny pants, casual pants, corduroy pants, leggings, dresses, wool skirts, sweater dresses, stockings, lace stockings, booties, snow boots, round-toed leather shoes, high heels, embroidered shoes, sneakers, walking shoes, lipstick, masks, deep hydration kits, skin cream, perfume, toner, Olay, car stereos, MP3s, MP4s, phones that play music, smartphones, touch screen phones, table lamps, gas stoves, range hoods, induction cookers, microwave ovens, rice cookers, stainless-steel pots, folding tables and chairs, brooms, mops, swabs, aprons, tablecloths, towels, bowls, plates, chopsticks, knives and forks, spoons, thermos flasks, glass bottles, dishwashing liquid, detergent, 84-brand disinfectant, tea-smoked duck, roast duck, tea seed oil duck, duck necks, duck tongues, Laizi's smoked chicken, Dezhou-style braised chicken, spring chicken, chicken wings, chicken feet, pig head meat, pig ears, pig liver, pig stomach, trotters, pig tails, chicken eggs, duck eggs, preserved eggs, dried tofu, five-spice tofu, brined tofu, cakes, pumpkin cakes, honey cakes, steamed buns, dry-flour buns, steamed twisted rolls, steamed stuffed buns, meat patties, sunflower seeds, 'toothpick' sunflower seeds, watermelon seeds, pumpkin seeds, boiled peanuts, pan-fried peanuts, salt-roasted peanuts, pistachios, pine nuts, chestnuts, easy-peel walnuts, pecans, Xinjiang walnuts, Hetian dates, raisins, hazelnuts, almonds, wood ear, meatballs, ribbon fish, frozen shrimp, baby shrimp, Wuchang fish, Wujiang fish, goldfish, carp, catfish, lifeless crabs, squid, cuttlefish, kelp, radishes, carrots, scallions, garlic, ginger, tomatoes, cherry tomatoes, onions, bean sprouts, taros, sweet potatoes, potatoes, cucumbers, red chilies, green peppers, mushrooms, spinach, celtuce, cabbage, bok choy, choy sum, lettuce, cinnamon-vine, strawberries, hawthorn berries, white pears, Asian pears, bananas, baby bananas, red grapes, kiwis, kumquats, tangerines, tangerines, navel oranges, blood oranges, pomelos, Fujis, Red Fujis, and Qixia Fujis she was dazzled.

(Once I talked with a man who wanted to be a woman. The lonely middle-aged man had been tense and restrained, until talking about the market. Then light started to flicker in his eyes. "You know what, once you go in, all your worries are gone, the feeling is fantastic you know, fantastic." He talked extremely fast, as if I would argue with him. He was so eager to persuade me. I told him I understood – the sacred light, the climax, the warm, electrifying feeling, the friendly and cohesive atmosphere, the everything-within-reach abundance, the ambition for a beautiful life and the joy of creativity, vividly in mind – I said I could totally sense God's arrangement and compensation.)

Those colorful products which came from all over the country, or at least all over the county, and needed to be sold promptly, were like the New World, shocking Widow's barren soul (many years ago, she had bent over the fields, familiar only with the regular grocery store which was converted into a small supermarket later – to her, the piece of paper pasted on the shopfront, *New Arrival: Dumplings and Rice Balls*, was incredible information). She felt the market was too long, no matter how far she walked, she couldn't reach the end. So she complained, like a girl about to lose her virginity, but also like a queen. All the shopkeepers, like slaves, called out to her. *I'll just have a look*, women warned themselves as they walked to the market. Then, after they went in, they sighed, *Just looking is enough, just looking*. Junfeng's mom grabbed a handful of wormwood, weighed it in her hand. This thing costs 6.98 a jin, that is, 7 yuan a jin, she was going to tell this incredible finding to Reai. Then, she eventually couldn't resist the constant temptation of the goods. In front of a brown scarf with a picture of the Taj Mahal printed on it, she swallowed.

"Try it on, you won't know what it's like if you don't try it on." The shopkeeper walked up, pulled it from her fingers, shook it open, draped it over her shoulders, then turned the mirror toward her. "Look." She seemed to be under the other's control. The feeling was very uncomfortable, but then she saw the self she had imagined. The shopkeeper, in her silence, found orange, red, blue, and other styles of silk scarves, which she politely rejected. This might increase what she had to pay. She couldn't bargain, so just mumbled throughout, looking clumsy and embarrassed.

"But what," the shopkeeper asked. "You tell me but what."

"But a bit too expensive," she said. "That's all I have, but that doesn't mean it's worth all I have." She was very sorry about it, and willing to bear the other's scorn. While she waited she said: "That's really all I have."

They parted on bad terms. With more or less the same disappointment.

When she was about to wander out of the lane, she remembered the purpose of the trip. Behind her was the sound of the skilled confession of a woman 20, 30 years younger than her. She paused but then walked on. At the end of this winding market, opposite a poplar tree, sat a white-haired woman, who wore an apron converted from a urea sack. She was shaving radishes nonstop. Whenever people came and asked, she would turn the knob lock, call the fortune-reader inside who was famous for his accuracy. Mr. Dong wasn't really blind, only had night blindness. Later when Widow gave him money, he almost stuck it on his eyes to look. That day, he seemed to profoundly sense the querent's sorrow. He said she walked in heavily as if carrying several corpses on her back.

After seriously singing a passage, he held the erhu, said:

"Really want me to say?"

"Please."

"The truth?"

"The truth."

"Then I will."

"Please, begging you."

"Your family will wear mourning clothes this year."

"Wore it last year, wear it again this year?"

"Wear it again."

This sentence was like a candy which Junfeng's mom chewed for a long time, before digesting it clearly. She gave a long sigh, remembered a curse put on her, also by a fortune-teller. "Sir, here's the money for you." After settling up, she went back the way she had come, but just couldn't find the shop, like a flower it had disappeared into the sea of flowers. She asked the price in another shop, which charged 20 yuan, so she didn't even have any interest in bargaining for a lower price. Then the previous shopkeeper, gripping poker cards, hurried over.

"Ten yuan, it's yours, can't do less."

"No."

"Look—"

"I only have seven yuan."

The shopkeeper folded the silk scarf. She said: "The brown one, orange doesn't suit me." So the shopkeeper got her the brown one. She went back to the lottery shop, examined the silk scarf for a long time with Reai. Reai said it wasn't even worth seven yuan, but it wasn't much of a loss. "Look at the texture, the texture is real good," Reai said.

"I also saw the texture is real good," she said.

When she rode off the paved road, rode onto the village road, feeling hungry, she went into Qiuchen's restaurant to have a solid meal. "There's no way," she said when Qiuchen didn't ask, while pulling down the hem of her hip-length shirt. She got on the bike, used her forefeet, or that is, her toes to pedal the pedals, advancing meter by meter, like a crow carrying a sword on its back slowly disappearing into that five-day, frighteningly quiet, seemingly ominous fog. Back home, she carried the bike in, put down the kickstand, locked the bike, then took down the half a watermelon wrapped in Saran wrap (it cost fifteen yuan and four jiao total – in town she had carefully kept Reai from seeing it), and went into the new house. "Hey Junfeng, never thought there'd be watermelon this time of year, huh? Shame it got beat up on the way, broke." She scooped a piece with a spoon, fed the other. "Mouth open."

He opened his mouth.

"Teeth open."

He opened his teeth.

"Swallow."

He started to swallow, but the food stayed there, didn't move at all.

"Swallow hard, son."

He tried hard, but it was in vain. She mashed that small piece of watermelon, pushed it in with spoon. He choked, started to cough. After that, she pounded the watermelon into juice, fed him with a spoon, but it always spilled out from the corners of his mouth. As usual, she said: "Junfeng, what do you want to eat tonight, whatever you want to eat, I'll cook it now." Then went on: "How about we eat fried egg soup. I forget whether it needs chives or not."

He didn't say anything.

"My brother doesn't even have the strength to agree or disagree." Zhifeng, gripping his mobile phone, walked in and said: "Mom, since you're back, I can go, I have some stuff to do."

"Go."

"I won't have dinner."

"I know."

Widow knew it was in vain but still meticulously made a dinner.

Every time a dish was made, she would pick up the kitchen towel, gently wipe her hand, find an empty bowl and cover it. She made some of his all-time favorites: bacon stir-fry, egg and chive stir-fry, spicy shredded potato, and fried egg soup. In the past, whenever he ate in front of her, she would carefully observe his likes and dislikes (what he disliked, she firmly disliked too), but in front of Zhifeng and Dongmei, she needed their constant reminding. After the cover was lifted, the hot steam and the smell specific to chernozem rice wafted out of the rice cooker. She scooped the rice into the egg soup, mixed them. "Eat as much as you can." She put a pillow at the head of the bed, lifted him up, settled him. He intended to say something, but decided the process of saying it was too complicated, and gave up. He turned his face sideways, fixed his eyes at some point, ignored her. Soon he closed his eyes. Wanted to sleep. She moved him straight, used the hot water in the thermos flask to wet the towel, wipe his face, wipe his back, then carefully tuck in the blanket. Then filled his thermos with a straw with water. Back in the old house, she put the dishes on the table (only the bacon stir-fry went in the rice cooker basket to heat up). Out of pity, she made a good bucket of pig feed, went to the pig shed to reward the two pigs which had gotten thinner since others fed them the past few days. When she struck the ladle, called *luo-luo*, they tumbled up, leaped up, stood upright against the wooden railing, anxiously twitching their pink noses at her. She also replaced the light bulb with a broken filament in the courtyard. After coming back, she kept tuning the radio, and the unique, bright, weak clamor of the signal came, which created an atmosphere where all the talented people had come, and the house was filled with distinguished guests: (*an alto singing*): so potent, took a sip, got drunk, got drunk – (*a middle-aged woman imitating a child's voice*) so Miss Glass Shoes played on the swing. When Miss Glass Shoes found Curious and Surprised Shoes, she shouted brightly: "Want to come and play?" – (*two-person crosstalk*) the audience is very enthusiastic, everyone knows you, (oh, familiar) the famous comedian from Tianjin – (*a movie soundtrack*) he didn't die... Why, why keep it from us, who gave him food – (*theater chorus*)??? (*Peking opera*) In the old days the family was too poor to feed. Of four sons two were frozen and starved to death. In the famine year they became horribly indebted to the Diao family. To pay the debt, his third brother worked in the fields. She walked under the dim light, sat at the dining table, poured alcohol, as usual, slowly, in the order of good to bad, picked at the plates, ate what was on them. The dregs went to the chipped, small, white bowl. What she couldn't throw away went to the small red bowl. She slowly drank the alcohol, slowly chewed. Her mouth, like a grinding machine, ground the food. Until all food was completely gone. In the process of chewing, sometimes she would stop, go into a long trance, then come to, and go on chewing. This is a common thing when one eats alone. The door was open, facing the fields. Night was gathering from all directions. The dark night, like lake water overflowing its banks, poured in front of her. She burped, picked up another bottle from the ground. The bottle was blue, covered with dust. She wiped it clean with her sleeve, shook it, shook it again, unscrewed the cap, sniffed the amber-colored liquid. After making sure that was it, lifted the bottle, drank down in one gulp. Perhaps thinking it was a private business, halfway though, she held the bottle, went to close the door. As she staggered, lurched, almost getting to the fir door panel (ten minutes later it would be taken down by a bunch of people jumping with anxiety) a shot of piercing, twisting pain like the one preceding delivery bent her waist. She crouched, let her head slowly lean on the threshold, clenched her teeth, tried to bear it. Sweat, like rain, dropped to the ground. But the gush of food pulp with its choking stench still violently prized her mouth open, spurted out from it.

It'd been 12 years since anyone drank pesticide.

The news alone was enough to make people's hearts pound and pound. The last time they were this tense was when Batu, who married into his wife's family, fell into a well a dozen meters deep. As if venerable Death, now dragging the sack (it rustled, scraping against the ground covered with wet pine needles and fallen leaves), was, from the near future, from the dense fog with branches and shadows,

228 • A YI

distinguishable, walking up. Her bewitched reactions – the muscle spasms, the exposure of the whites of the eyes, and the animalistic howls – shocked the few people who arrived first. Hurry, hurry – anxious shouts with indefinite content were everywhere – hurry. A bunch of people holding emergency lights, flashlights rushed to the houses of the barefoot doctor and the driver. Unspoken coordination. The driver Anfang was informed by mobile phone. When he drove the truck, hurrying over, there were still people running toward his house. Even though the car lights already shone on them, they backed away to the side to let it pass. Someone took a shortcut through the fields, ran to the village committee a kilometer off, kicked the door open, found the *First Aid Manual for Pesticide Poisoning* from a pile of documents.

Shouts and reproaches abounded. Someone who simply thought doing so might help a little moved her away, stripped off her outer clothing, and kept pouring water on her forehead, neck, upper body, while at the same time wiping off the food sludge and foam spilling incessantly from the corners of her mouth. Some people fanned their shirts to circulate the air. After the door panel was taken down, they carried her into the car. Someone held a flashlight to light the stone heaps and wild grass by the road, while running ahead of the car, as if doing so would help the driver see more clearly, until the car easily passed him. By then, people felt a bit relieved, panted, and, along with the barefoot doctor who arrived late, watched the car skid this way and that (like a car stolen on TV, driven by a fleeing robber) as it rushed toward the emergency health center.

After Widow was conveyed back alive, it was broken.

Anfang parked it by the back door of Widow's house.

Of course he could push it home – that meant convenience in fixing it, many people offered to help – but he still used fatigue as an excuse, left it there. It was a small demonstration: to see if there would still be people willing to save the dying and heal the injured in the future. He pushed away the toll money Zhifeng offered, he said: "Later." And the women watching over Widow, while she was fast asleep (now her breathing was even and smooth), started talking: there were several ways to drink pesticide, the first was to not drink, the second was to drink, the third was to drink in front of others, hers was to drink not in front of others but knowing others would find out. The door was open. The lights were on. There was only a little at the bottom of the bottle, which had been drying for so long, exposed to the absorbing sun, the poison long decomposed. *She, well, does need to let something out, needs to be cleansed, but doesn't want to die for it.*

This was some kind of ceremony.

They took turns going on watch, watched over her for several days, until she could get out of the bed. She leaned on the walking stick, helped by another, to check on her son. Still the same. A little shrunken. She said to everyone she saw, "Nothing to be done, really nothing to be done." Saw someone, said it once. Fearing the cold, they set up a coal stove in the kitchen, used a poker to make the fire blaze, gathered around her for warmth. Someone said coal smoke was bad for recovery. She said it was no problem. She drank hot water, shivering, then spread her hands over the coal stove to get warm, sadly said: "There is nothing at all I can do."

They remained silent. She was the only one constantly and routinely singing of helplessness and desperation, her rising and falling cry tearing their hearts. Eventually, to lead her out of weeping, Mrs. Ju said: "Auntie, you still want to die?"

"No."

"Why not?"

"Pain."

"Pain how."

"A lot of pain, heartbreaking pain."

"I'm afraid you still want to."

"No, I don't."

Judging by her eagerness to argue, she had lingering fear about the tormenting experience. So everyone laughed. She didn't laugh, though, but didn't cry either. "You shouldn't worry about me." Widow nodded at them, then asked: "Ah, you eat candy or not." All said they don't. "No, no, Auntie, don't move, I don't eat it." But she still got up. Someone stood to help her but was refused. "Better to walk a little," she said. She stumbled over, opened the cupboard door, pulled out the middle drawer, dug around. People went on spreading their hands over the coal stove. Some were in a trance. Some looked at her. She dug out a cleaver with a red plastic handle and yellow rust, stared at it for a while, as if judging if it belonged in her house. She touched the teeth of the edge with the top part of her index finger, then aimed it at her neck, made a sudden cut. Like cutting a handful of straw, cutting a handful of wheat, she cut herself again and again, cutting without getting to the point, until finally cutting a main artery. There was simply nothing they could do to get up. Their faces were deathly pale, whole bodies trembling, sitting there frozen, no way to stand up at all. For a week afterward, they were all like that, as if paralyzed. Fresh blood, like the nation's flag hoisted in the morning, was suddenly thrown out by the guard's white-gloved hand. Humans have so much blood – from the blood streaming out endlessly you could tell if she hadn't committed suicide, she would have lived for many years – like endless water gushing out from the hole of a plastic water tube, the enormous gushing force made the water tube wiggle crazily like a snake. This was a suicide method unheard of for a very long time, it belonged to the ancient times: throat cutting.

No need to think. No way to rescue. No possibility at all.

With one hand Widow held on to the kitchen, the doorframe, walked heavily out. As if walking out would give her relief. She covered her throat, pushed down the empty bamboo scaffolding outside, then threw herself at the white truck, which had been repaired and was driving away. Anfang slammed on the brakes. The truck thereby stopped there again. More and more people gathered around. They stood carefully, from time to time lifting a leg to let the red, bubbling blood flow away under their shoes. The body lay prone there, twitched for the last time.

Junfeng lived out his remaining days, died punctually.

About Mother's death, he had no opinion. Cleaning his body for the last time, his younger brother Zhifeng couldn't take it anymore, cursed him cruelly. Zhifeng gripped the toilet paper stained with his excrement, moved up to him, shouted: "You killed Mom. You know you killed her." He had no response. No anger, and no grievance, no fear and no shame. He died when he got as thin as he could possibly be. The skin, already like a soaked shroud, clung tightly to his protruding skeleton, showing the prominent gaps between his ribs, made people terrified – or that is, like a rubbing, the appearance of a skeleton was rubbed out. His beard, like a handful of grass, grew on his proud chin. His eyeballs were particularly big. Almost as big as billiard balls, Zhifeng said.

In the moment of farewell, Dongmei came, she wanted to pry into the details of people near death. His lips slightly open, she put her ears closer to listen and guessed his obscure plea from his breath. She asked him about it, but there was no response. She moved to the other side of the bed, found the mobile phone under his pillow, plugged the charger connected to it into the wall socket. During this process, her older brother died.

Around that time, two strange incidents happened one after another in Laoyangshu Town: one, on the icy surface of the Yao River, a giant, one-meter-long lizard was found. Although human beings issued more than one hundred calls to it (they believed it was like an alien, could understand friendly signals from human beings), it still dared not go onshore. After busily spinning round and round on the ice, it simply died. Two, a truck slammed into the auditorium. The driver was killed, dozens of dogs jumped off the truck, ran east in packs like wild horses. These two incidents weren't as shocking as Widow's suicide. Many people said, "I really want to have a good long cry over this incident."

FLAME TREE PRESS
FICTION WITHOUT FRONTIERS
Award-Winning Authors & Original Voices

Flame Tree Press is the trade fiction imprint of Flame Tree Publishing, focusing on excellent writing in horror and the supernatural, crime and mystery, science fiction and fantasy. Our aim is to explore beyond the boundaries of the everyday, with tales from both award-winning authors and original voices.

•

You may also enjoy:
American Dreams by Kenneth Bromberg
Second Lives by P.D. Cacek
Vulcan's Forge by Robert Mitchell Evans
The Widening Gyre by Michael R. Johnston
The Blood-Dimmed Tide by Michael R. Johnston
Kosmos by Adrian Laing
The Sky Woman by J.D. Moyer
The Guardian by J.D. Moyer
The Goblets Immortal by Beth Overmyer
A Killing Fire by Faye Snowden
The Bad Neighbor by David Tallerman
A Savage Generation by David Tallerman
Ten Thousand Thunders by Brian Trent

Horror titles available include:
Snowball by Gregory Bastianelli
Thirteen Days by Sunset Beach by Ramsey Campbell
The Influence by Ramsey Campbell
The Haunting of Henderson Close by Catherine Cavendish
The Garden of Bewitchment by Catherine Cavendish
Black Wings by Megan Hart
Will Haunt You by Brian Kirk
We Are Monsters by Brian Kirk
Hearthstone Cottage by Frazer Lee
Those Who Came Before by J.H. Moncrieff
Stoker's Wilde by Steven Hopstaken & Melissa Prusi
Ghost Mine by Hunter Shea
Slash by Hunter Shea
The Mouth of the Dark by Tim Waggoner
They Kill by Tim Waggoner
The Forever House by Tim Waggoner

•

Join our mailing list for free short stories, new release details, news about our authors and special promotions:

flametreepress.com